ACES AND
ETERNITY

ROBERT RICHMOND FARRELL

ACES AND ETERNITY

SOUTHBEACH BOOKBINDERS
NEWPORT BEACH, CALIFORNIA

ISBN: 0983694508
Library of Congress Control Number: 2015916865
SouthBeach BookBinders, Newport Beach, CA

Edited by Robin Quinn – www.writingandediting.biz

ISBN-13: 9780983694502

V1.0

"Every man takes the limits of his own… vision for that of the world."

Arthur Schopenhauer
"Further Psychological Observations."
Studies in Pessimism: A Series of Essays
[*Parerga und Paralipomena*] (1851)
Translated by Thomas Bailey Saunders

∽

"The soul attracts that which it secretly harbors; that which it loves… and also that which it fears."

James Allen
"Effect of Thought on Circumstances"
As a Man Thinketh (1902)

Catherine Rosina Farrell

DEDICATION

The Blessed Mother

All blessed mothers

Author's Note

This book is a work of fiction and fantasy. Names, characters, powers or abilities of characters, officials, families, entities, businesses, organizations, governments, agencies, militaries, places, locales, events, incidents, or occurrences are the product of the author's imagination or are used fictitiously and are not to be construed as real or having any basis whatsoever in fact. Any resemblance to actual persons (living or dead), families (living or dead), officials (living or dead), entities (past or present), businesses (past or present), organizations (past or present), governments (past or present), agencies (past or present), militaries (past or present), places, locales, events, incidents, or occurrences is entirely incidental and thus is not to be construed as having any relation to reality. The author has no knowledge of any individual, being, entity, process, or technology with the power to restore human life.

ACKNOWLEDGEMENTS

——

Jon and R.J.

~

Dr. Louis Batmale
Father John Kavanaugh
Uncle Bob Perasso
Dr. Henry Cuniberti

~

Peter White
Sanford Hull
Terry Bissell

"Who knows… whether the common sense, that we take for the judge of truth, can be the judge of that which has created it."

Pascal
*Conversation of Pascal with M. de Saci
on Epictetus and Montaigne* (1728)
Translated by O.W. Wright

Aces and Eternity

——

Crime and cruelty is the most conspicuous couple on these hard-boiled streets. Hustlers, pimps, prostitutes, thugs, and boulevardiers gone bad all have their share of turf on scruff sidewalks. The decaying neighborhood of East Bethune, an inelegant city out Interstate 10 from Los Angeles, is for the leathered, hardy, and borderline foolhardy.

A black pimp in garish dress argues with a beefy prostitute; the spat geometrically escalates. The pimp sharply slaps the prostitute's face. She retaliates with a punishing kick to his groin. Enraged, the pimp collects himself, snaps an antenna from a parked car, and takes to whipping the woman. She screams for help and appears to draw none... as well as little more notice.

But then sirens break close, muggy air. A patrol car, lights whirling, screeches to a stop. Trina Lewis, fortyish policewoman, pistol drawn, jumps from the passenger's side. "Drop it!" This night her sharply cast cheeks and tribal jade eyes radiate considerably more gravity than beauty.

Defiant, the pimp spins and menaces her with the antenna. "I don't lay down for no bitch, *bitch*."

Trina's partner, Cronin, a stout cop of 45, midsection slabbed by a five-course appetite, hands fleshy mitts, is cold efficiency as he pops out of the driver's side, props a shotgun on top of the patrol car roof, and takes a bead on the pimp. The pimp's taste for confrontation demonstrably wanes; he unhands the antenna, which drops to the street.

Trina flicks her revolver toward the black and white. Without further prompt, the pimp steps to the car, spreads his legs, and hugs the hood with outstretched palms as though he was well practiced at it. Trina begins to pat him down. The prostitute, knotted on the sidewalk, sneaks a hand inside her purse.

Cronin cocks a barrel. "Hold it!"

When Trina swings her head toward the prostitute, the pimp throws a stinging right fist across the policewoman's face, jolting her to the ground and knocking away the revolver. The prostitute clears a handgun from her purse. Cronin unflinchingly unloads a barrel into her thigh, dropping the prostitute prone on the sidewalk where, clutching her leg, she writhes and brays in pain. The pimp, shielded from Cronin, reaches to his ankle for a holstered automatic pistol. Trina balls her lithe, finely cut body; nimbly rolls to her weapon; and comes up on a knee with barrel pointed at the pimp's face. "Show it... *please*, show it." The pimp has a notion, but chooses to test the policewoman not.

Brendan Hopper, forties, powerful torso, Spartan features, watchful instructor, walks behind a paired line of largely ill-conditioned, gi-clad men and women on the hardwood floor of a chichi suburban health club. At the end of one row, a fiery-eyed, chunky woman, strapped with a blue belt, stands apocalyptically across from a frail man, a wisp of a white belt.

"All right, basic front snap-kick," Hopper barks to his class. "Counter with a downward block and reverse front punch. Strong *kiai*!"

The white belt's line kicks. The man lands awkwardly and lurches forward into the blue belt's counterpunch, delivered with a primal shriek. The white belt folds to the ground, gasping for air. Hopper quickly moves over him, grips his belt, and raises his mid-section. "Deep breaths... deep breaths," Hopper ministers his student.

After several moments, the felled white belt finds air and then rubs the blue belt's impress on his throat. Hopper helps him up. "How are you feeling?"

"Better," the man reports without conviction.

"What do you need to do with your blocking hand so that doesn't happen again?"

"Sign up for the low-impact aerobics class?"

"You may have something there."

The movie set is frantic with a crew readying for a shoot. Bill Stackhouse, 260 pounds of ill-defined, middle-age mass parked beneath a ball cap, stands with other stuntmen near several rigged cars. A sniveling production assistant, Laird Parkins, walks briskly from cameras to Stackhouse.

"Brock rewrote the scene last night so the chase car comes screaming around the corner into a three-sixty roll, landing straight up." Laird frames his hands and crouches slightly, looking through his impromptu finger camera. "We smash-cut to Brock in the driver's seat, rivulets of sweat running down his face."

One of the stuntmen raises a cynical hand. "Say, Laird, any chance we can just smash Brock? Since when did he become a scripty? What does a fucking actor know about pulling off a stunt like that?"

Laird is oblivious. "House, can you make it work?"

"Roof of the Chevy doesn't have a roll bar," House duly reports.

Laird canvasses the remaining stuntmen. "Anyone else?"

No takers.

Laird heads back toward the set. "All right, we'll bring in Simkins and pay him his rate," he spits over his shoulder.

In an austere, big-city courtroom presided over by an austere, big-bellied judge, a doughy bailiff, whose neck tests the collar-button stitching of his stern blue uniform, leads 12 jurors, unified in impassivity, into the courtroom and jury box, where they efficiently seat themselves. The fidgety, crowded spectator gallery rights itself with decorum. The defense table is an uneasy amalgam of lawyers; computers and wires; long, yellow, ruled tablets of hieroglyphic legalese; waters, Altoids, and antacids; and suited corporate types. At plaintiff's impeccably settled table, Greg Hardisty, dark hair tinged with gray, serious eyes, compelling features, properly presides over his nervous client who exudes 60 years of excess in his face and questionably gotten affluence in his eyes.

The Judge angles to the jury box. "Mr. Foreman, have you reached a verdict?"

"Yes, we have, your honor."

The Judge nudges back in his chair. "You have been instructed. Please proceed."

"With respect to Causes of Actions One through Five and Eight through Fifteen, the jury finds in favor of defendants."

The announcement stirs the spectator gallery, yet only intensifies defense-table anxiety. Greg is stoic, his client near apoplectic.

The Foreman continues. "With respect to Cause of Action Six for interference with contract and Cause of Action Seven for interference with prospective business advantage, the jury finds in favor of plaintiff in the total amount of twenty-eight million dollars."

The Judge permits not a moment to tick. "Thank you, Mr. Foreman and members of the jury. You are dismissed." With a rap of his gavel, he is on his way to chambers.

The twittering spectator gallery is in full motion. Those at the defense table look as though someone had just gift-wrapped their intestines with baling wire. Greg's client fairly leaps to the gallery to be congratulated, hugged, and esteemed by his supporters and intimates. After a moment of glorification, he breaks away to lean over the shoulder of Greg, who is deliberately closing shop. "How much of the verdict can I write off against my carry-back losses?"

The eyes of the two do not meet. "I'll email you on that."

Greg walks into "Primo's," a downtown bar whose wooden walls, tables, chairs, and indeed some regulars all bear a similar scarred history. Blaring rock music punishes partitions and patrons alike. Primo, a Polynesian with a marquee smile and fire hydrant for a neck, whoops over the throng of folks rinsing away the workday. "Greg, what's up?"

"D.D. tonight, so a Diet Coke it'll be."

Primo handily splashes the order from a soda gun into a tall glass bedded with ice and pushes it across the bar. "Be here long?"

"No, we're making a run to the Indian casino."

"They recovered from last time the crew was there?"

"That's the purpose of insurance." Greg signs off with a wave.

At the back, Trina, Hopper, and House, near a row of dartboards receiving spirited play, have staked out a table appointed with beer glasses and a dying pitcher.

"Just gettin' back from the courthouse?" Trina, with a smidge of sympathy, asks Greg, he of slumped shoulders.

Greg wearily nods as he drops his coat on a chair.

"You need to loosen the tie, lose that tie tack, and bring aboard a new social director, buddy," Hopper notes.

"Need a new something," Greg acknowledges.

House raises his hand, presenting a small bouquet of feathered darts. "What he *needs* is to unloose the Bill Tell in him." A tipsy House stands and presents darts to Greg. "You ready?"

"Take it I'm your partner."

"Yep, and you got a damn good draw. Trina's hand is still a little shaky from that gunplay night before last."

"That'll explain it when one of my darts ends up in your fucking ear," Trina retorts as she scrapes away her chair.

Hopper sweeps a set of darts from the table. "Don't get her too fired up. Big night in front of us. Can't have her flaming out early."

"When was the last time you matched me shot for shot, big boy?" Trina offers up.

"Tonight." Hopper stands on his chair. "Primo," he shouts exuberantly, "three shots of mescal and a bottle of Tabasco."

Primo is immediately to the task.

Greg opens his arms and looks to the heavens. "Tell the Donner Party they may have company."

Bright, glitzy signs irradiating casino fantasies, retail outlet stores, and fast food fare are but a dim coral glow in a dark, quiet desert sky. Few vehicles course the four-lane highway. Greg is behind the wheel of a convertible BMW humming along at an easy clip. Trina snores away in the passenger's seat. House, heavily inebriated, decimates a bag of French fries. Hopper, across from House in the backseat, most capably apes a rusty meat-grinder as he shrilly sings along to a Tom Petty and the Heartbreakers track.

Suddenly, the car behind the BMW ignites with red and blue roof lights. Hopper spins around, then back to Greg. "Were you speeding?"

"Nope."

"Maybe they want to issue a community citation for all the money we just left the Indians," House nonchalantly manages between mouthfuls.

Greg dutifully pulls over to the shoulder, extracts vehicle documents from the glove compartment, fishes out his driver's license, buzzes down the driver's window, and looks straight ahead.

A buff Sheriff eases from behind the wheel of a black-and-white rig, rights his Western uniform hat during a brief mirror check, then parades to Greg's car. His affected walk is somewhere between that of an elderly John Wayne and arthritic Daffy Duck. He raps his flashlight against his proudly holstered, six-inch-barrel .41 Magnum as he approaches the BMW.

The Sheriff stops at the rear of the car and hits, first, House and then Hopper in the eyes with the flashlight. Hopper shields his face. "Hey, this is the back of a car, not back of a fucking coal mine."

The swaggering highway heat relishes his quarry's aggravation. He steps to the front and executes the same routine with Greg and Trina, stirring her but slightly. He then puts a pretentious arm to the driver's door, leans down, and asks (rather judgmentally, one might well conclude) of Greg, "Have you been drinking?"

Greg's delivery is as flat as that of a lip-weary professor. "No, sir."

"Boy, I sure have," Hopper chimes in. "How 'bout you, House?"

"Yep. Fair to say I was over-serviced this evening," the big fellow piles on as he cracks open a box of candied popcorn.

The Sheriff manages to restrain his amusement. "Step out of the vehicle," he disparagingly orders Greg.

Greg, disbelieving, responds, "Me?"

"Someone else driving?"

Hopper snaps at no one in particular, "Can you believe this shit?"

Greg, documents in hand, rotely removes himself from the car. The opening of the driver's door rouses Trina. She quickly assays the situation, removes her badge, and presents it to their anointed martinet. "East Bethune P.D., Officer."

The Sheriff re-engages his flashlight on her. "Have a makeup mirror on the other side of that shield, lady?"

As Trina lurches for the door handle, Greg extends a hand. "Trina, we can't afford another one." Trina stops, venomously stares at the high-handed patrolman, then reluctantly stands down... sits... and seethes.

Greg quickly dispatches a field sobriety test and reseats himself, which gives occasion for House's displaying to the officer a miniature toy compass dredged from the bottom of his popcorn box. "Looks like our man aced the balance thing. Wanna see how he does on direction?"

The Sheriff glowers at House. "You a funny guy?"

"Been known to turn a joke or two."

Hopper takes House's stead. "Live guys like you just bring out the stand-up comedian in him. They call you 'Charmer,' something like that, back at the OK Corral, Officer Earp?"

The mighty keeper of the road arches his back, pans the desert, then returns his attention to House. "Appears as though you haven't missed many meals in your time, lard-ass. What was the main course tonight?"

"That would be a Senor Salsa Blazing Burger."

The Sheriff beams his flashlight on his car. "If I could ask you lamebrains to take a look at the black-and-white."

In unison, the four turn and inspect the spotlighted crime scene—a police roof light bar unusually, but nonetheless neatly papered with a hamburger wrapper stuck in a mounting bracket. The group slowly returns its attention to the finger-tapping-on-the-butt-of-his-pistol lawman, who is inquisitorially glaring at House.

House prepares to take the fall for the inadvertent transgression of wind-tricked, fumbling, alcohol-addled fingers. "Ah, that would be my... "

"That's *my* wrapper, Officer," Trina acerbically intercedes.

The scrubland enforcer sticks his chin across the line Trina has drawn. "Think I won't cite a cop?"

"Won't have to. That's from my burger," Hopper adds to the conspiracy.

The Sheriff peers down at Greg. "Anything you want to say?"

Greg extends over the driver's door for a clear view of the patrolman's feet. "Sure do. Could you tell me where I could procure a pair of those cowboy boots ... without the embroidery and elf toes?"

The Sheriff pulls out a citation book.

Trina and about 20 other police officers sit on folding chairs in a small briefing room bordered by tired, institutional yellow walls, where a whiteboard, cluttered with police codes, street addresses, and officers' names, occupies position front and center. A Sergeant, whose red facial veins could serve as a directional map to most any groggery in town, stands sentinel at the board while reading from a notepad. "Jones, Grammatica… Vidulich and Frankel, command needs relief at that standoff in the mountains. The Chief has thrown our hat in the ring. You're swing at the scene the next week… unless someone there gets their goddamn act together first."

Several cops scribble notes, a couple make entries into their cell phones, most parry boredom.

The Sergeant flips a page on his pad. "Cronin, Lewis… we have legwork for the D.A. on the Brasner trial. Today, Friday, and Saturday you need to… "

Shifting uncomfortably in her seat, Trina pipes up, "Sarge, there's that thing I talked to you about this weekend."

Before the Sergeant can reply, a policeman in back breaks into song. "Don't you know, that's the sound of the men working on the chaaiinn gaaannnggg."

Amateur hour has kicked off. Half the room then joins in rickety unison, "THAT'S THE SOUND OF THE MEN WORKING ON THE CHAAAIIINNN GAAAANNNNNGGGG."

Trina more or less shrivels in her seat as the chorus mounts, sweeping the entire room and gushing into the corridor.

In the staid, near antiseptic office hallway, Greg, in suit pants, crisp white shirt, and correct business tie, intently reads a file after stepping from a law library, whose orderly shelves would do justice to the Smithsonian.

Sutter Nance, a man of 60 with regal gray hair, suit of fine artisanal detail, and air of superiority, walks by. "Ready for the Streeter depositions on Monday?" he inquires in passing.

"Nearly there."

"I'll be in the office Saturday," Nance boasts, if ever so slightly, "should you need run anything by me."

"Won't be in Saturday."

"Thornberg will be," Nance jabs.

"I'll catch up with him Sunday night."

A disenchanted Nance receives the news of Greg's unthinkable sloth by brusquely moving on.

Wind whips sand and solitude across high chaparral and a lone desert freeway, dotted on either side by motley members of an orange-outfitted road crew of 70 or more. Greg, Hopper, Trina, and House work as a group apart from others, spearing trash from the ground and roadside brush.

Trina spikes a paper cup. "Hey, House, a Wild Whip shake cup from Senor Salsa. Guess somebody musta missed a sheriff's patrol car when he chucked it."

House bounces it back to Trina. "I told you the wrapper blew out of my hand. I coulda tossed your badge—for all the good it did us."

"Mussolini, at this very moment, is trying to kick out of his grave to enlist that dickhead cop," Hopper intermediates before drifting to an area of particularly high growth. He spots something in a small clear area inside the thicket and quickly forges inward. "Holy shit, there's a body in here!" he calls out.

Trina, with practiced efficiency, arrows in behind Hopper. House and Greg follow step. A shriveled aged man with deep, heavy wrinkles and soiled clothes lies listlessly in the dirt. Trina bends down and reaches for his wrist. Hopper kneels at the man's head and presses a finger to his jugular. House and Greg, warily eyeing the highway shoulder, stand behind Trina.

Trina: "Whadya got?"

"Nothing," Hopper replies. "Have anything?"

"Nope."

Trina waits several beats before standing and turning outward.

"Where are you going?" House asks.

"To notify the supervisor; he needs to handle this."

Hopper drops his head and mouths words of prayer. Trina decides to stay to take a moment with the other three.

Hopper's head jerks up. The aged man, propping himself on an elbow, is weakly tugging at Hopper's pant leg. The man is whispering something to him; Hopper leans over to listen.

Hopper looks to Greg. "He wants water."

Greg charges outside the cluster of bushes as Trina takes off her jumpsuit to make a headrest for the aged man. Greg quickly returns with a large jug of water and hands it to Hopper, who puts it to the man's mouth. The elderly one drains it unfathomably quickly. The group exchanges quizzical looks, then those of amazement as wrinkles miraculously vanish from the man's face.

The man sits up, eyes bright, alive, and speaks in an unrecognizable accent. "You came in here to help. No one else would. Others have seen me and walked by. You cared. For that, each of you will pass death—once."

As the old fellow sprightly rises, Hopper studiously probes, "What do you mean 'pass death once'?"

"You will have one chance to die and come back to life."

Greg steps forward. "Everybody dies."

"And so shall you," the man responds, "but not the first time."

House joins the panel. "Do you mean that we... like... resurrect?"

"In a manner."

"How long do we have this 'chance'?" Trina asks.

"Until you tell someone about it beyond you four," the elfin man firmly answers. "Then you shall have it no more." He bustles out of the thicket. The stunned assembled stare at one another, quickly gather themselves, and scuttle after the man.

Outside the large clump, they see absolutely no trace of the enigmatic interloper. Without prompt, the four take off in different quadrants, each a carbon of the other in lean and gait. After a thorough search, they convene at the cluster of brush and inspect one another's faces as though they had just been transported to a lunar picnic.

House is the first of the exasperated to speak. "**Whiskey Tango** mother **Foxtrot**."

"What in the holy hell was that?" Greg asks before House voices all his words.

"Best damn spook we've *ever* come across," Trina dryly notes.

"Jesus Christ," Hopper exhales.

"His take on this we could dearly use," Trina observes before she steps into the bushes to retrieve her jumpsuit.

"Whatever that just was," House offers in a lost voice, "we're not gonna figure out here and now. If we don't fill these damn bags, we're back on this highway for another weekend."

Four querulous miens return to the litter hunt.

A fusty, yellow county bus drives away from a fenced, worn industrial building as the road crew of sun-soaked, penitent civilians trudge sluggishly toward cars parked in the lot. Greg, Hopper, House, and Trina stand alone outside the chain-link gate.

"Let's take everything you say as true," Greg posits. "The man had a very low pulse."

Hopper is adamant. "He had *no* pulse."

Trina: "That old man didn't have any sign of life."

"OK," Greg says, weighing the evidence, "he had no detectable pulse or heartbeat. That doesn't necessarily mean he was dead."

"What are you when you don't have a pulse—bored, out of touch, lackadaisical?" Hopper retorts with a heap of sarcasm. "You're not telling me the old guy didn't disappear, are you?"

"We couldn't find him."

Trina antes up. "He either went across the highway, up or down the roadside, or out to the desert. We asked nearly every one of the other people," Trina declares as she points to the dispersing road crew, "didn't we? No one saw an old man—in any shape, size, or form. I didn't find a single footmark in the sand leading away from that mess of brush. Did you, House?"

House reluctantly shakes his head in the negative.

"And how about the wrinkles on his face?" Hopper appends to his case. "They disappeared. I mean, they just plain-ass disappeared. Tell me the last time you saw that on an infomercial."

"All right, all right," Greg capitulates. "There's no denying they're all strange events, maybe even otherworldly. That doesn't automatically translate, first, into uncategorically accepting something magical happened; second, that the old man has the power to pass along a supernatural gift; and last, that somehow, someway we've received a one-time hall pass on death. Even if the old guy *was* able to resurrect himself, does it follow he can confer the power to someone else? Assuming he could, why us? For giving him water? Come on. It isn't like we went through the March of the Bataan for the man. And face it, how the hell are *we* deserving of a gift like that old coot claims? How can four people who've taken life be given life? I don't know about you all, but when I kick, I'm not expecting a big hootenanny at the pearly gates. To think we were, out of the blue, chosen for some storybook fantasy is letting logic take a complete jump to hyperspace."

This gives Trina pause for consideration, but Hopper is not to be dissuaded. "Think of the voodoo shit we've seen on our missions—Philippines, Burma, Cartagena, Guatemala, and those fucking H.A.L.O. drops in Somalia and Sudan. Did we ever, and I mean *ever*, see anything like we saw this afternoon?"

Hopper stumps the audience. After reflection, House is the first to speak. "It was strange mojo, I have to admit. But what all those years of ops taught me is one thing: trust my gut—nothing else. I'm not sure what happened out there, but I know if there's something I can't explain, I won't just accept the next reason that comes along. Nobody will convince me that any person, being, or thing has the power to bring me or anyone else back from the dead. I don't care if a bottle of water turns that old man into Cary fucking Grant."

"When it's a matter of faith, one doesn't have to be convinced," Hopper apostolically argues. "That man gave us a message."

"Yes, he did, Hop, and here it is: Because we have an unusual experience with a bum out cold in the high desert, it doesn't necessarily track we've been beamed into a *Twilight Zone* episode."

Trina is unpersuaded. "Can't just write it off that easily, House."

"Well, I don't plan on cashing out my union life insurance policy tomorrow," House counters.

"Let's sit on this a few days," Greg suggests. "There's a lot to think about. We have plenty of time to figure out what all this means."

"Maybe a very long time," Trina adds.

The only sound this afternoon in the unremarkable neighborhood church of plain stucco walls; squeaky, varnished pews; stained glass; cloistered baptistery; and venerable alcoves of candles fronted by kneelers is that of Hopper's sanding a newly installed confessional door. He has a carpenter's hand and craftsman's patience. His work is expert; his mind distant.

An older priest with a bone-honest face, clinician's eyes, and sure carriage steps from the sacristy, followed by a chubby altar boy as well as a wiry, meek Hispanic one. Father Raymond leads the two to Hopper.

"Ryan, Honorio, this is Brendan Hopper."

Hopper shakes the boys' hands. "Nice to meet you, Ryan... Honorio."

"Hello, Mr. Hopper. You're the flag-football coach, right?" Ryan bubbly inquires.

"Yes, I am."

Father Raymond rests a hand on Hopper's shoulder. "Brendan was one of my first altar boys here at Our Lady of Perpetual Hope. His second year, he served all three weekday morning Masses for the whole of Lent."

"All of Lent?" young Ryan asks, nearly reverentially.

"Yes, but Father Raymond's sermons weren't as long as they are now," Hopper jokes. He sizes up Ryan. "Have a good set of arms there. Are we gonna see you out for the team this year?"

Ryan puffs his chest. "Yeah. Been working out with my brother, improving my hands. Wanna be a tight end."

"You look serious enough for a tight end."

Ryan fills himself with the compliment.

"How about you, Honorio? Do you play any sports?"

Honorio manages a weak reply. "I like soccer."

Father Raymond takes the shy one's part. "Honorio's father was a great soccer player from Uruguay."

"Do you play for a team?" Hopper gently prods the youngster.

"Not anymore," Honorio answers, somewhat despondently.

Father Raymond preempts the moment by gesturing to the pews. The boys immediately take to the task of collecting stray hymnals. The priest stands back to admire Hopper's carpentry. "That's as fine a work as you've done for the church, Brendan."

"Thanks, Father. I can stain it tomorrow or wait until Monday so there won't be any odor during Sunday services."

"Whatever is better for your schedule."

As Hopper surveys the door for an unusually long time, Father Raymond looks knowingly through pince-nez glasses. "It took about twice as long to sand that door as the one near the altar last month, Brendan. Something on your mind?"

Hopper lifts his eyes to a Station of the Cross, The Second Fall, above the confessional. "You believe the Lord has performed miracles?"

"He has and He does."

"Ever seen one, Father?"

"No, but that doesn't lessen my faith in them."

"Do you believe anyone else can perform miracles?"

"You mean a human being, Brendan?"

"Anyone other than the Lord."

"That's a large question."

Brendan rotates to the cleric. "Large questions have always been in your wheelhouse, Father."

The priest studies Hopper's beset countenance. "You're a good man, Brendan. The goodness of the Lord is in your heart. He has seen you through difficult trials, many despairs. Only He can provide an answer you will accept. Mine will not, because you already know what it is."

Hopper turns back to the Station.

Greg, buttoning his shirt, sits on an examination table in a compact patient room presided over by Dr. Klein, a sweater-vest physician in his sixties who delivers candor to match his estimable medical skills. "This is the third time in fourteen months we're raising the dosage on your blood-pressure meds. That, in combination with your statins, is not a happy situation. Plainly stated, Greg, if you don't do something about your hypertension, your health will be at risk... a *very significant* risk."

"I understand. Should I discontinue flying lessons?"

"Not unless you're experiencing unusual symptoms in the air."

"No, nothing like that. I actually feel most relaxed up there."

The doctor drums his clipboard. "Is it your father, Greg?"

"That's part of it... I think."

"You understand we have the best possible man on it."

"Yes, and you know how much I appreciate it."

"You never did make an appointment with either of the two counselors I recommended to talk about your overseas experiences."

"Think I've worked through that."

Dr. Klein, unconvinced, nevertheless moves on. "What is it then—caseload, hours, clients, senior partners? I know it can't be Diane. They don't come any more genuine than that young lady."

Greg knots his tie and shifts himself on the edge of the table... to yet another uncomfortable position. "Wish I knew for sure."

Dr. Klein rumbles through documents on his clipboard. "Blood work continues to be negative. This spike in your pressure started just about two years ago. Any turning points come to mind?"

Greg swivels his gaze toward the window. "The job... it just doesn't seem to produce much positive anymore... outside the check. Please understand, Doctor, I'm not ungrateful. I'm lucky to be where I am. My parents gave up a lot to provide the opportunities I have. God bless my mother for the sacrifices she made."

"From what I hear, your practice is going exceptionally well."

"It is. I'm very fortunate." Greg considers further articulating his thoughts, but sees little sense in offering more inconclusiveness.

"Perhaps, as the stakes have risen in your cases, clients are now more overbearing?" Doctor Klein supposes.

"I don't have the cheeriest bunch on the books, I'll say that."

"Has your ratio of difficult clients to good clients changed with your success? Lord knows I have my share of crotchety patients these days."

Greg smooths his fully smoothed tie. "Sadly enough, it's mostly difficult, litigious ones who end up in court... and my end of the hall."

The resourceful physician has no prescription for that condition.

Greg, Hopper, House, and Trina sit at a window as tables around them thin with approach of closing time at Primo's.

Greg has the floor. "We're talking about this as if we have a fix on exactly what it means. One chance to die... what is that? Say you kick and do come back, what are you? An infant? Same age? If you're killed in an accident, do you live the rest of your life as a cripple?"

Hopper brooks no equivocation. "Now you're being the attorney, Greg. We're talking about a matter of conviction here, not a matter of legal interpretation. You either believe or you don't. As far as I'm concerned, there's only two ways to explain that old man and what happened with him: he was either some sort of alien or a higher being."

"I didn't see a strong resemblance to Predator," House remarks as he looks over his shoulder to Primo and gestures for a last pitcher of beer.

Trina leans into the conversation. "You know, House, you've a right to be a cynic. With all the inhumanity we've seen, there's reason enough to have lost faith."

"You don't believe we were given something, too, do you?" House peppers Trina. "You honestly think the old guy holds the deck of life in his hands and just dealt us aces and eternity?"

"I do think we were given something," she answers. "But the question I've been asking myself since Saturday is whether I have gumption enough to take on the belief."

Hopper stands firm. "That old man was there to bring meaning to our lives."

House ladles on cynicism. "Well, seeing as your career path since we cashed in after Sudan has more or less been along the lines of a game of 52-Card Pickup, I would have to conclude that's a good thing."

"No matter what any of us say, believe, or don't believe," Greg opines, "something *is* certain: we won't have a definite answer in the short run... unless one of us decides to test it, and I can't see the sense in that. If we've been given something, it's an insurance policy that we hopefully won't need for a long, long time."

"Yeah, and what if we did come back younger?" House conjectures. "We'd be pissed if we used the chance now instead of when we are a bunch of old hacks."

Seeing that Primo has filled a pitcher, House, obviously having sampled his share of the establishment's spirits, unevenly rises to retrieve it. As plods back to the table with his prize of suds, Trina suddenly bolts past him and out the door.

"Where the hell are you going!" House hollers.

She is not taking inquiries.

Abandoning the pitcher on the bar, House chugs to the front doorway where Greg rushes to join him. Hopper drops down from his seat, crouches below a window ledge, and scopes the scene. They see a runt, tattoo-infested gunman in his late teens backing out of a convenience mart across the street, his revolver dragooning a clerk and two patrons cowering near the cash register.

Trina, badge in one hand and drawn automatic in the other, takes a position behind a car parked in front of Primo's.

"East Bethune Police!" she shouts. "Drop your weapon!"

Greg and Hopper both mouth the word "Shoot." The young armed assailant whirls and unleashes a barrage of bullets in Trina's direction. Only then, does she return fire. The clerk draws a pistol from underneath the counter and wildly blasts away at the robber's back. Caught in crossfire, the thwarted teenager catches a bullet first in his leg and then stomach before collapsing to the ground.

Trina, automatic poised, steps from behind the car and walks gingerly across the street. She motions for the clerk to stay inside. Trina reaches her bloodied attacker, kicks away his revolver, and hovers over him. She removes her cell phone, and as she is punching in numbers, glances at Primo's. Greg, House, and

Primo are frantically tending to a wounded, bloodied Hopper, freckled with glass, draped over a window table.

As the sun announces its presence on a horizon interrupted by dreary institutional buildings, Greg is walking with two paramedics. The attendants are returning to their van from the emergency unit entrance of a solemn hospital complex bustling with arriving staff.

"I don't know how to thank you guys. That was one helluva response time," Greg says in a voice one click above a rasp.

"That's our job," the first paramedic officiously replies.

"Glad we were so close," the other adds.

House, frazzled, dried blood marbled on the front of his shirt, steps outside the emergency unit automatic doors and calls to Greg. "He's on his way to I.C.U. I'll see you there."

Greg spares his vocal cords and raises a hand in acknowledgment. House steps inside.

When they reach the van, the first paramedic hops in the rear to ready for another run. The second slips into the passenger's seat and starts pecking at a laptop in the dash. Greg has an inclination to soldier back to the hospital, but lingers at the van door.

"That was close," Greg says with a somewhat convincing offhandedness.

The attendant releases his fingers from the keyboard. "There's not much I can say about treatment of the patient, sir. We're bound by a strict set of confidentiality policies."

"I'm Mr. Hopper's attorney," Greg fudges as he reaches for his wallet. "Be pleased to show you my card."

"That's not necessary." The man prudently gathers his words. "I'll tell you this: I've seen people come back from that deep a condition, but always in there..." He points to the hospital. "... after a very large jolt."

"How far down was he when you arrived at the bar?"

"Off the record?"

Greg nods.

The paramedic ventures on. "That guy had the vitals of a grapefruit when we first hooked him in." He throws his thumb over his shoulder. "The patient flat-lined right after we strapped him. Then, just before we reached this hospital, he lit up the screen. How... I have *no* idea. Never seen anything like it... anything."

Greg inspects the paramedic's face, finding only verity.

The large ranch house of taupe, grays, and beige occupies expansive, finely landscaped frontage on a cul-de-sac of yuppie-on-the-rise homes nestled in wooded foothills. In the backyard, Greg is at the task of planting shrubs next to a wrought-iron fence separating his acreage from rogue hill brush. His baggy gardening attire appears to be a varicolored assemblage from a fashion refugee's garage sale. Sitting in spotty shade of freshly planted jacaranda, a Panama-hatted House sips a beer with the aplomb of your garden-variety armchair observer.

Diane, Greg's wife, late thirties, pert, attractive, strides with little wasted motion from kitchen French doors to the patio, past flower beds of white-capped gardenias and jasmines, around several exactly manicured topiaries, and underneath blooming violet crape myrtles to the back fence. She stops at Greg's work station. Arms akimbo, she flashes a Pattonesque glare. "Why are you planting hydrangea there?"

"Because that is your wish, my dear."

"I asked you to plant *hibiscus* along this fence, not *hydrangea*."

"Well, at least I'm not planting Miller *High Lifes*."

"Greg!"

"Honey, I asked you to go with me to the nursery."

"The splendor of strolling through annual color while you talk litigation strategy on your cell phone was far too resistible." Diane spins on her heels and ploughs back to the kitchen.

House waits a couple of polite seconds before commenting, "Hope you're presenting better cases for your clients than you are for your hydrangeas."

"It's my dad, Diane's trying to get pregnant… " Greg spikes the shovel into the dirt. "And having to keep a lid on this thing with the old man isn't helping." Greg retrieves a can of soda from the ground and plops next to House. "So what does our boy have to say?"

"Hopper's absolutely convinced he died and came back to life. He has been saved; now it's his turn to save the world."

"You say he wants to take up *missionary* work?"

"Yep."

"Where?"

"Knowing Hopper, somewhere he'll be ducking poison curare darts."

"My guess is a place we've dug in."

"Probably not far off."

"Well, maybe that's the one thing he hasn't tried in the last nine years." Greg tosses the near-empty can. "There's nothing to prove he clinically expired, you know." Greg had long ago mastered the art of politic concealment.

"Well, someone will have to convince Hopper."

"What about his wounds? It isn't like the bullet hole and lacerated ribs have mystifyingly disappeared."

"Doesn't want to hear it. He's a believer. Guess he's convinced himself we're somehow worthy of this gift… whatever in the hell it is."

"Last time I checked the Vatican sainthood watch, I didn't see us favored to win, place, or show."

House extends an upturned palm of resignation. "I'm tapped out with Hopper, Greg. Whatever I have to say, he definitely isn't a buyer. You should probably talk with him yourself."

"Think it'll make a difference?"

"Can't work out much worse than it just did with the bride."

Greg takes a pondering view of his garden. "House, you believe there's anything to it with the old man?"

"Well, I gotta tell you, buddy, though I have no plans to do a swan dive off a tower crane to test the theory, it does cause you to think."

Trina marches down a long corridor lined with photos of decorated police officers radiating little frivolity. Anita Galton, a tall, strapping policewoman with swarthy skin and meaty hands jointed by bulging knuckles, walks in the opposite direction. Her buoyant step belies 51 years engraved in her face. When she comes upon Trina, she slows and leans into Trina's ear. "Solid work out there."

"Thanks, Galton."

Trina permits a smile to crest before she turns into a small reception area of government-issued furniture, metal file cabinets, exactly arranged manuals, dated law enforcement magazines, and sparse invitations for lounging. A dowdy secretary presides over an efficient desk of manila folders, message pads, and general inhospitality. She offers Trina a rehearsed smile. "Go right in, Officer."

Captain Doolin, late fifties, square shoulders, squarer face, uniform perfectly pieced together, sits stiffly at his desk, signing documents and methodically assigning them to a rear credenza. Trina enters the Captain's office and stands immediately behind one of three chairs, none of which she is invited to occupy. After churning through a batch of stapled pages, the Captain breaks from his task and offers Trina a mildly relaxed expression... but no seat.

"That was top-flight police work in the field last week."

"Thank you, Captain."

"You followed department procedure to the letter before invoking deadly force. This should be through Internal Affairs in twenty-one days tops. *And* you gave the media absolutely nothing to feast on."

23

"Appreciate that, sir."

"How's your friend?"

"Recovering."

"Freak that he caught a ricochet bullet off a steel column in that bar."

"Between the perp and that crazy-ass clerk, there was heavy lead flying."

"Thanks to you, there's one less trigger-happy maniac out there. He'll be locked away at Folsom until they have saunas in the cells. Keep it up."

"Shall do."

The terse Captain Doolin returns to the orderly cycling of documents. Trina takes a soft pivot and is out the door.

Greg, tie unloosed, sits at his desk in a spare but tastefully appointed corner office whose floor sprouts stacks of files. He is transfixed on his in-basket.

Paul Thornberg, a balding, hard-charging sort of 30-plus in a lackluster brown suit accessorized with a mismatched tie and pocket square, blows into the office. "Can we finish exhibits for the Streeter pre-trial today?"

"Paul, what do you think of your in-basket?" Greg quixotically asks.

"Stupefying; it has no bottom."

Nearly oblivious to the reply, Greg immediately advances, "You know, if we slave here day and night, our reward is a bigger in-basket for business we generate."

Detecting a welcome non-shop conversation at hand, Thornberg takes a seat. "Any other bubbly observations to carry me through the day?"

"Let me ask you a hypothetical," Greg airily inquires. "If you were to acknowledge the existence of otherworldly beings, what would you presume to be the extent of their physical capabilities?"

"Who are we billing for this? Obi-Wan Kenobi?"

"Seriously, Paul. I'm interested in your view."

Thornberg tugs at his collar and his psyche. "OK. What do you mean 'physical capabilities?' Could they play jai alai with their hands tied? Is that what we're talking about?"

"No, I mean empowerment over life."

"Such as?"

Greg lazes in his chair and permits his eyes to tour the ceiling. "Do you think they would, for example... could they realistically have the power to bring a dead human being back to life?"

Thornberg scrutinizes the wastebasket to the side of Greg's desk. "Been pepping up the morning coffee with a jigger of firewater?"

"No, seriously."

"You honestly think that's a serious question?"

"A serious hypothetical question."

"All right. Are we asking if an alien could raise big Bill Custer from his grave?" Thornberg pauses. "Does Custer actually reside in a grave?"

"No, I'm talking about more like what Jeff Bridges could do in *Starman*."

"I personally thought he had greater power in *The Big Lebowski*."

Greg, a bit agitated, grumbles "You know, Paul, if I... "

"OK, OK. Let me put it to you this way. We have it way over weeds in terms of empowerment, right? But if a weed is hit with a shot of Roundup, there's nothing you or I can do to bring it back to life."

"That's your analysis?"

"That's it. If there are aliens out there, they may be advanced... even incomprehensively genius. That doesn't make them avatars or angels."

Greg looks contemplatively away.

The small park of winding paths, stone benches, bit-sized ponds, and measly floral touches is bereft of visitors. The noon-hour crowd from surrounding mundane office buildings has returned to work, leaving their trash brimming in receptacles and demarcating the way to the street. Greg and Hopper, hunched and pale, walk deliberately side-by-side.

"I respect the belief that your life has been blessed by a miracle," Greg says, avoiding any trace of skepticism or condescension. "I understand you also believe you must do something about it... something in recognition. That's the way good turns work. But does it mean you immediately throw your life into a somersault and jump into missionary work? Haven't we done our share to put things aright in places most of the world forgot?"

Hopper keeps his eyes ahead and defenses upright. "You either have conviction or don't."

"There are all types of convictions. We've already marched off across the globe to the Crusades. There's plenty of people right here in our own backyard that need help." Greg stops and puts a reassuring hand to his friend's shoulder. Hopper glances at Greg, then avoidingly past him. "Be honest with yourself, Hop. Since we shelved our fatigues, how many times have you jumped headfirst into this life-changing experience or that?" Greg grips Hopper. "You're a good man, a phenomenal person. You laid your life on the line a hundred times over for people you didn't know. You do the world a service just by being who you are."

"I could do more. I always could've done more. When we left places, I knew that. Now I have to."

"No one hit it harder when we were in deep... no one. You were the bravest son-of-a bitch I've ever seen." Greg glimpses at his watch before a final appeal. "Can we do this: talk more before you commit to some sort of service? A couple of days aren't much in the total scheme of things when you're considering throwing your life into a spin."

"Helping other people isn't throwing my life into a spin," Hopper protests.

"That was an unfortunate choice of expression. But can we please talk about this more? You still have healing to do."

"Sure," Hopper replies more out of impatience than concurrence.

"Great. I'll come back Thursday. We'll have dinner."

"OK."

Before releasing Hopper's shoulder, Greg sermonizes, "The good Lord willing, we all have a lot of years ahead to accomplish what we need."

Hopper faintly nods in agreement.

"And take it easy on the pain pills. You know how goofy you and I got on those in Guatemala."

"Sure it was Guatemala?" Hopper spoofs.

After an earnest smile at his friend, Greg spirits off to the street.

Hopper watches Greg leave and then turns away. Head down, he tramps toward the other side of the park. He passes a bench and seated figure to whom he is drawn not by notice, but by the sudden draining of aching from his body and entanglement from his mind. Hopper is now staring into the eyes of the aged man who, with his causal, cultured attire and beaming complexion, bears little resemblance to the disheveled lump in high-desert freeway scrub.

Hopper takes a tentative step toward the aged man. "Is that you?"

"Yes, it is, Brendan."

"How do you know my name?"

"Shouldn't I know the name of one who prayed for me?" the man socratically responds.

"The gift was real, wasn't it?" Hopper nearly pleads.

"It was."

"I came back from the dead, didn't I?"

"Yes, you did."

Hopper seats himself a secure distance from the cryptic man.

"Why was I... were we graced with the gift? Who are you?"

"Does it truly matter?"

"Hell yes... heck yes, it matters."

All Hopper can wring from the aged man is a kindly smile; yet the student will not be stonewalled. "What do you want from us? Should we do something in return for the gift?"

"I have no wants," the man defers.

Hopper takes a turn at irreverence. "Why are you here? I don't see popcorn for pigeons."

"I am here to reinstate your chance."

"Why?" Hopper asks, suspiciously.

"You were the first to help. You were the one who had true faith, who earnestly tried to understand the meaning of what you were given. You are deserving of the chance... again... this final time."

The aged man rises.

"How should I use it?"

"It is your conscience that brought you this chance, Brendan. It's your conscience—not an airplane or boat—that will enable you to use it wisely."

"How did you know I was planning on... "

Not to be further detained, the man takes off toward a stand of trees.

Hopper calls after him. "Will I see you again?"

The aged man steps spryly on. Hopper is sure this mystic disappeared before he reached the trees.

Absent inmates' prison garb, uniforms of two meandering guards, and razor wire articulating the top of chain-link fence, one might think he had landed in the midst of a rehab center for the incurably morose. Among buildings vaguely resembling noir motels, convicts numbly go about their appointed tasks, acknowledging one another when recognizing prison hierarchy or overcome by a burst of impetuous goodwill.

Behind a large structure off an entry road, visitors and inmates huddle at outdoor metal tables. House occupies a seat across from his brother Cord, a body double of himself, whose spirit appears to have been run through a rubber buzz saw. Cord presses his thumbs into a can of Dr Pepper, folding it into a mangled tin hourglass.

"What are the chances of Marianne going out of state?" House voices with compassion.

Cord fiddles with the can. "The thing with Darcy is drivin' her crazy. She's feelin' the walls closin' in. If she takes our girl to Michigan, then at least she has her family to help."

"I had a guy I know at the studio make some calls. The news isn't terrific. To pay for what it will really take to put Darcy right, we're talking well over a hundred grand... maybe closer to one fifty. Moving to Michigan won't substitute for that kind of treatment."

Cord anchors his bowling-pin forearms on the table. "Marianne has her old man in the joint, daughter on the edge, and a ten-year-old boy that needs stability. I can't do anything for her in here, Willie Buck. Her people in Michigan are good folks. If that's what's best for her and the kids, then that's where she has to be. Hell with everything else."

House studies despair wrenching his brother's face. "Maybe there's something we can do." Cord mechanically nods, admitting little encouragement. House tries another flank. "Things are OK in here?"

"Yeah, I'm still takin' care of some corporate types that need protection. A few weeks ago they moved in a cyber-crime nerd and freak, high-end drug boiler, PhD in chemistry or some fuckin' thing. They both were jacked up as soon as they hit the yard. I straightened things out for them, so they slipped me a nice wad of cash after their first visiting day." Cord briefly views the premises. "The guys in here are mostly all right... for being degenerate criminals and all."

"Seventeen more months, and we're done," House says with a burst of bright.

"The world I know will probably be gone in seventeen months, my brother."

Greg is lodged in front of a computer terminal in the den of his house where blowups of framed fighter jets patrol the walls. Outfitted in shorts, paint-stained T-shirt, and pilot's cap, he catches bits of a baseball game on a wall flat screen as he hammers out a legal document. Law books and files serve as his footstools.

Diane steps briskly into the room and dispassionately reels off the course of forthcoming events. "I'm taking the package to the nursing facility. I'm stopping by to see my sister on the way home. The landscaper will be here in a half hour. You need to show him where to trench for irrigation lines near the fence."

"Don't the plans show that?"

"No, they don't." Diane dangles car keys. "You can take the package, and I'll meet the landscaper."

"No, Dad likes spending time with you. Besides, I'll be there with him next weekend."

"Lot more time than you spend with me." Diane's brusque about-face takes her down the hall.

Greg draws a long breath, registers his wife's pique, digests it, and is again at his keyboard. Shortly, the phone rings; he answers.

"Hello." Greg attentively listens. "What do you mean 'second chance'?" Agitation crawls up Greg's face. He studies the TV screen. On instruction, he works the remote until he hits a newscast; he clicks up the volume.

Mitch Arnett, a television reporter with a nasal delivery and bad comb-over to match a bad sports jacket, pumps urgency into an uneventful status report from a command post in mountain terrain. "Today, the standoff between authorities and this cult—one that has allegedly harvested marijuana in these peaks for years—drags on for yet another day, further threatening hiker hostages. One has to wonder when negotiations must give way to an expedient exercise of force by law enforcement officials before..." Arnett histrionically lingers. "...the thread that holds the lives of these teenage hikers snaps." The drippingly melodramatic reporter allows himself a momentous, theatric turn to ridges behind before squaring to the camera. "This is Mitch Arnett reporting live from the San Bernardino Mountains."

Greg laments into the telephone, "He's going to engage, isn't he?"

As House's vintage, wide-bodied Pontiac GTO tests all the asphalt and a good part of the shoulder of a hilly road, Greg, on his cell, balances himself in the front passenger's seat.

"OK, understand," Greg rattles into the phone. "I know you're busy. Thanks for your time." He closes the call and wipes his tongue over teeth that taste like he had just sipped nectar squeezed from a car-wash chamois cloth.

"That the forestry guy your client knows?" House inquires from the helm.

"Yep."

"Any change?"

"No. Did Hopper respond to *any* of your texts?"

"Not a one."

"Me neither. He's carrying that throwaway, right?"

"That he is," House confirms.

"Did you ever consider installing seat belts in this beast?"

"Takes all the adventure out of it."

"You have a wheel to hang onto there, Hollywood."

"You're the one that's always wanted to be a jet pilot."

"Yeah, but they have ejection seats."

A straightaway releases Greg from the role of contortionist. He tries a number on his cell. The call and Greg's patience fail simultaneously. "Shit." He jams the device into his pocket.

"Who are you trying?" House asks as he exacts a handful of stale cashews from a crinkled bag in the console.

"Trina."

"I told you I talked to her. She made a call to one of the East Bethune cops on duty at the command post... guy named Frankman... " House plucks a piece of paper from his shirt pocket. "Frankel... yeah, Frankel. Have his number here."

"What kind of uniforms are at the site?"

"According to Trina, full monty — local sheriff, county, state, feds."

"Which agencies?"

"She's checking."

Greg processes the data, assays the blurry stream of rocks and twiggy brush outside the passenger's window, then bangs the dashboard. "What in the holy hell is Hopper thinking!" Shaking his head, he looks restlessly ahead.

"Fair to say he probably isn't doing a whole lot of thinking."

"If the government wanted ops, they'd be on the case."

"If that was your daughter being held by those goddamn lunatics with all that ammo, would you sit back until someone finally gives the green light? How many times were we crammed into some fucking rat hole or another, bottled up on cork, standing down, waiting for a first shirt to let us execute? Seems to me we spent forty percent of our time on the Thai-Burma border doing just that."

"We didn't have to worry overseas back then about the law, House. Bit of a different situation here, wouldn't you say?"

As House muscles his car into another set of turns, he replies, "Tell me which Mountie is going to spy him? Ever seen an op that could move in and out without a trace like Hop?"

"When he's right. At the moment he has a bullet hole in his gut and cracked ribs, remember?" Greg passes a hand over his stomach. "Or did the old man pull pixie dust from a Merlin cap he wore into the park and cure all that?"

"Don't know what happened, Greg, but when I saw Hop yesterday, he was fit enough to give Darth Vader a serious bitch-slapping."

Greg anxiously combs a hand through his hair. "You know what happens if he slips up, House? I end bailing him out again."

"Let him take care of it himself. He's a big boy."

"Is he? Is he really a big boy? Because you sure couldn't prove that by me... or Trina... or the Pro."

House takes steam from the pedal and lowers eyes on Greg. "You have enough friends to be so picky about them?"

Greg has a riposte of his own. "You have any idea the equity I use at my firm when I step into these legal messes? Our executive committee threw a damn shit-fit when I took off those days for Trina in Vegas. And you don't want to hear what they had to say about my filing an amicus curiae brief in your brother's case."

"He'd be doing a hard-time jolt of eight years or more if it wasn't for what you did, Greg. Everyone knows that."

"He didn't deserve the Q for defending what was his." Greg reduces his scrunched eyelids to slits. "I have stroke at the firm for dollars I bring in, but that only goes so far, House. If Hopper gets into a fix up here, I don't have carte blanche to represent him... particularly if there's a lot of publicity. There's only so much I can do."

"No one's ever asked for more."

Greg lets the moment spend itself before wrapping up his peeve. "You understand how much Apostoli, the Pro, and I have put into making sure our past is buried so we don't lay awake at night worrying about who's coming after us or our families. A move like this could blow the whole damn thing."

"We've *all* sacrificed a lot to keep the lid on, but you can't ask a man to forsake his heart."

Greg is absent a reply. House gives the gas to his gnarly engine, the burst consuming a stiff silence.

The turnout off the serpentine, two-lane blacktop leads to a gravel road cutting through dense trees and brush to a large, oval dirt clearing high on an imposing mountain range. On an ordinary day, this area hosted little more traffic than did the Marianas Trench. But this is no ordinary day. The kidnapping of teenage hikers by cultists of a bent generally undefined, save a devotion to marijuana and havoc, had captured the public's imagination and, thus, media saturation. This day the clearing is a cabled labyrinthine of law enforcement camps, communication tents, and television vans, topped by a buzz of circling helicopters.

Greg and House park some three-quarters a mile from ground zero, talk their way through two separate sets of security barriers, and eventually find East Bethune Police Department Sergeant Hoyt Frankel, a cop in his forties with a thin mustache, thick mid-section, Clark Kent eye glasses, butterball cheeks, and waning enthusiasm for the business of bureaucracy. They manage to sequester Frankel some distance from the reporter/paparazzi/gadfly epicenter.

"Trina says you've been here on and off for most of the last four days," Greg says without scent of gratuitousness.

"About the four longest days of my fucking life," Frankel despairs over an uninspiring plastic cup of coffee.

House nods toward the top of the range. "Any movement in the situation?"

Frankel throws a glance to the media camp. "Nothing more than they're reporting."

"Trina told me the kidnappers have sharpshooters in trees on the way to the encampment near the crest and that they're holding everyone back."

Frankel slips a pack of Camels from his uniform jacket and gives flame to his nicotine fix. "Let me tell you something," he pontificates, one eye closing to the first curlicue of smoke. "The deal here is pretty simple: bring in some wet-work guys, take out the sentries, drop down a TAC team to secure the bunker, and that's a take."

"What's holding it up?" Greg queries.

Frankel points his cigarette to a tent teeming with brass of one stripe or another and gets down to decimals. "Well, first of all, have some jurisdictional issues. Big fucking surprise, eh? It's federal land, but there's a state easement on the trail to the top. This area is patrolled by the local sheriff's department. Since the Sheriff is short-handed, you have guys like us filling in. To top it off, some forestry department or other has mandate for this range."

House sends a told-you-so look Greg's way. Frankel continues, "But the big sticking point is level of offensive to bring. The freaks up there have serious firepower. That bunker is loaded with *major* ordnance and materiel. Add in the fact that they're all hopheads — I mean real unstable types — and you have a formula for potential mayhem. Make a wrong move, and those maniacs could light this whole place up. The big hats here calling the shots don't want dead teenagers or an out-of-control forest fire on their hands because they didn't check down through all options."

"Think they're being overly cautious?" House questions the officer.

"You tell me." Frankel nods toward the ridges. "Those motherfuckers in that bunker aren't 'cultists.' That's the spin the dickhead reporters over there are giving it to pretty up their stories. They're marijuana traffickers. They're growing hundreds of acres of the stuff. Our intel is that they have at least five million cash stashed in the bunker. If it wasn't for that, there wouldn't be any hostages. They would've surrendered right off. People do crazy shit for that kind of dough."

"Some deal," Greg mutters to himself. He then turns his consideration to Frankel. "You're busy. We appreciate your time. We'll let you go."

"Good enough." Frankel moves to a group of police officers, leaving Greg and House to sort through their situation.

"What do you think?" House asks for lack of alternatives.

"Don't know there's much we can do." Greg eyes antennae sprouting from vans and tents. "If we dial out, it'll end up being at least a five-party call."

House inspects the slopes. "Wonder where he is."

"Doing his recon."

Forty yards from Greg and House, reporter Mitch Arnett is in caucus with his assistant, Roland Brandt, an undersized fellow in his late twenties with a wiry frame, wily ways, mess of curly hair, smart mouth, and cell phone in tune with fast-twitch finger muscles. Arnett stops his discourse when his muckraking eyes settle on Greg. Arnett tugs on Roland's sleeve. "See the one there with brown hair and the fatigue jacket?"

"With the big guy?"

"Yep."

"He's an attorney… won a huge verdict in a telecom merger case last year. His name is Hardaway… something like that. Tried to interview him after the jury came in, but he blew me off."

"Just exactly how much of your charm did you drop on him?" Roland the Cynic deadpans.

"Why would he be here?"

Roland continues his banter. "Maybe you should breeze over to renew acquaintances."

"Did you come into an inheritance in the last hour or so, Roland, where you don't need this job anymore?" Arnett suggests with little velvet.

The assistant backs off. "What are you thinking?"

"The attorney only handles heavyweight corporate litigation. He wouldn't have anything to do with a mess like this. He has absolutely no use for publicity."

"Maybe the guy he's with has somebody involved."

"Could be. When they leave, follow them to their car. If the big lug is driving, nail the plate number. We'll do a check on him. Maybe there's an angle."

"I'm supposed to head back to finish post-production on that L.A.P.D. internal affairs piece."

"Good for you to be out of the goddamn studio. News is in the field. That's how we'll pump back up ratings. Besides, don't have to worry about catching a Belvedere when you're banging it out on the streets."

"Right you are," Roland requisitely concedes.

The four men stand a little too tall, a tad too confidently on thick branches near the top of soaring trees. Their faces evidence greater hubris than angst; their eyes a mist of cannabis. The assemblage of military garb is more state of the art and statement than efficiency. Their laser-scope rifles are overly encumbered with camouflage. As Hopper studies them, he notes their binoculars trained well on every possible route to their positions and bunker above, but, to their rue, not the impossible one.

They go down serially and identically. Hopper first fires from a tranquilizer gun a ballistic syringe and hypodermic needle into the neck area that instantly jets an immobilizing drug into each guard's bloodstream. Before the sentries can purge the needle or grasp a communication device from their belt, Hopper whistles a blunt arrow to the side of the head that sends them into a free fall to ground, where they land as lumps of splayed bones and lost cognizance. A master of the assailant's protocol, Hopper makes short work of the vaunted sentries in just under six minutes.

As Greg and House alternate between canvassing trees on high, grousing over the obvious, debating the unobvious, and performing a vigorous post-mortem on why they hadn't made a pit stop for grub-to-go before hitting the mountains, Hopper appears. With his windbreaker, pressed khakis, and pleated smile, he comes across more as a badminton groupie than vanquisher of four accomplished paramilitaries.

"How was the hike?" Greg asks with manufactured light words and darkened face.

"Enjoyed the sights—in between taking in all your texts," lightly responds Hopper, plagued little by his friend's demeanor.

House nods at electronic equipment bolted onto roofs of nearby vans. "They have enough channel running through the air here to pick up squirrels squabbling."

"Let's drive down the hill," Greg says as he turns away, awaiting neither consent nor conscription.

While Greg, House, and Hopper are leaving toward the road, Agent McManus, a 50-year-old man wearing an inconspicuous field outfit and mien of experience, stands apart from a group of government types in muffled debate. As he reviews printouts, an aide-de-camp rushes to him. "Sir, the sentries have disappeared from the trees."

"Since when?" McManus contests, flicking a finger at sheets he holds. "Motion sensors show positive human readings in all these areas. This data is no more than twenty minutes old."

"Sir, we have confirmed reports of at least two heavily armed targets down. We strongly believe we have two more."

McManus takes a moment to braise this revelation in furrowed reflection before intensely scouring the immediate area. His eyes settle on three men exiting the encampment.

On the way down the mountain, House veers the Pontiac onto a deep shoulder and locks the brakes. Hopper settles his

Jeep in the GTO's dust. Greg is out of the passenger seat as House is setting the parking brake. Face uneven with anger, eyes toxic, Greg stamps to the Jeep and is on Hopper before his seatbelt is released.

"Mind telling me what the fuck that was about?"

"Doing what I could to save innocent people," Hopper routinely replies as he steps from the Jeep.

"What do you think will happen because of that?"

"I'm hoping those hostages will be with their families tonight."

"I don't mean about them," Greg spits out. "I mean about us. You know how much time the Pro, Apostoli, and I spent communicating with generals, admirals, commanders… just about any salad shirt you could think of… making sure our tracks were covered, files wiped clean so we wouldn't wake up in cold sweats worrying about who might be coming back at us or our families." Greg cranks up the staple-gun staccato. "What was it all ten of us agreed on that last flight out of Sudan — to keep a low profile… a *low fucking profile*."

Hopper examines his wrists, then cynically observes, "Gee, handcuffs must've slipped off on the way down the hill." He motions to his vehicle. "The Jeep is clean. No problem there. Somebody plant a bug on House's hog?"

Greg turns to House, vying for an ally. "Can you believe this guy? Did someone airlift him in a time capsule from the Pepsi Generation?" Greg wheels to Hopper. "Did you see all those helos in the sky? How many of them do you think are surveillance? When they find out those sentries have suddenly disappeared from the trees, you think they'll just chalk it up to all the shooters having collective migraines at the same exact moment and passing out from pain? You don't think they'll have prints on you over the wire within an hour?"

Hopper chooses not to match Greg's vitriol. "Unless they have some new camera lens that films through tree branches, camouflage gear, and a mask," Hopper calmly debriefs his friend, "I don't think we have an issue. Besides, only reason I showed my face was to circle back with you. Why did you come up?"

House taps the trunk of the Pontiac. "Drag bags in here ain't exactly filled with broomstick handles. You caught fire not that long ago. Who knows what could've happened to you. Wanted to make sure we had your back."

Greg drops it down a notch. "Help me with this, Hopper. You're convinced we were all bestowed this gift from that old man for a purpose, to, in one way or the other, do right with it. I'm with you to there. But how does that make it your assign-ment to save the world before the next U.N. General Assembly? Haven't we all taken up arms enough in our lives? Couldn't you just, over time, wage war against a disease threatening humanity or knuckleheads who paint their faces for croquet matches? What about that?"

Hopper, proudly, replies, "I did something really good to-day... and it's been a long time since I could say that."

House weighs in without reservation. "You're a hero, buddy, just like you've always been."

Greg throws a sharp glance at the seditionist before returning his attention to Hopper. "House is right. You did a great thing. You may have given some kids long lives they deserve. But what if a year from now, you could save a hundred lives? What if ten years from now, you need this chance you believe in to save the life of the son you may have? If you possess the gift, does it mean you have to risk it this week? You can only take so many chances like just now before you cash it in. None of us would've ever tried a one-man cowboy move you just did. We made it through all those shit-storms as a team. You know that."

"I understand. But the thing is, you're more conservative with your life since we've come back. I'm not. It's up to you how to manage what the old man gave us. You do it your way, I'll do it mine."

"Let me tell you something, Hop. You're not in this thing stand-alone. How long do you think it will take for a stunt like today to draw attention to the rest of us? With this kind of high-profile stuff, someone eventually will start putting pieces together. I don't need it. My legal practice doesn't need it."

Hopper's ire shows its first pulse. "I know what you need. What you need is to keep your world safe and cozy. That's what you're so worked up over, what you're drumming about. You're more concerned about yourself than any of us. What you're not thinking about are teenagers in a bunker with shotguns rammed down their throats. And I can *guarantee* the other thing you're not thinking about now: me… what it means for me to take those kids — frightened to death — out of harm's way." Hopper abruptly steps to the solace of several nearby somber trees.

Greg is left standing with words to issue, but without object. He casts eyes on House, who offers, "He was the brave one today — somebody special. He's been searching for a day like this since we stashed our gear. Nothing wrong with his wanting time in his own sun as long as he keeps us clean, Greg — nothing at all."

House trails after Hopper. Greg stands dismayed in a gravel court with neither witness nor jury to address.

A bedraggled Greg lumbers into the unlighted den and sags into his desk chair. He inspects the floor covering of files and legal books blued by the computer screensaver. His brain an ashtray overflowing from the day's fallout, he cannot remotely process tasks he hastily left to deal with Hopper.

Diane, in nightgown, robe, and patent irritation, appears at the doorway. "What time did you get in?"

"A bit ago."

"Sutter phoned, said he couldn't call through on your cell. You were supposed to meet him this afternoon at the office… a discovery briefing or something on the Streeter case."

Greg shelves this along with other distress and looks aimlessly into the terminal.

"Are you having an affair, Greg?" Diane asks without preamble.

"No. Why would you say that?"

"Because the past few weeks, you've been somewhere off in space… as if I'm not here."

"Part of it's my dad," Greg hollowly replies.

"It's something more than your dad."

"It's *not* another woman. House needed help. That's it."

Greg's explanation evidently carries the day. "I saw another bill from Dr. Klein's office. You're not at risk of having your father's condition, are you?"

"No, just a small adjustment to my medication. Nothing major."

Diane holds out a hand. "Come to bed. You can't possibly work now."

Greg's day needs no more dispute; he switches off the screen.

It really doesn't matter if someone in the health club is ripping off sit-ups, grinding through military presses, or suffering a spin class. Any view through the glass wall into the racquetball court tells the same story: the woman is far superior to the three men with whom she is playing doubles. It matters not if a deep corner shot comes screaming off a wall like an unloosed proton, she charges after it… and, most the time, chases it down. In stark contrast is her partner, whose midsection is a half-step behind his feet, which are usually a full step behind the ball, and who is given to waving at passing shots with the vigor of a parade-fatigued celebrity.

One can tell from subtle head dips and brief exchanges of players milling outside the glass walls that all is not entirely kosher on Court 4. At crucial points, the woman's two wide-bodied opponents, virtuosos neither, take up sphinxlike positions in the middle of the court, making it all but impossible for her to return direct shots off the front wall. If the maneuver is legal, it certainly isn't cricket. Undaunted, the woman plays on, admirably acquitting her team, but eventually falling to the inequity before her and indolence to her side.

When she retires from the court, the female player does so alone. Her partner buddies up to the other two fellows, and, consumed with man-speak spawned by sweaty competition, he slumps off with them to the men's locker room. When they exit 20 minutes later in casual clothes, gym tote in one hand and clothing bag with police uniform in the other, Trina is alone on a vacant court, driving backhand after incendiary backhand into the wall.

There is nothing quite like a neighborhood bar... as long as a soul is free to pick his neighborhood. This particular spot, Tailspin & Tonic, is nestled in the shank of a district where gather folks who do heavy lifting in the production end of the entertainment industry. The alcohol-minded patrons here don't view the movie business as particularly arty, glamorous, trendy, select, or compelling, but rather the source of a hard-earned paycheck... and an inconstant one at that. Drinks are rarely ordered with ice and without certitude. Island getaways, haute couture, and trending show biz celebs are rarely conversation pieces at Tailspin & Tonic.

House is a regular here. He likes the fact that the joint isn't lousy with lover boys, looky-loos, or losers... well, at least not too many of the last. He is ably surviving a disastrous day at the establishment (the disaster, of course, being a broken window shade letting in sunlight). House is about to call for another Tangueray Ten on the rocks with a Grey Goose float, but countermands himself and reduces it a grade to Tangueray and soda. He is pretty damned looped, he judiciously admits to himself, and he's yet to celebrate approaching sunset.

As House scrolls through a newspaper article about the mysterious and chivalrous rescue of teenage hostages held by mountain cultists, a stocky man takes a wide berth as he bellies up to the bar next to him. Tully Simkins, whose dark olive skin is the product of a Cajun father from New Iberia, Louisiana and Cherokee mother from parts of Oklahoma basically unknown, is one to countenance little fluff. His 50-plus years on this vale have left him less wrinkled and leathered than corded. Muscles run up from his Hawaiian shirt, course his neck, and set his jaw and cheekbones in unforgiving, hard lines. His battered and scarred fingers sprout in more directions than summer crabgrass. It is a mild surprise that his black hair has shown the nerve to reveal gray.

"Hey House," he says in a burry voice.

"Thanks for coming out, Tull."

Tully reaches under his shirt, pulls an envelope from his waist, and sets it on the bar. "Most I could come up with is thirty-five."

"Can't tell you what this means."

"Know it doesn't get you where you need to be."

"It'll take my niece somewhere past where she is now."

Tully nods to the bartender who, in turn, makes a Pavlovian reach for a bottle of Wild Turkey.

House slips the envelope into his pocket. "I'll put together a promissory note and bring it to the lot Tuesday."

"No need to paper it; we're cool."

Tully turns the barstool with his rump, trying to keep his torso parallel to the bar. This ad hoc shot at lower-back alignment produces more wincing than righting and relief. When his neat double Wild Turkey arrives on cue, Tully has a handful of pills ready to throw down the gullet. He tilts back slightly to digest his preemption of the sinister onset of pain.

"For the back?" House inquires.

"Back, neck, groin, knees, headaches… " Tully pounds down the last of his glass and displays it to the bartender for refreshing. "Know more doctors than I do directors in this god-damn town."

"But the business has been good to you."

"Good for my family."

"Wearing down, compadre?"

"Can only trick fate so long, House. You know that."

House takes a strong sampling from his cocktail. "And fate can be damn tricky."

Hopper scrapes cream paint from stucco walls beneath eaves of the Spanish tile roof of Our Lady of Perpetual Hope Church. As he takes a moment to swab sweat dripping from his spongy ball cap, he views the schoolyard. It is no longer the occidental province of Irish, Italian, German, and Polish kids of his youth. Now for every ruddy-faced youngster, there are three of dark complexion. Yet the collective exuberance, jocularity, mischievousness, and wealth of abandon from Hopper's time are an unmistakable legacy.

He rubs cloth of his shirt on his streaked sunglasses and gazes at his old neighborhood, where square footage was meager, but hope ever bountiful. The future then was a crucible where seemingly any admixture of determination and effort might well meld into starry reward. Hopper wonders when the last of that idealism had leaked from him. It is, he now thinks apt to conclude, sometime after he rationalized taking human life for just cause and before he tied his last knot on a makeshift cross over a grave of an innocent in some hellhole of humanity.

Hopper's eyes settle beyond a marquee softball game, conclaves of chattering girls, rogue rounds of grab-ass, and roaming teachers to a lone figure bouncing a soccer ball from his feet to shoulders, head, and back down as if on a magician's tether. It is Honorio. While Hopper knows more about the inner workings of the Church's gabby sodalities than he does soccer, it is clear that this young boy displays an extraordinary talent. It isn't so much his fluidity and coordination as his precociously stolid expression while controlling the white ball in uncanny orbit around him.

About to re-employ his scraper, Hopper notes a blacked-out SUV parked a short distance from the schoolyard. Greg's admonitory words of snoops getting a line on him creep into his mind. Hopper had been certain that he was too well masked when among the trees to be identified. He'd even changed the plates on his Jeep so he couldn't be tracked on the way up or down the mountain. But he had learned early to never discount what he might not logically suspect.

He peels off his sunglasses for an unimpaired look. No unusual antenna from the SUV... at least not clearly visible. Since Hopper had come to know few uncertainties confrontation didn't clarify, he scales down the ladder.

As he hastens toward the SUV, it abruptly starts and takes off. Hopper records the license number.

If one of the uninitiated were to speculate on office décor of a high-profile metropolitan television reporter, he might spot walls with industry awards, antiqued photos of Mr. TV and the telegenic, glossy shots from notable field reports, and glowing reviews of media cognoscenti. Well, there is some of that around Mitch Arnett, but more prominent are framed first pages of lawsuits served on him by a host of plaintiffs, ranging from celebrities to police captains to basketball centers to clerics. The journalist Arnett permits not decorum, protocol, good taste, or baseline civility to deter goosing of ratings.

Roland Brandt sits across an outsize desk from his boss as he reads from a computer tablet. "The big guy's name is Stackhouse. He's a stuntman—fairly well known around town. Not an elite guy, but pretty good. He went to a small college in Northern

California, had some odd jobs as a cook to pay his way through school… "

"Roland," Arnett snaps, "I'm looking for a fucking *news* story here, not a narrative of his family photo album."

Roland halts his fingers. "Well, there's not much more to tell."

"You have guys in what, their mid-forties? There should be reams of data on them from our sources."

"Should be, but from the time just after Stackhouse and the attorney graduated from college until their mid-thirties, their screens are virtually blank."

"Blank? What in the hell does that mean? No credit transactions? No email traffic? No air travel? What?"

"No anything."

"For ten years?" Arnett objects with an open, poised hand. "Come on. What did they live on? Shekels dug from the earth? They had to bank somewhere."

"Nope. Only explanation I can think of is that they were out of the country, but the bitch of it is there are no records of their even having passports during that period."

"You check with Pfannel?"

"That I did. He couldn't find a log of either the stuntman or attorney coming in or out of the country back then." Anticipating Arnett before he can speak, Roland adds, "*And* I had him contact Brashier. Brashier reached out to his people overseas. Nothing anywhere about the two being stamped… Canada, Mexico, Europe, South America, Middle East, Africa, China… you name it."

"What the fuck?"

Roland returns his attention to the computer nestled in his lap. "Since they came back on radar, both Stackhouse and Hardisty have kept very low profiles. Hardisty went to law school, then straight to the firm he's with. Has a wife. No blips. Stackhouse fell into the stunt business after bouncing around. Had a marriage that lasted a couple of years. He and his wife did the divorce themselves… no lawyers, no debris." Roland responds to Arnett's souring face. "But there *is* one thing."

Arnett shoots a glance at his desk clock, then to Roland. "Hope it's a helluva lot better than what you've served up so far."

"Three years ago, Stackhouse got into a beef at a bar outside Santa Barbara. Supposed to be a pretty laid-back place… mostly mellow, middle-age people. Five bikers on the way to Mexico from the Bay Area stopped in, had a few pops, and started jacking up patrons. Stackhouse, who was pretty well oiled himself, took exception."

"Stackhouse like his cocktails?"

"Oh, yeah. Anyway, the stuntman squared up with all five bikers."

"Big brawl?"

Roland noses the screen. "No, closer to a summary execution. Stackhouse laid them all out inside a minute… and two had blades."

"Reading from the police report?" Arnett asks.

"That I am."

"Good man."

Roland traces his finger under lines of print. "According to one witness, Stackhouse went after the bikers like a fat Bruce Lee… eyes cold as death."

"Well, our guy clearly has chops in hand-to-hand combat. Anything else?"

"Hardisty was at the police station within an hour of the incident. No charges were filed against the stuntman."

Arnett spins in his seat and peers out the window at a plaza fountain spawning elaborate water gymnastics. "Let's see where we are. Our third guy, the mystery one, who looks like he could get the better of an earth-mover, appears on the mountain, meets with what appear to be two friends who have been hanging around for some while, and, in an instant, they depart together. By all evidence, just before the guy we have yet to I.D. rendezvous with the other two, well-trained coverts take out four expert riflemen that the sum total of law enforcement agencies and military in the entire area couldn't budge. The coverts do this *without* casualties and *without* anyone remotely fixing on them, even though there are more helicopters in the sky than Coppola had in the Philippines. Now, it sounds like one of the three we spotted, this Stackhouse, is a very serious hand at martial arts. So you'd have to say that if the mystery guy was the one of the coverts that cleared out the mountain, he and his buddy the stuntman have skill sets. Couple this with Hardisty and Stackhouse being espionage-type dark for ten years or so after college, and what pops out of the hopper?"

"With those kind of trades, have to say you're looking at spec ops, likely very high-end," Roland concludes for the chief.

Arnett turns back to Roland. "But why does the third guy risk exposure when you tell me his two friends have a blotter on their past and made a career keeping their heads down? Doesn't sound consistent with their DNA. And why would he be the only covert to show his face? What happened to the others who erased the sentries?"

"That's the rub. Can we put someone on these people?"

"With what we're laying out for Palladian on the Brentwood prostitution ring, I'd have to make a real strong case to mahogany row, and I don't think we're there yet. If our numbers were up, I could probably swing it." Arnett bounces his fingers on the desk. "Stay on the stuntman... as much as you can."

"I was on him yesterday... *my day off*," Roland retorts.

"Any leads?"

"He spent the afternoon and early evening in a North Hollywood bar, then went home after his friend, another stuntman, piled him into a cab. So far, the third guy is nowhere to be seen."

"What about the attorney?"
"All he does is work."
"Lay off him for now."

Greg glares at library shelves of bound legal reports surrounding him on a day that was thankfully passing with relative calm. Sometimes the tomes' oppressive presence makes him long for a swarm of locusts with a palate for parchment. He steps over to a window and cracks it open. Fresh air does little to stem blood pulsing up his neck to his forehead. Dr. Klein's increase in medication is proving largely ineffective, but, then again, it probably wasn't formulated to contend with frayed marriages, rattled friendships, a pressure-cooker caseload, and assimilating the prospect of resurrection.

As Greg surveys commute traffic snaking to the suburbs, Sutter Nance, suited a click down from formal wear, hurries by the door to the law library. He stops and, discernibly displeased, observes Greg gazing out the window. He extends his neck inside and sharply inquires, "Working on Streeter?"

Greg, a mite unsettled, turns to Nance. "Thinking through strategies."

"With what this firm has riding on the case, I would have hoped you'd be fixed on that by now. Had you been here this past weekend as we had discussed, I might've been able to review the matter with you."

"I'll manage," Greg curtly replies. The Monday mea culpa should have been contrition enough, he thinks to himself.

Nance covers Greg with steely eyes before moving on.

The young man and woman, Allan and Greta, both in humdrum business attire, sit at a long panel with enough dials, switches, buttons, and gizmos to have been a transplant from Houston Ground Control. (While Greta bears understated Scandinavian beauty and eager eyes, Allan has the nerdish, retreat-to-big-data comportment of one who values a search button above a beer.) On the counter below the panel are blunt arrowheads, ballistic syringes, and hypodermic needles with a tailpiece. Before them in the blackish room are four large wall screens comprising a perfect square. On each are separate aerials shots of the mountain range where Hopper performed his handiwork. Agent McManus, carrying the expression of a disgruntled process server, strides purposefully into the room and stands behind the two.

"What do we have?"

Greta braves an answer. "We'll run Screen Two in quartertime." She switches on a slow-motion video of a mass of very tall trees and zooms to one with dense branches. No discernible movement is evident until, after several seconds, there is a partial image of a man in paramilitary gear falling in a heap to ground.

McManus momentarily waits for more, then harshly issues, "That's it?"

"We've been over every aerial photo and frame of film the day of the capture, and that's the only visual of sentry activity we're able to recognize. As I told you, we have absolutely nothing on the perps."

"How long have you been at this?"

"Since 6:00 a.m. yesterday morning, sir."

Hoping to stymie further dissection by her superior, Greta nets out the situation. "The sentries chose for their stations those trees with extreme cover. That's the reason air recon was ineffective and a top-down offensive against them infeasible. When the sentries fell, it was more or less a straight drop, so nothing appears outside the perimeter of the trees, except," pointing to the image, "that. Whoever took them out stayed completely off screen."

McManus digests this information as happily as he would a cement bon bon. "Any change in the condition of the sentries?"

"Two are out of I.C.U., but they all have a long way to go—cracked vertebrae; concussions; broken ribs, legs, and arms; and severe contusions. Long-term prognosis, though, is good."

"Too bad," McManus tartly notes. "We learning anything from the wires in their hospital rooms?"

"They have no idea what happened. Their stories are exactly the same. They felt a stinging sensation in their neck, a thud to their heads, then they don't remember anything until they were coming down the mountain in paramedic vans."

McManus selects a seat next to Allan. "What's your take?"

"In my view," Allan opines in an oddly concocted basso profundo voice, "it's next to impossible for a shooter to fire a dart gun and then follow up with a club arrow that quickly and accurately. Four sentries down inside ten to fifteen minutes... had to be a two-man team... at least."

McManus looks to the comely Greta, who nods in unanimity. "Executing under all that surveillance without detection, it's definitely a team, and one with true craft."

"So we likely have two or more assets of high accomplishment on the ground and you have nada on them or who they might be? Is that where we are?"

"Sir," Greta says less out of apology than exasperation, "we've been over and over every air record we have. We do have findings of some motion in target areas, but we really can't be sure if it's human or animal life." In reaction to McManus's stone face: "I don't know what to say other than it's a kind of deployment we just don't see in a domestic civilian situation."

McManus churns considerations in his mind. "Did you drill down on the three men I described?"

"The copter shots were way too opaque for any kind of I.D.," Greta advises McManus. "But you're right. Two of them came into the encampment together, spent about an hour and a half mostly talking to each other. The third one joined them, then almost immediately after, they all left. We have no footage or photos of the third until he met with the other two."

"Did he come out of the woods or from the road?" McManus queries.

"The road," reports Allan.

"And only the third one was entirely off surveillance while the sentries went down?"

"Yes."

McManus's face winds tighter. "Bring up what you have on those three."

Playing the instrument panel with nimble dexterity, Greta quickly has on Screen One an enhanced, albeit nondescript, overhead shot of a huddled Greg, House, and Hopper. Identification is hopeless.

"That's the best you have?"

Greta and Allan demurringly nod in unison.

McManus moves around the control board to the screen, studies images, and then points to the bottom of the shot. "See this? There are two vans from local television stations. They were issuing live reports every couple of hours. Review their film that day. Maybe they caught these three... or at least one of them in the background. Slim chance, but worth throwing out a line."

"Might take a bit of time," Allan hesitantly forewarns his superior.

"Oh, no rush," McManus sourly replies. "I only have one phone or another lighting up every twenty minutes with D.C. grilling my fucking ass on how this complicated situation I so painstakingly described in my dailies was defused in a half-hour by a team of cowboys."

McManus is quickly out the door, leaving the young pair to hammer the telephones.

Greg, wilted and pallid, appearing to emerge from a guest slot in the Spanish Inquisition, exits a courtroom, lugging a large briefcase in one hand and scrolling through emails on his cell phone with the other. He finds the respite of a hallway bench, where he begins knocking out responses on his cell. As he busies his screen with print, a shadow settles over him. Trina, fully uniformed, smiles down on her friend. "Look a little preoccupied there, counselor."

"Hey, what brings you here?"

"Had to testify at a preliminary hearing on the shooting outside of Primo's."

"Did you tell them you received my vote for the Wild Bill Hickok Award of the week on that one?"

"No, told them that's how I skip out on a bar bill when it's my night to buy."

For the first time in the day, Greg's face finds a novel dynamic: a smile.

"Headed back to the office?" Trina asks.

"I should."

"No, you should deep-six that load you're carrying and meet me at Primo's," Trina peppily advises Greg.

"I should?"

"Most definitely."

Greg and Trina are squeezed into a small table near the service corridor at Primo's, prospering with patrons, dart enthusiasts, lager devotees, and purgation of employee angst. As is often the case, revelry is bunny-hopping with bravado throughout the premises. Greg has his mitts on a beer mug while Trina is well into a cocktail with decidedly little frou-frou.

"Honestly, Greg, I think you're way too wound up over this thing. If you don't think the gift is real, just ignore it."

"I can, but I can't ignore what it's doing to a friend, can you?"

"Yes. Hopper's drummer has always had a helter-skelter beat."

"Do you really believe that old man has some special power?"

Trina permits the conversation to skip a moment, then, "I tracked the paramedics who treated Hop." Trina potently eyes Greg; he momentarily walls off his conscience so not to buckle. She continues. "They told me the same thing they told you: Hopper flat-lined in that van, then came back to life—no stimulants, no jolt, no jump-start injections. They were convinced he was so far gone that none of that would do any good. The word one of them used to describe Hopper's reviving was 'miraculous.' How do you explain that?"

Greg quickly moves off the spot on which Trina has placed him. "I didn't have all that much time with the paramedics. They really convinced you Hopper came back?"

"I convinced myself."

"What are you going to do about it?"

"Not get worked up about it is what I'm going to do about it."

"You agree, then, that you don't have to turn your world around today or tomorrow because of it?"

Trina, used to Greg's ringmanship, will have none of it. "I agree that whatever we were given is personal to each of us."

Greg, not easily derailed, comes back, "But we need to help each other. There are huge ramifications to how we interpret this thing. One of us could end up dead."

"Maybe it's less a gift and more a challenge." Trina allows the consideration to settle in before tacking on, "But that's something you the trial attorney probably have run through your mind how many times, how many different ways?"

Greg exercises his practiced art of query-deflection. "Does that mean we just let each other go, even if we see disaster around the corner? We've always covered each other's six, haven't we?"

Trina rattles down some of her cocktail and then throws a shoulder into her logic. "Apostoli and you have handled civilian life better than any of us... House, Lucci, the Pro, me, everyone else. Judson and you dove into law school and lost yourselves in your careers. I couldn't be happier for the two of you. The rest of us couldn't go cold turkey on the adrenaline. That's why Nello and I wear a badge, House does those crazy stunts, and the Pro and Emma do whatever in the hell they do. Hopper, the Deacon, and Lance have just never found their niche... or their fix. I'm not sure Lance ever will, but now at least Hopper has something he can latch onto."

"We all have a lot riding on keeping our missions dark."

"There are huge consequences for any outsider that tries to pry open the lid on our history. You and Judson made sure of that."

Greg lets some air from his campaigning. "That's true. I just don't want to see Hopper... or you or House do something you don't walk away from."

"If we do, that's our choice. It goes wrong, we're the only ones who suffer. We don't have a Diane waiting at home."

"You're not going to try anything crazy, are you?"

"Wasn't it in Libya that you said I was the craziest woman you've ever known?"

"Actually, it was Mali."

"Well?"

"You make a point."

Working on a movie location, particularly at night, has its advantages, e.g., a regular working stiff who's not on immediate call can rather easily find a place to lose himself from your typical pain-in-the-ass production assistant. However, Laird Parkins is not the average nettlesome set P.A. Despite the fact that for some time House has been under the hood of a stunt car in a warehouse a couple blocks from the city street that is blocked off for a shoot, Laird manages to root him out.

Taking a moment to dig through his toolbox on a workbench a reach away, the stuntman notices the assistant approaching. He edgily asks, "Hey, Laird, what brings you here from video village?"

"House, we have a problem," Laird informs with a collegiality that simply doesn't wash.

"What do you mean 'we,' chief?"

"Brock wants to change the stunt."

"The stunt tonight?"

Laird nods.

"I just spent two hours lining it out."

"The scene needs more punch."

"We both know who needs the punch."

"Take a look at this."

House snatches Laird's clipboard. He does not have to delve far into the workup to arrive at a verdict. "Has this fucker been in Makeup sniffing fingernail polish?"

"It's not something you can do?" Laird reacts with a bewilderment worthy of cameras on the set.

"Sure, it's something I can do… if you bring in the pope to part gravity during the stunt."

"You know how much we have at stake on this film."

House looks up from the clipboard, events of the past few weeks carbonating his mind. "Yeah, I know. Brock's last two features have tanked, and the dailies on this one aren't exactly bringing out pompoms over the hill at the studio. We're behind schedule to boot. Way I see it, you boys are up against it."

"Brock is perfectly certain this stunt can help turn the film around," Laird resolutely declares.

House scratches a number on Laird's papers and flips it around. "Does he believe that much?"

After Laird has his properly paralytic moment, he is immediately on the offensive. "That figure is outlandish… grossly over market. I'll call Simkins… "

House steps on Laird's pushback. "No, you won't, because he's on a redeye to a family funeral in Breaux Bridge. Capidonica is on location in North Carolina, and Reed's concussion is so bad he still thinks his head is on a fucking pogo stick. Outside of those three, you have no other way to go."

"What will you do with that kind of money, House?" Laird scoffs.

"I have plans."

"What? Install hotplates in the dashboard on that monstrosity you drive?"

House delivers the clipboard to Laird. "That's the sell. Your star and his producer buddy don't want to ante up, my guess is that Brock's leading lady on his next film will be a chimp in a hoop dress." House returns to his tools.

Even at 1:30 a.m. on a cordoned-off street in a lightly traveled commercial area etched into the northern outback of the San Fernando Valley, the still is unusual, punctuated only by a crew readying to roll cameras from multiple angles. Extras, technicians, those without immediate function, and cast groupies are pinched into cracks and crevices along the street out of filming range. Most had been stationed some while to witness the stunt that couldn't be; the hum of their anticipation is now nearly mute.

Soon enough, the director, of Orson Welles girth and Hitchcock jowls, with Brock Branning, movie star and script improvisatore, at his side, calls for action. A flatbed truck, its cab pocked with faux bullet holes, takes off from the far end of the street under fabricated repair. When the truck has gained speed, House guns a souped-up stunt car in pursuit. As he quickly gains ground, the flatbed veers to the edge of the street. House steers his car close to the sidewalk, sending a stunt vagrant diving into a doorway. He comes up on a pile of dirt and asphalt chunks (disguising a heavily fortified ramp), gives gas to his car, hits the pile squarely, and takes off for the back of the speeding truck. Bystanders are mesmerized as they watch House in flight.

Astonishingly, House lands squarely on the truck deck. His car rams violently into the cab and caroms backward, sending the rear of the car off the edge of the flatbed at a slight angle... secure, but still exposed. The set raucously erupts in hoots of approval and applause; Brock and the blimp director breathe deeply of air filled with relief, redemption, and the prospect of tidy box-office receipts. As the flatbed starts to decelerate, it courses too close to the sidewalk. The bumper of House's car catches a light pole, jerking it off the flatbed and sending it into an uncontrolled roll in the wake of the truck. Paramedics, on ready-alert, tear to House. Those not numbly aghast sprint after them.

A forlorn Hopper sits alone in an antiseptic Intensive-Care-Unit waiting room. His drained, olive complexion neatly complements drab custard furniture. He absently removes his cell phone and checks it, for what purpose he is wholly unaware.

Greg barges through corridor doors. He looks first at Hopper, then at vacant chairs next to him, hoping, one might guess, for a palatable alternative.

"What do we know?" Greg asks, accusation powdering his tone.

"He's in critical condition... highly unstable," Hopper thinly responds.

"Where's Trina?"

Hopper motions to I.C.U. "In there with the surgeon."

"What form of human sacrifice was he trying with that fucking stunt?"

"Something they cooked up last night. Trina talked to the director's assistant."

Greg drops his carcass into a seat, takes an irritated breath, and again hollowly pans the room. "Can we see him?"

"That's what Trina's trying to arrange."

"Anyone spoke to the paramedics?"

"They were gone by the time I arrived."

Greg rests his head against the wall and shutters his eyes.

Trina emerges through swinging doors from I.C.U. "Not good," she murmurs.

"Have faith," Hopper responds.

Greg is not to be heartened. "Have faith! Are you expecting the old man to waltz in here, paint a road of yellow brick to House's bed, and magically put him back together?"

"I believe House will come out of there."

"I know you do. House knows you do. You think he'd be in there if you hadn't decided to make this thing with the old man your life mantra?"

"That's bogus and bullshit," Trina objects. "Nobody pushes House's button. *Nobody.*"

This does little to stanch the rush of Greg's aggravation. "If that's true, then why did he all of a sudden try something so absolutely fucking lunatic?"

"Because Cord's daughter needs money for treatment," Trina spits back.

"Why didn't he ask me? I could've helped raise it."

"Because he said we all already ask you for too much," Hopper lets out without rancor.

Greg's words to House on the mountain road boil to his brain, acidically drip to his conscience, and foil any rat-a-tat response. Guilt immediately squelches his ire.

At that moment, Diane enters the waiting room from the corridor. Before she can digest the scene, a buttoned-up I.C.U. nurse appears and announces in a clipped voice, "You have three minutes, no more."

Trina, Greg, Diane, and Hopper trail the nurse into the Unit. An aisle divides 20 beds. Doctors and nurses efficiently move from one station to another, where patients, some of whom appear to be little beyond freshly wrapped mummies, are laced into webs of I.V.s, monitors, breathing apparatuses, and restraints.

When they come upon House in Bed 14, Diane grabs Greg's arm and folds into her husband. The sight is not for the fainthearted. The right side of House's bruised, blue cheek is so swollen it's flush with his nose and reduces his eye to a slit. Stitches zipper a long, deep gash on his forehead. His heavily bandaged right arm and left leg are slung and immobilized. Greg, Trina, and Hopper spunkily maintain their composure; Diane cannot harness tears.

Greg asks the nurse, who is standing behind a monitor tracking House's fragile hold on life, "Has he been conscious at all?"

"No sir, he has not," the nurse responds with military efficiency before shuttling to another patient.

Hopper leans over House, whose breathing is largely generated through a ventilator tube lodged in his mouth. "We're here with you now, buddy."

As eyes of the group bounce from House to the monitors to one another, the seasoned lead doctor approaches. His angular face and thin, square wire-rim glasses bespeak more analytics than emergency.

"Thank you for giving us this time, Doctor," Trina says.

"Does the patient have immediate family in the vicinity?" the Unit chief managerially inquires.

"Only a brother; he's unavailable," Greg responds.

The doctor presses his lips.

"He has a sister-in-law," Trina offers, "but she's not ready for this."

"Has she been notified?"

"Not yet."

"She should be." The physician deliberately circles faces of the visitors. "I cannot overstate the criticality of the patient's condition."

Tears stream down Diane's face; Greg holds her tight. "Doctor, we are prepared to spend any and all monies on Mr. Stackhouse's recovery," he stoutly declares.

"Quite frankly, it's not a matter of technology, care, or resources. The patient has suffered extensive internal injuries; his trauma is extreme."

As the doctor is about to step away, a low buzzing sound emits from House's set of monitors. He spins and reaches for needles on the tray latched to House's bed. "You must exit the unit immediately," he orders the group. The first nurse rushes back to assist. Another sternly states to the four, "This way." She systematically shepherds Greg, Diane, Hopper, and Trina to the outside area.

While they await further word, Greg consoles Diane as Hopper and Trina exchange obscure mumblings. The arc of their collective anxiety is quickly truncated. The first nurse reappears. "The doctor will be out to speak with you shortly."

"Did House die?" sobs Diane, her body fading to limp.

Though the nurse avoids downcast eyes for scarcely a second, it is proclamation enough.

"Oh, my God!" Diane cries out.

The nurse is instantly back behind I.C.U. doors.

As Diane presses herself into her husband's chest, he, House, and Trina, all oddly stoical, fairly gape at one another. When Diane looks up to Greg, she is taken back by his dispassion. She turns to Hopper and Trina. Seeing the same seeming suspension of emotion, Diane bellows, "What's the matter with all of you! Your friend just died! Don't you care!"

The three would have done well with a rehearsal for such interrogation, for they offer but confounded expressions.

Meanwhile, back in I.C.U., an attending doctor reads from the Bed-14 chart whilst dictating particulars of the patient's death. Oddly, he becomes distracted from his task by a blinking green light reflecting on his glasses. House's vital signs have reappeared, pulsing quickly upward.

When Hopper enters Our Lady of Perpetual Hope Church hauling his carpenter's toolbox, he somehow feels closer to his roots and religion. Trooping towards the confessional door on which he had earlier worked, he notices Honorio, doing his darndest to muffle crying, kneeling before a lighted candle at a devotional area in one of the Church's transepts.

Upon Hopper's deliberate rattling of his tools in setting them down, Honorio dries tears on his white cotton school shirt, makes a hasty sign of the cross, and stands. As he skirts the pews to cordon off his fragility, Hopper rings out, "Hi, Honorio."

The young boy stops and haltingly replies, "Hello."

"Do you have to go right home?"

"Ah, no, not right away."

"I could use some help… if you have a few minutes."

"Sure," Honorio responds, largely because he cannot feature another answer.

Hopper points to a side door. "Could you please open that so we have more light?"

"OK."

Though Hopper needed no more light than he did help, this gives Honorio a chance to step outside and settle himself. After Hopper had extracted a hand plane and level from his toolbox and is placing newspaper underneath the opened confessional door, Honorio, hands in pocket, shuffles over to Hopper. "How can I help?"

"Have to shave the edges of this door a little, maybe move the brackets a touch. Father says it sticks a bit when it closes. Want to make sure the door stays straight when I adjust it." Hopper exhibits the metal spirit level. "Need you to hold this against the side of the door and keep an eye on the tube. Gotta make sure the bubble in the green fluid stays between the two black lines. Do you see them?" Honorio nods. "Just press it against the side," Hopper instructs. Honorio secures the level in proper place.

"Is the bubble between the lines?"

"Pretty much."

"Good. Keep an eye on it for me, OK?"

"OK."

Hopper lets the comfortable silence of men at work bridge the boy's uneasiness before offering, "Saw you practicing with a soccer ball during lunch recess. Have you been at it a long time?"

"My uncles started practicing with me when I was two," Honorio, with a slight show of pride, advises Hopper.

"Could they play like your father?"

"They are very good, but my father was a professional." Honorio points to his heart. "He had *garra*."

"That's really something," Hopper comments. "So you're not on a soccer team?"

"No, my mother won't let me." Honorio's disappointment is palpable.

"I'm sure your mom is doing what she thinks is best."

The youngster gazes politely and distantly away.

Hopper runs his hand along the top of the door to inspect his workmanship. "How's that bubble?"

"Still pretty much in the middle," Honorio reports.

"Why don't you set it down a minute."

"OK." Honorio lowers his arms.

Hopper backs up to view the young boy more than the door. "Have you ever played football?"

"Never really been taught how."

"You wouldn't have to pick up much to be a kicker for Our Lady's team."

"I don't know how to kick a football."

"Well, since this is the first year your class will have a flag football team, most everybody will be learning new things."

Honorio permits a glimmer of enthusiasm. "I guess I could try, but you'd have to talk to my mother."

"Does she not want you playing sports?"

Honorio lets the level sway in his hand. "She's been talking about moving us to Uruguay... to live with my grandmother."

"Let me speak with your mom."

"OK."

Hopper stoops over and places the hand plane into the tool-box. "I can finish here later. I have footballs in my Jeep. Why don't we go to the schoolyard and let you boot some."

"Have to be home soon."

"We won't be long."

"OK."

Honorio, toting a knapsack on the back of his white uniform shirt, playfully tosses a football in the air as he bounces down the sidewalk of a street of bandbox, but well-maintained stucco homes. Hispanic children playing in the street eye Honorio respectfully as he passes. The blacked-out SUV that Hopper had seen parked in front of Our Lady of Perpetual Hope swings around a corner and rumbles behind Honorio. The passenger's window zips down, revealing a slickly attired Hispanic in his early twenties with swept-back black hair, shifty smile, darting eyes, and slimy demeanor. Honorio ignores the SUV as it putters next to him.

"Honorio," the Hispanic tries to engage the boy in a voice more syrupy than friendly, "what's with the football? You're never gonna get famous kicking field goals."

Honorio, eyes straight ahead, tucks the ball under his arm and picks up his step.

The Hispanic hangs from the window a dazzling powder-blue soccer jersey embroidered with ornate emblems, the number "10," and name "Fernandez" boldly stitched across the back. Honorio's resolve appears to wither in the face of the magnificent jersey with his emblazoned name.

As the boy's gait falters ever so slightly, the Hispanic spots an opening. "Our team is playing in a tournament in Pico Rivera this weekend. We need a striker." The Hispanic extends the jersey to Honorio, jiggling it so the lustrous threads reflect late afternoon sun. "There will be a lotta coaches from Mexico and South America there."

Honorio stops, seemingly in the trance of the shimmering jersey and enticing prospect. The Hispanic continues to pitch. "We have a bag in the back. It has your name on it. There's a warm-up suit, shoes, iPod, headphones… even money for meals." Honorio appears to be listening.

The SUV stops. When the Hispanic gets out and opens the rear door to display the player booty, Honorio suddenly bolts down a side yard, hops a fence, and is quickly out of sight and range.

Mitch Arnett, his coat the creation of a designer goofed on killer cannabis, stands behind TV-studio cameras as a makeup artist does her best to soften his harsh, hawkish features. As the reporter scans several pages, Roland blows into the studio through a side door. Like a cock of some grand walk, he boldly swings his shoulders as he parades to Arnett. "Have something that might interest you."

Arnett strays not from his pages. "I'm on in four minutes," he says rather dismissively. "Whadaya have?"

"Seems the Stackhouse guy from the mountains bought it on a hellacious stunt east of Simi Valley yesterday."

"Bought it. How can that be? We have people at the studios who would've piped us into that right away."

"He made it to the hospital before he kicked."

"We still should've got a line on it. Why in the hell are we paying people?"

"Well, there's a twist. After he died, he came back to life."

Arnett lowers the pages. "Are you looking to move into public broadcasting, Roland? Patients come back after they flat-line all the time. Why in the hell do you think they manufacture defibrillators?" Arnett reinstates the pages in front of his face.

"Didn't go down that way."

"How do you know?"

"Greased an orderly at the hospital where it happened."

Roland now has the full spectrum of Arnett's attention. "Greased somebody!" his boss exclaims. "We have enough ditched out to our regular sources and on the prostitution ring. Why weren't you at the hospital? I told you to stay on the guy."

"The shoot was at one in the morning. The stuntman was on the table until 7:45 a.m. I do sleep," Roland exonerates himself. "There were four visitors at Stackhouse's bed after the surgery. I think one of them may've been the mystery man from the mountains."

Arnett slowly releases himself from his snit, rolls the facts over in his mind, then waves off the makeup artist. "Look, I'm not against sifting through hospital records for the right story, even though if our risk management people got wind of it," Arnett nods upward, "they'd hang both you and me from one of those booms. But the cult hostage rescue is turning stale fast from all the coverage."

Arnett immediately addresses the mope coming over his assistant. "The piece that'll sell isn't so much what these people are doing now... even if one of them just pulled a Lazarus... it's what they've done—what they're all about. Since the Bin Laden thing, people can't get enough of the SEAL/sniper/special ops/snuff-the-terrorist stuff. We crack that with these people, tie in the cult angle, and we have something with major legs."

Roland perks back up. "That's what I'm thinking. They wouldn't do all they've done to blanket a decade of their lives if everything they did then was copacetic."

"To cover themselves in that way, these are some smart heads. But now it appears they're acting out of type." Arnett pauses a beat, then continues to steer his charge. "We have to exploit that to see what they have under their fingernails."

Roland edges toward a plead. "Any way we can put a tail on 'em?"

Arnett shakes off the suggestion. "The cufflinks would have to pull jack from someone else's line item, and I don't see them doing that... not with another dip in our ratings last week." Arnett primes Roland with a buccaneerish smile. "You just have to be creative... if you want credits on a piece, that is. I have a lot of segments competing for air time."

Arnett dishes the pages to Roland, rejiggers his expression, and, camera-ready, is off to his rightful place before the red lights.

House's brother Cord, face awash with reprieve, is at one of the prison outdoor visitor tables. Billy, his 10-year-old son, sits on his lap. Dad has a beefy arm slung around his waifish, sallow-faced teenage daughter Darcy. His wife Marianne, a full woman of 40 whose careworn facial features had long ago become impervious to the magic of makeup, is across from Cord, dabbing at tears from eyes daring a glimmer of optimism. If there is one thing evident in this family dynamic, the fellow on the other side of that table is most clearly her man.

In the parking lot, House, his battered face a mosaic of jaundice yellow, streaky purples, and red swatches, slumps in the passenger's seat of his Pontiac. Scars from stitches flank a nasty, healing notch dominating his forehead. Casts lock his right arm and left leg.

"Cord is a great guy. Kinda cute the way he calls you 'Willie Buck.'" This passes over House, not in a particular cutesy mood. "You did a really fine thing for your brother," admires Trina, relaxing behind the wheel as she imbibes the affection of Cord's family.

"Yeah, there's enough money for my niece's treatment and to keep Cord's place out of foreclosure until he's released."

House fidgets with his leg cast; relief is elusive.

"How's the peg?"

House winces. "Not as bad as the last couple of days."

"On happy pills?"

"If I wasn't, they have to cage me like the guys down there."

"Still having problems with sleep?"

"No more than usual, really. Shit, haven't had a straight eight hours since our first op."

"With you there. Never get more than three or four hours at a time myself."

"It's what we signed up for... I guess."

Trina, sparing little candor, notes, "Seems like this thing has you in a pretty mean funk."

"Yeah... maybe."

"From the pain? Because it stalls your work?" Trina brings up no lights. "Because you used your chance?" she further tries.

House shifts in his seat, attempting to ease discomfort from his injuries and a nettlesome truth. "Kinda."

Trina opens a hand toward the visiting area. "Look what you did. You kept your brother's family together with the money you made. From where I sit, that's a pretty damn noble thing."

"I guess," responds House, feeling no inclination to rub down the goose bumps. "When Greg came by yesterday, he was sorta pissed I didn't go to him for the dough."

"We can't keep tapping him whenever we're up against it," Trina counters. "Besides, even for Greg, it would've taken some time to assemble that kind of cash, and from what you said, your brother was on the clock."

"That he was."

Trina offers another perspective. "Correct me if I'm wrong, but by your pulling off that stunt, didn't you put yourself in line for some pretty sweet gigs?"

House ably harnesses his enthusiasm, "Yeah... if I want to sign up."

"Why wouldn't you?"

"I'm a good stuntman, Trina, not a great one. The real money is in the dicey shit like I tried out in the Valley. I keep at that stuff, and best that happens to me is I end up buffet meat for some surgeon's knife... just like this last time. Worst is I buy it."

"You took it to the edge under a black rain of AK-fire more times than I can remember, House. Risk never made you blink."

"I was a helluva lot better soldier than I am stunt driver." House emptily takes a gander at the prison yard, then exhales his malaise. "When I was laid up, I had a lot of time to think about things… first in a long while, really. You know, the fact that we made it out of all those scrapes, especially the two in Angola and Culiacan when we had thousands of rounds and all those fucking flashbangs exploding around us day and night, I think I came to believe I was kinda invincible… that we all are. I had no idea a body could be in this kind of agony." House slowly swivels his rigid neck to Trina. "How the hell did all ten of us survive so many missions… and walk away with all our parts intact? Were we just the luckiest sunvabitches ever to zip on cammies?"

"We planned, we executed" is Trina's pronouncement.

"The other side planned and executed."

"Not the way we did. There wasn't a contingency that didn't hit Greg's or Apostoli's computer screen. The Pro would put us through so many dry runs I still get sick to my stomach thinking about them. Ever remember seeing anything in the field that took us by surprise?"

While House may not have been entirely convinced, a retort he had not. "Can't argue with that." A moment passes between the two, then House fesses, "I think that gift in my back pocket was a lot of things… security, sense of being special, bit of magic, a high, I don't know what else. Now all that's gone."

"Would you rather still have it and your brother's family on the other side of the country?"

"No."

"Outside of being racked up pretty good, are you any worse off than before we met the old man?"

"No, I'm not."

"Well, then," Trina summarily concludes, "there you have it."

House traps a response in his throat.

Trina cracks the window, takes a sniff of country air, then follows her scent. "House, you're not expecting that old man to appear again the way he did for Hopper, are you?"

House, without invention, admits to her, "Think maybe I am."

In the cockpit of a single-engine plane, Greg takes in the expanse of desert below, an undulating, burlap carpet melding into an azure, cloudless sky. Knowing his cell phone is dead to barking clients and imperious senior partners serves as better medicine than anything Dr. Klein could peel off his prescription pad. Unspectacularly piloting this ordinary plane makes Greg feel spectacularly alive.

"Everything OK?" Marek, his fiftyish flight instructor with a military look, asks in a slight Polish accent.

"Couldn't be better."

A moment passes, then Greg casually asks, "When's your next run?"

Marek efficiently clicks off the schedule. "Wheels up tomorrow night at 7:00 p.m.; load going to Boise."

"Full cargo?"

"No, about three-quarters... and it's light—lamps with a lot of foam packing. Easy run." Marek peers outside his window. "Where do you want to have lunch... Palm Springs or Vegas?"

"How about that restaurant with all those crazy misters off Palm Canyon Drive?"

"Good enough. Bank when you want."

As the two luxuriate in the solitude of unfettered space, Greg asks a question out of the blue. "Marek, do you ever regret not going commercial after you finished your tours?"

"Once in a while."

"Is it the dollars or tarmacs in Rio and Stockholm that gets you to thinking?"

"Rio always has me thinking," Marek banters.

"You had offers from European lines, didn't you?"

"Yes, I did. When I was filling out applications, I made sure I didn't write anything about my association with your crew."

Greg smiles at Marek's jest. "You'd probably be retired now if you had chosen commercial."

"Yes... retired from a regular life."

"Nothing wrong with that, is there?"

"No... if you're a regular guy." Marek swivels his head. "Any regular guys aboard?"

"Not last time I checked," Greg logs in. He ponders, then starts a turn.

After Greg enters the kitchen from the garage and tosses his pilot's cap on the table, he suddenly feels much like game entering a suspiciously too quiet and comfortable clearing. Something is amiss; all unsettlingly still, symmetrical. Greg's eyes hop from the sink to pans over the cooking island to the montage of photos and magnets on the refrigerator to dinette chairs. No giveaways. Just where was Agatha Christie when a guy needed her?

With level eyes, a flummoxed Greg circles the entire kitchen. His three-sixty produces not a clue. Just *what is* the very orderly that is out of order? Greg draws a bead on the counter. There *it* is... the mail. It is stacked so fastidiously—as if someone had rammed the envelopes on the tile into a concise pile before leaving them perfectly parallel with the rectangular counter edges.

All too soon, "someone" comes upon the scene. Diane, countenancing no greetings, stalks to the counter and taps a forefinger on top of the mail. "Your phone bill is here."

"Still think I have a woman on the side?"

"No, I'm thinking you have another *life* on the side."

Breaking his own cardinal trial rule, Greg submits the question whose answer he does not already strongly surmise. "What one is that?"

Diane is supremely prepared for the prompt. "The Saturday you missed your afternoon appointment with Roland, you said you were off with House."

"I was."

"That afternoon you made a call to area code two ninety-nine."

"If you say so."

"You know where two ninety-nine is?"

"Haremville, USA?"

Greg's wit goes unappreciated. "*That* happens to be the area code where those mountain cultists held hostages for a couple of weeks. The day of *that* call to *that* area code," Diane digests for her audience, "was the day those hostages were suddenly freed because some phantom operatives took out four riflemen. I think the exact term the papers used was 'super soldiers.' It was you and House, wasn't it?"

"No, it wasn't." Greg doesn't relish a tango with the truth in the courtroom, let alone his own house. Yet he knows well that if he does otherwise, Diane's penchant for penetrating questions would eventually lead them to the old man, and that is verboten lest Greg forfeit whatever he and the others were given.

Mrs. Hardisty, on the other hand, is seasoned enough in verbal sparring with her husband to discern that if he isn't geared up on the offensive, then he's defensive about something. She presses. "If it wasn't you and House in the mountains, then it was Trina and Hopper. Am I right?"

"No."

Diane slams an open hand onto the counter. "How many goddamn questions are you going to make me ask!"

Greg emerges from the weeds. "It was Hopper."

"Just Hopper?"

"Yes."

"Bullshit! Everything I saw on TV said there were at least two unidentified assailants… probably more."

"I'm telling you, it was just Hopper."

If Diane were not so angry, welling in her eyes would have produced tears. "You promised me that life is behind you."

"It is."

"Then what in the hell were you doing there!"

"Trying to get Hopper to stand down."

"Why did he go there in the first place... to take on four marksmen by himself? I thought your sacred team, *your band of family* did everything together?" Diane is succeeding remarkably at winding herself up. "Why did House put his life in jeopardy with that lunatic stunt? How did he recover after he flat-lined?" Greg swings his gaze to the backyard, which only incites Diane to keep peppering him. "Why were you all looking at each other outside Intensive Care like you were expecting something to revive House? He was declared dead, but none of you acted like it."

"We were in shock," rejoins Greg, now truly glad he had kept mum on Hopper's providential turn in the paramedic van.

"Horseshit! Unless I'm sadly mistaken, you and your friends faced your share of deaths overseas... some very ugly ones, I would imagine. The doctor inside Intensive Care all but said House was a goner. You should've expected the nurse to come into the waiting room to tell us, but it was like you all were denying it."

Greg falls uncharacteristically silent; Diane will not allow the drawbridge to rise. "Hopper and House took maniac risks. I've never known them to do that. After years of quiet duty on the police force, Trina suddenly guns down an armed robber in the middle of the street. That's way off the screen for her too... not normal in any way, shape, or form. *You* haven't been normal for the last two months. What's happening with you all? Are you having some delayed, coincident post-combat trauma? Talk to me, Greg! I'm your goddamn wife!"

Unfortunately for Diane, Greg is canny in his ability to neatly step through a barrage of sharply pointed questions. "They're unpredictable people, Diane. If they weren't, they never would've been the line of work they were. I'm not taking any risks. You don't see me juggling Ginsu knives, do you?"

Unfortunately for Greg, Diane is in no mood for his invocation of this particular ability. "That's such a crock-of-shit answer."

Diane stomps back in the direction whence she came. "When you decide to include me in your life, give me a holler," she pitches over her shoulder.

Greg grabs his cap, puts it on, removes it, ruffles his hair. He feels he should busy himself; he does not feel compelled to open the mail.

The break room is an ensemble of Formica, chrome, and vinyl in the form of yellowed tile floor, nicked counter, outmoded eating tables, and dinged chairs, most in angled supplication to a row of antique vending machines. Clearly, no cadre of celebrated software engineers or snack zanies are on the payroll here. In this homage to bare-bones, cost-efficient amenities, McManus sits alone, fortifying himself with a bag of gaily garnished chips and cup of coffee with scant spunk.

As McManus dips into his munchies, Greta, eyes fatigued, enters the room. She subtly sizes up her boss for indication of mood. Sensing no harbingers of unusual ill will, she settles across from him.

"Been to the studios?" McManus asks in mid-munch.

"Yes, sir."

"And?"

"Absolutely nothing. Best we could find was a few frames... remote shots of the big guy's back."

McManus takes a jolt of coffee. "Between all the agencies and media on that mountain, there were enough cameras rolling to film the entire fucking Normandy invasion. How in the world did we miss them?"

Greta's monotone reply: "We just did."

"So we're bust?"

"Not exactly. You know Mitch Arnett, right?"

Bitterness contours McManus's face. "That prick was personally responsible for blowing up an op that was fourteen months in the making and permanently destroying the cover of one of my go-to snitches… who I actually happened to like… which I know you might find unusual."

"How did he do that?"

"Laid out more money than I had available to keep him at bay. We had bigger cases on our plate at the time."

Seeing little purpose in a further rehash of her superior's grudge, Greta cuts to her lead. "When we were at the studio watching the channel's film from the mountains, Arnett's production assistant always found a reason to be in the room. For as much time as he was with us, he didn't have a whole lot of questions."

"Because he didn't want to come across as interested?"

"That's what I'm guessing."

"Think maybe Arnett's onto something?"

"He had the opportunity to see what you did."

Without hesitation, McManus instructs Greta, "Put an asset and equipment on him and his assistant."

"Anyone in particular?"

"The Mick."

Greta, somewhat surprised, asks, "The Mick? Isn't that pretty top end for something like this?"

"Whoever those ops are, we've gotta secure a fix on them. If they can clean out a position that quickly without a trail, there's no telling the extent of their skills. Because they did something very good doesn't mean they aren't fully capable of doing something very bad. At this point, we can't make any assumptions as to their intentions. We have to open all channels."

Greta steadily eyes McManus, not taking that as the whole answer. He pauses, then details, "I'm taking it hard in the nuts for that fucking cult fiasco. I can't afford a replay."

"OK."

The streetside café across from the hospital has so many people in scrubs of muted colors, one might think an Impressionist painting is about to break out. Brent, lanky, long curly hair in the fashion of an alpaca lampshade, pitted complexion, sits alone at a small table out of a modest afternoon sun. His earphones are wired into a small laptop on whose keys he fluidly raps. Unexpectedly, Roland Brandt slides out a seat next to him. Brent stiffly unplugs from his hardware.

"Hey, Brent," Roland chirpily opens.

"What's going on?" Brent scans his memory banks. "Ronald, isn't it?"

"Roland."

"Right... Roland. What's up?"

"Taking care of a few things before I head to King's Road tonight... party for some folks at the station."

"Don't you kinda wanna get a break from people at work?"

"Normally, but a lot of potential weather girls supposed to be there. Can't pass on that, you know."

"I'll bet," Brent says with a tinge of envy.

"Any plans for tonight?"

"Not really. My shift finished at two."

"Why don't you come by?"

A chary Brent floats, "Seriously?"

"Sure."

"What's the address?"

"I'll text it to you. I appreciate what you did for me," Roland responds without evident caginess. He lets an appropriate moment expire before going to the well. "Could really use your help on something."

Brent warily responds to the TV bagman, "There's only so much patient information I can let out."

"No, no, not here to put you on the spot," Roland says in an even, premeditated tone. "You guys have strict confidentiality laws; I respect that." Roland inches his chair toward the table. "This one's easy. I'd just like to have a quick look at some surveillance film of your parking lots."

Brent loops his earphone cord around a finger. "Don't know. They're in cans in a security room in the basement... real tight place."

Roland senses negotiations have joined. "All I'm trying to do is pin down some license plate numbers. If a car's parked in a public lot like yours, there are no privacy issues — are there?"

Brent lets the bait dangle, then replies, "A good buddy, Denny, is basement janitorial on swing. He's knows some security guards down there. He might be able to work it out... but everyone has to come away with something, you know."

"I can cover it." Roland pops up from his seat. "Denny working tonight?"

"He's off yesterday and today."

"He cool?"

"Yeah, Denny's cool."

"Then you and Denny both come by the party. We'll talk it out."

"Some deal, bro."

"All right, I'll text you."

"OK."

Roland is off. Brent, confirmed wheeler-dealer of the first water, smugly looks at the mundanity in tables about him.

It's hard to believe a wispy 12-year-old could generate such leg speed. When Honorio whips his right foot through the football Hopper holds to the asphalt, it explodes toward white irrigation pipes jerry-built to the front of the maintenance shed. In a seeming instant, it bisects the impromptu goal posts and disappears behind the bite-sized structure.

As Hopper extracts a ball from the depleted canvas bag to his side, he suggests to Honorio. "How 'bout the last one with the left leg?"

"OK," Honorio says through a toothy smile.

Honorio and Hopper change sides. Hopper places the ball, and the boy rips it with his left foot through the goal posts. As they admire the trajectory, Trina, riding an imposing motorcycle, turns off the street onto the Our Lady of Perpetual Hope school-yard and circles to Hopper and Honorio. The youngster's attention is quickly diverted from goal posts to handlebars.

As Trina kills the engine and sits straddled on the bike, Hopper extends a hand toward her. "Honorio, this is my friend Trina."

"Hi," Honorio says a little clumsily.

"Hi."

"Trina, I told you about Honorio."

"Yes, you have," Trina sprightly responds. "How are you, Honorio?"

"I'm fine, thanks."

"Trina's a policewoman in East Bethune."

"Do you ride that motorcycle for your job?" asks Honorio, daring a step forward.

"No, I ride a patrol car."

Trina shows a questioning expression to Hopper, who subtly nods.

"Can I take you for a spin?" Trina poses to the boy.

Honorio retreats his step. "No, my mother doesn't let me ride with anyone."

"You have a very caring mother."

"Honorio, why don't you gather the balls. You probably should be heading home soon."

"OK, Brendan."

Hopper's eyes follow Honorio as he hightails it for the stray footballs.

"Been a while since I've heard anyone call you 'Brendan,'" Trina muses.

"Mariah called me 'Brendan'… sometimes."

Trina drops her head in mock contemplation before asking in a feigned puzzled voice, "Mariah?"

"She's the one I dated last year."

"Before or after Julia?"

"After."

"Oh yeah, the lusty Portuguese gal who buttered both sides of your toast... and then some. As I remember, she only called you 'Brendan' when she was angry with you."

Hopper allows some self-deprecation. "Which, at the end, was most the time, wasn't it?"

Trina, not one to let a sidekick easily unpin himself, responds, "That's certainly my recollection."

Hopper points in Honorio's direction. "Brendan will be helping Honorio with the footballs."

"Why don't you run off and do that, Brendan."

Lazing in the serenity of late afternoon, Trina sits on the ground, back against the schoolyard shed, eyes shut, lips offering a smile to a sun bestowing enveloping warmth. Hopper, football tucked under his head, lies prone on the asphalt next to her. Save a groundskeeper and a few rogue crows scavenging lunch remnants from bench-area garbage cans, they are alone.

"If that black SUV is owned by an offshore trust, does it mean the owners have to be domiciled offshore?" Hopper asks Trina.

"No, I hit up a couple of detectives about it. Anyone can create a trust in the Seychelles. They just have to pay a resident there a fee to represent the trust locally. Even if we could get our hands on the trust document, which is really difficult, the beneficiary of the trust could be a shell corporation or another trust from somewhere else... like The Bahamas, Panama... one of those."

"What about the car registration in Beverly Hills?"

"It's an executive suite... basically just a mailbox. Same entity that paid D.M.V. fees on the SUV paid the rent for the suite... two years in advance."

"Think it could've been a government vehicle?"

Trina shoos away an itinerant fly buzzing about. "If it was quiet government, the vehicle search would've come up blank or blocked. The way I see it, no alphabet soup involved."

"Who was it then?" asks Hopper, puzzlement lifting his eyelids.

"I think Greg is wearing everybody out on this. You said you changed the plates on your Jeep before you hit the mountains, had a mask on until you slid back into civvies, and stayed under tree cover when you were engaged. How could anyone I.D. you?"

"They couldn't." Hopper lets the exchange momentarily stew, then adds, "If the vehicle wasn't government, what was it doing here?"

"Could've been kidnappers, but this isn't exactly their student profile. Maybe drug dealers, but from what I understand, Father Raymond uses every ounce of influence he has in town to keep that shit away from Our Lady."

"Yeah, he's relentless about it," Hopper confirms.

"Doesn't leave a lot, Hop. Might just've been a guy on a cell who pulled over because he wasn't hands-free or someone who made a quick stop at church."

"Didn't see anyone go from the church to the SUV."

"Thought you said you had your head under the eaves while you were painting?"

"Yeah."

"Well? Could be the driver picked up a friend when you were working and they were talking before they drove off."

Hopper releases himself from espionage triangulation and permits his eyelids to fold down. "You're right. I think Greg has me skittish on the surveillance thing."

Silence briefly settles in before Hopper airs a fresh thought. "What do you think's happening with House? I can't convince the guy to come out of his apartment to meet me at Primo's…

when I promise to buy. I woulda bet our Israeli friends to take a summer cottage in Tehran before House would turn down an adult beverage on my tab."

Trina shifts her rear to a more comfortable swatch of pavement. "I think it's a couple of things. He's really banged up. Greg is the one who put that unknown out there. I'll give him that. The old man never said how we'd come back. Don't believe House had really thought that through."

"I didn't."

"And there's that House used his chance, which, no doubt, is a downer."

"But he used it for a real good reason."

"So I said to him."

"Does he have a schedule to go back to work?"

"I think he has disability as long as he needs it. His union has great coverage."

"I would've figured he'd want to return to the job. He's gotta have bounced up his brand big time with that last stunt... which means a lot more cake in his pocket."

Trina reckons, "He may have the yips."

"House? No way. That fucking guy was ice in the field."

"Yeah, but he was never torn up like now. Worst I recall was him catching some of that Bouncing Betty in Kosovo, and he was right as rain after what... less than a month?"

Hopper rises on a forearm. "Are you saying that a guy who was pinned down for almost three days by a shitstorm of R.P.G.s, Mk-211s, and tracer rounds is afraid of a back-lot stunt? How many times could he have been killed during that stretch? How many times could any of us there bought it?"

"But we didn't. We were never even ripped up really bad. None of us had to go through what House is now, so it's hard to judge. He's popping Vicodin like breath mints."

"OK, I'll give him a call. It's about time for him to change his number, isn't it?"

"He did — two days ago — like clockwork. I'll text it to you."

"Man, old habits die hard."

"Yeah, they do." Trina crinkles her toasty face. "What time do we start tonight?"

"Need to head over to the kitchen in about forty-five minutes for food prep."

"Too bad House isn't here to treat us to his cooking."

"We don't offer American prehistoric."

Trina smiles at the recollection. "How many dinners like this does Our Lady have?"

"We do one every couple of weeks. We rotate the theme... corned beef, brats, Italian... try to switch it up."

"Not many Italians, Irish, and Germans in this parish anymore, are there?"

"Not a lot. We do it that way so it doesn't seem like we're giving away meals to families that need them. Hell, we send away some people with three or four times as much food as they eat here."

"You're a good man, Hop."

"Hopin' to get there."

As far as cafeterias in antiquated denominational grammar schools go, this one isn't bad. Some parishioners with a few bucks in their pockets and others with plumbing skills in their hands had turned the kitchen into a sleek assembly of stainless steel appliances, sinks, and counters. The seating area is significantly less avant-garde, though still clean and crisp. Lighting throughout, however, passed code, inspection, and only the most humble expectations. Electricians in town evidently sought eternal reward at other hallowed haunts of God.

As folks get up from padded metal benches flanking long tables, Father Raymond and several altar boys, including Honorio, standing near the door are handing out Styrofoam containers of cheese ravioli, pasta primavera, chicken cacciatore, and a couple other dishes of representative Italian fare. Trina is part of an aproned crew clearing dishes from tables and ferrying them on carts to restaurant-grade dishwashers. Three chirpy teenage girls, doing the songwriting of Adele little justice, rinse and stack dinnerware in the machines.

Hopper, a festive tomato-based sauce dotting his apron and crewneck white T-shirt, sits across a table from Florencia Fernandez, Honorio's extremely overweight mother whose pouchy face, discolored eyes, and labored breathing give evidence of a debilitating infirmity. Her resolute voice, though, suffers no waver. "You want Honorio just to be the kicker for the football team? That's it? Kicker and nothing else?"

"Yes, but he could play other positions if he wanted. He's an incredible athlete."

"But he doesn't know anything about the game."

"He's such a talent, he could learn almost any position very quickly."

This clearly does not wash with Honorio's mother. "No, I don't want that. If he plays, he would only kick."

"That's entirely up to you, Mrs. Fernandez."

Realizing her response a bit harsh, the Latin woman tempers her tone. "I really don't want Honorio playing on any teams. But he talks so much about time he spends with you, I can't deny him that."

Hopper is somewhat taken back by the compliment. "Your son is a fine young boy. He has a lot of potential. Father Raymond has told me how well he does in school."

"Grades are most important, Mr. Hopper."

"Can we go with 'Brendan'?" Hopper requests with an accommodating smile.

"Sure, Brendan. I want my son to make a living with his brains, not his feet."

"I understand and agree, but I must tell you that your son has an extraordinary gift."

"So did his father," Mrs. Fernandez sniffs.

Hopper lets the subject float. After a pause, Mrs. Fernandez cannot resist giving it wind. "I'm sure Father has told you about Maximiliano, Honorio's father."

"Very little. Father keeps his counsel quite close."

Mrs. Fernandez begins a seemingly familiar litany. "When Maximiliano was a young boy, he was a great soccer player in Uruguay. If his family had stayed in Montevideo, he would've played for the national team. But they were very poor, so they moved here to find jobs. To bring food home, everyone had to work… Maximiliano, too. When he went to high school, the family had saved enough that his father could let him play on the soccer team. He turned heads right away. He had college scholarships waiting." The recollection sparkles Mrs. Fernandez's filmy eyes. "One day Maximiliano came home and said he had a chance to play professional soccer in Mexico. I was pregnant with Honorio. I told Maximiliano I wanted our child born in America, not Mexico, and I wouldn't go with him. He said he could work his whole life here and never make the money he could playing soccer there. He went alone." Mrs. Fernandez's face tightens. "Three years later, he was dead."

"How did he die?"

"We were told pneumonia, but we never saw his body."

Hopper, anticipating a seamy side to the story, does not prod.

A deep sadness shadows Mrs. Fernandez's face, her breathing becomes more strained; nonetheless, she closes the parable of loose ends. "We later found out the team Maximiliano played for was owned by a Mexican cartel. We think they ordered him to smuggle drugs when he came home to visit and he refused. For that, we believe they killed him… to set an example."

Hopper needs no more arrows on the diagram. "So you're concerned that if Honorio becomes a well-known athlete, he'll be lured the same way as his father?"

"Maximiliano was a good player in Mexico, but not like the stars who won World Cups for Uruguay." Mrs. Fernandez hunches forward slightly to clamp down her position. "Honorio can be a much better player than my husband ever was. Heads of drug cartels like Pablo Escobar can be crazy about soccer — just like they're crazy about everything else. They'll pay any amount for a great team. To have someone with Honorio's skills, there's little they won't do. They'll spend all the money it takes on coaches and lessons to make him the best, but then he's tied to criminals the rest of his life. I won't let that happen. If I have to, I'll take my son to his grandfather's village in Uruguay where they'll never find him."

"Honorio's a very sound boy," Hopper assures the mother.

Before Mrs. Fernandez can reply, Trina comes over to the table and extends a hand, "Hi, I'm Trina Lewis, friend of Brendan's."

Mrs. Fernandez reaches out. "Hello. Thank you for this wonderful dinner."

"I'm strictly plates, knives, and forks," Trina pleasantly shares with Mrs. Fernandez. She crooks her body to Hopper's ear. "I have graveyard tonight; got to run."

"Thanks for pitching in," Hopper says.

"See you later, Mrs. Fernandez. Nice to meet you."

"Nice to meet you, too."

As Trina is shedding her apron on the way to the kitchen, Mrs. Fernandez inquires, "Is that your girlfriend? She seems very sweet."

"If you only knew the half."

Trina stares from the patrol car at blighted sidewalks, boarded storefronts, scruffy drifters, petty criminals waiting for patsies, and a smattering of roughly painted women of the evening. She wonders at what point hopelessness becomes less a condition and more a legacy.

"Pretty quiet tonight," Trina's partner Cronin observes from behind the wheel.

"Yeah," Trina vacantly replies.

Cronin drops a dipstick. "Folks around here must've known you'd be in an off mood."

This draws Trina from her disquietude into earnest conversation. "I'm not in an off mood."

"Well, that's kinda right. Compared to the off mood you've been in the last few weeks, tonight you're not far off from that off mood."

Cronin's slight smirk douses Trina's tension. "Just been thinking through things," she confides.

"Anything between us?"

Her eyes soften. "Nothing but that belly I've been telling you to lose for two years."

The level of banter brings atmospherics of the patrol car within proper range. The still is abruptly broken by an urgent cackling over the car radio. "Ten-double-zero! Repeat: ten-double-zero on Aleta between Lincoln and Mission! Two-eleven-A; four-four-four."

Nothing puts the jolt to a patrol more quickly than an alert that a fellow officer is down. Cronin stomps on the accelerator; Trina draws a shotgun from a rack bolted to the passenger's door and snaps it open to check ammunition.

The scene at the jewelry store of cinder block, steel-gated doors, and barred windows in this hardscrabble neighborhood is not boding well for the good guys. Two rooftop snipers, perched on an industrial building across a back alley from the jeweler's, have pinned down Anita Galton behind a large iron dumpster. A uniform leg is soaked with blood. Whether her ballistic vest or flesh had caught a round in her drooped shoulder isn't clear. Bullets are skipping around her so fast she's barely able to fire a shot. In back of her stands a slug-riddled patrol car that had rammed into the parking lot brick wall. Behind that black-and-white, one patrolman tends to another whose stomach gushes gore.

Trina and Cronin screech up to the rear of a second patrol car, equally pocked with gunfire, slanted against the curb. O'Dowd, a paunchy policeman in his fifties with rumpled uniform and personality, kneels on the street and barks into a fully stretched car radio microphone, "Bring TAC Unit! Repeat, bring TAC Unit!" Ammo-dense street wars do not appear to be the riled cop's cup of tea.

Cronin crawls from behind the wheel of his black-and-white onto the asphalt. Her door facing the snipers, Trina, cradling the shotgun, bellies over the console and driver's seat onto the ground next to her partner. Staying low, Cronin and Trina, drawing a cannonade of sniper fire, quickly crab from their car to join O'Dowd. "Whadawe have?" Cronin pumps out.

"One perp, maybe two inside the jewelry store... tripped a silent. Cover is across the alley on top of that machinery shop — two of 'em. Sounds like they're firin' M40s or some damn thing. Galton and Pressey were first to respond. Pressey caught rounds in the gut... wasn't wearin' his fuckin' vest. Looks bad. Galton took one in the leg, maybe another in the upper body. Can't tell. Her shoulder unit went down when she dove for that garbage bin. Have no comm with her. Paramedics are rolling. Called for TAC."

Correctly reasoning that poking her head up above O'Dowd's vehicle would cast her a tin duck in a lethal carnival shooting booth, Trina lies flat on her stomach and squirms underneath the patrol car until she has view of the scene. Several feet across the alley from the dumpster where Galton is pinned sit four large industrial drums. Trina spots oil leaking from one. She quickly pushes herself back from under the chassis. "We gotta get Galton outa there," she raps at O'Dowd.

"That dumpster'll hold. The rounds aren't even piercing one side," rebuts the unheroic old cop.

"Yeah, but one could skip up off the concrete underneath the dumpster and catch Galton," Cronin counters.

"No," O'Dowd quibbles, "the angle from the roof is too high."

Trina, sharply, alerts both, "It's not that. There are oil drums outside the building across the alley from Galton. If one of those shooters figures it out and starts blasting rounds into them, he'll blow up the goddamn alley and Galton along with it."

"Drums could be empty," argues O'Dowd the Gallant, clearly not budging from his hold.

"They could also be full of fairy glitter, but I'm not counting on that to save Galton's ass," Trina fires back.

"We told Pressey and her to wait on the street for backup. But she wouldn't listen. She had to do what she always does — show she's got stones. Look what it did to her partner."

"Galton has a bead on the back door of that shop from her fix," Cronin sounds off. "If she doesn't hold it, the perps will be outa there and gone."

O'Dowd stakes his position. "Well, she's gotta stand her ground for five minutes more, 'cuz there's too much field between us and that dumpster to get to her. Those shooters will drill us as soon as we clear the car."

Trina allows herself but an instant to register disgust with O'Dowd, then scoots to the rear of his black-and-white. She quickly scans the parking area and notices that Galton's crashed patrol car has knocked off the top of a second iron dumpster. She turns to Cronin. "If we crawl into our car, can you back it up and turn it so it's facing the alley?"

"Yeah... as long as we stay down. They can't shoot through the engine block."

"Whaddya want to do?" O'Dowd asks with a skeptic brow.

"Angle the side search lights at those shooters... blind them for just long enough for me to make it to Galton."

O'Dowd: "So how's it gonna help to have two of you pinned down?"

"I'll snatch the top of that second garbage bin over there. I'll use it as cover to walk Galton to the street."

"What about locking down the rear of the jewelry store?" O'Dowd unwelcomely cross-examines Trina.

"By the time I clear her from those drums, TAC will have shut off two square blocks around here. Those fuckers on the roof... whoever's inside... are chum."

"All right," Cronin signs on, "let's hit it."

A flurry of slugs chases Trina and Cronin as soon as the snipers see the cops' movement to their patrol car. Trina, then Cronin, scrambles inside through the driver's door. As Trina scrunches down on the passenger's seat, Cronin, his upper body prone over the console, starts the car. Bullets rip through the windshield and shred the top of the seats, smoking the interior with stuffing.

Experimenting with a modicum of bravery and proving not a total shirker, O'Dowd angles his gun toward the top of the industrial building and cuts loose. Though he probably had a better chance of nicking the ghost of Buffalo Bill Cody than snipers, it does momentarily draw fire in his direction. In that instant, Cronin and Trina reach to searchlights bolted to the front doors, point them at roof level across the alley, and turn them on. The glare of light catches the snipers flush and sends them back.

The moment rifle fire ceases, Trina sprints to the parking lot, grabs handles of the dislodged dumpster top, sets it front of her, and negotiates the heavy, awkward iron slab toward Galton. As she is about halfway there, the snipers reposition themselves and, after making their first order of business shattering the patrol car searchlights, next open up on Trina. Her cover proves impenetrable.

However, just before she reaches Galton, she is undone by a chuckhole in the parking surface. It catches an edge of the dumpster top, drawing it away from Trina. In that moment, her upper torso is completely exposed.

Unfathomably, a fusillade of bullets zings by her, only one grazing an arm before she has righted the iron plate. She reaches Galton, who indeed is hit badly in the shoulder. In short order, Trina has Galton on her feet. Propping the wounded officer, she totes Galton backward behind the dumpster top, off of which sparking bullets furiously ricochet.

Frustrated at the release of the captives, one of the snipers stands to continue firing. His eyes momentarily drop and catch sight of the oil bins. He immediately unloads rounds into them, causing rapid-fire explosions that violently blast apart the dumpster that had protected Galton. The force blows back the top shielding Trina and Galton and slams them to ground beneath it. Smoke from the alley ablaze envelops the jewelry store and parking lot as swirling red and blue lights converge on the scene.

Roland seems all but impervious to the fact that by squatting his zippy, though worn and dinged, Lotus Elise in the middle of the restricted bus zone, he is forcing disembarking passengers to clump around a long waiting bench and string of single-copy newspaper stands to reach crosswalks of the keystone intersection. After the disbursing band of admirers had expressed the entire panorama of their feelings (some with an internationally recognized hand gesture) to Roland, Brent the hospital worker walks hurriedly around a corner and to the Lotus. Roland buzzes down the passenger's window.

"Hey Brent, thanks for making it out."

"No worries."

Brent dredges a computer disk from one of a patch of cargo-shorts pockets and hands it to Roland. "Denny made a copy for you."

"Great. Did he have a good time at the Kings Road thing?"

"Still talking 'bout it."

Roland fingers the disk. "This the whole night we talked about?"

"Yeah, from midnight until noon the next day. All of Stackhouse's visitors were gone by about 11:00 a.m., I think."

"That's great, Brent. Really appreciate it." Roland forks over a small roll of cash which Brent furtively slips away.

"Have a date with a station hottie this afternoon?"

"No, have legwork on a story."

"The station ties you up on Sunday?"

"Yeah, but this one could have a nice payoff." Roland starts his car. "I'll give you a call after I run through the disk, OK?"

"Sure."

Roland bounces off the curb, tests a yellow light, and cuts a sharp left on Sunset Boulevard. A bulky man on a motorcycle who had been parked across the street from the bus stop takes off in Roland's direction. His thick, reddish blond hair flaps from beneath his helmet onto sturdy shoulders as he weaves through traffic behind the Lotus.

The cacophony in these close hills of dense brush, lank trees, ragged ground cover, and rutted dirt roads is not of frisky, territorial wildlife, but rather cracking gunfire. The source is a hollow where an outdoor shooting range, evidencing the construction sophistication of a ramshackle tree house, had been niched into the base of a slope covered with thickset scrub. The place appears to be a not-so-wondrous resurrection of castoff lumber.

The shooting stand is a creaky deck of worn planks. (The carpenter in charge apparently had been broadly unaware of the miracle of a framing square.) One can surmise the control tower to be an unoccupied, threadbare chaise lounge plopped atop a cashier's shack. Targets hang from splintered posts awkwardly driven into the ground down range. Notwithstanding the back-woods nature of the operation, shootists, eclectically outfitted, have more than a fair handle on their guns.

In an enclave separated by high bushes from the main range is a railed timber platform where Tully and House, he battling a leg cast just to stand fully erect, are shredding body targets. With each discharge of heavy load from Tully's six-inch, blue Colt Python, flames spit from the barrel, echoes fairly leaping surrounding hillside. While Tully's shooting is clearly practiced, though unmetered, it's a poor country cousin to House's. Shots blaze from of his SIG Sauer P226 as if governed by a timepiece. One precision slug after another piles into holes of the target's eyes.

After they finish, Tully and House stow their pistols. As Tully gathers spent shells from the ground, House, a thin film of sweat covering his scabbed face, corrals crutches leaning against the front railing, swings to a bench at the rear of the platform, and plants himself. Tully soon joins him. He slides from underneath the bench a cooler and extracts two cans of beer, which is a manifest violation of the range's rules and regulations, unposted though they be. Even in the jurisdiction of outlier gun ranges, evidently some are accorded their privileges.

As he savors his suds, Tully inspects the long, stitch-marked, red notch on House's forehead. "That's coming along OK."

"Yeah, I should start auditioning for romantic leads in a couple weeks."

Tully smiles. "Crash sure didn't do anything to your hand. That's as good as you've ever shot."

"With all the trigger time I have in, oughta be second nature."

As House dries his sweaty face with the sleeve of his shirt, Tully drops an additive from a chrome snifter into his beer. He offers some to House. "Just a touch," House cautions. And, without objection from House, more than a touch his confederate in arms and spirits administers.

"Thanks for repaying the money so fast, House. Never said anything about interest. Didn't have to do that."

"That's fair."

Tully digests House's equanimity along with a thorough slug of his impromptu boilermaker. "When does the doctor say you'll be back at it?"

"Tell you the truth, I'm not all that sure I will."

"*Really*? With the years you have in?"

House casts eyes on his battered body. "Just don't think I want to go through something like this again."

"You could drop to lower profile stuff. Pay's not all that great, but at least you're still in the business."

"I'm finished writing checks to the wife next year, so I don't have any big obligations. I'm thinking about going back to the kitchen—kind of stuff I did before... maybe a little more upscale."

"You could make more marking scenes for me and rigging explosives. Christ, you're the best in town at that."

"Don't know."

"Let's stop in at 'T' and 'T' before I drop you off. We can talk about it over something serious."

"My afternoon happens to be open."

As Tully sweeps damp dollars bills from the bar of Tailspin & Tonic, House does his best to collect fragments of his consciousness.

"Sure you want to stay?" Tully solicitously checks with his friend. "With those Vikes you're on, you could find yourself asleep right where you sit."

House slurs a response. "Tired of looking at those goddamn apartment walls."

"Come to my place. I'm grilling pulled pork for the family and a few neighbors."

"Don't feel much like eating. Thanks, though."

As House fights a drooping head, lame bar stool, and anchor of a leg cast, Tully nods to the bartender who joins him at the end of the bar. "When he's ready to go or passes out, bring around a cab and pay up front. Put it on my tab." The bartender understandingly nods.

"Take care, House," Tully calls out before finding the door.

House waves a wobbly hand.

Roland, who had been seated alone at a table near the back wall, waits an appropriate moment before transporting his drink to the bar and settling a stool away from House. Another patron by himself, he with a mop of reddish blond hair and scraggy face corrugated by harsh Irish winters and harsher still brute encounters, lifts his cell phone as he continues to text... evidently. A motorcycle helmet is at his side.

Paul Thornberg sits at a desk in a cramped office. The walls appear to have been the loose target of a near-sighted slingshooter armed with wall tacks and quiver of illegible notes. As Thornberg sifts through a heap of legal briefs on his desk, Greg lumbers in and sinks into a chair. Thornberg parts a couple of manila stacks for an aperture to him.

"Been looking a little worn lately. Everything OK?"

"Nothing out of the ordinary," Greg responds with thin conviction.

"Sutter was in yesterday... " After a weighty pause, Thornberg focuses over half-mast reading glasses, "... to talk about you."

Greg flexes his back as if acknowledging a twinge of lumbago. "What about me?"

"Wanted to know if you had sufficient focus on Streeter?"

"And?"

"*And* I told him my honest, unexpurgated opinion."

"Which was what... I've become fixated on crop circles?"

Thornberg releases his colleague from the lurch. "I said that... as always... you're nails."

"Appreciate that." Greg's shoulders soften.

"Just speaking the truth." Thornberg eases in his seat. "Caught a clip of that shootout in the Lincoln District night before last. Jesus, looked like a combat zone. Must've rolled six or seven engines."

"Couldn't tell you," Greg tartly replies in hopes of short-circuiting the anticipated conversation.

It was not to be. "Wasn't it your friend who saved the life of the other policewoman?"

"Yes."

"Man, she must've been channeling Schwarzenegger. Took a helluva chance diving into all that sniper fire."

"Sure did."

"What was her name again?"

"Lewis."

"That's right... Tina Lewis."

"*Trina* Lewis."

"Was she the one you had to travel to Vegas to bail out a couple of years ago?"

Greg shakes his head slightly, earnestly wishing the moment would spend itself. "Yes, she was."

"Got into a scrape, didn't she?"

Greg nets it out as succinctly as possible. "A security guard at a casino was manhandling a prostitute. Trina took exception."

"Woman has some momentum, has she?"

"That she does."

"Where do you know her... from the patchy time we don't talk about around here?"

Greg's eyes skim Thornberg's desk. "If you can locate your egg timer, I believe you'll find sands have run out on the subject."

Thornberg grapples with momentary silence. A secretary, holding an expression of extreme urgency, appears at Thornberg's door. "Greg, may I speak with you, please."

Greg, face running with grief, nostrils sated with an ineradicable disinfectant smell, rests his back against a corridor wall of an acute-care nursing home. He stares into the patient room where a respirator and attendant apparatus circle his father's bed, above which death has most clearly hung its warrant. Approaching footsteps take Greg's attention down the hall.

Dr. Farrin, a stately 63 years, unimpeachable in a finely tailored suit, professionally strides the glazed terra cotta hallway floor to Greg. Seeing that the good doctor holds not clipboard, files, or paperwork, Greg immediately recognizes that the message about to be delivered requires no pathological reference points.

"Good evening, Greg," Dr. Farrin says in a pleasant, but prudent tone.

"Evening, Doctor."

"How is my friend Dr. Klein?"

"Showing me patience... as always."

"Bernie has been in the business too long to be otherwise." Dr. Farrin's eyes bore in on Greg. The physician assumes a tone both sympathetic and final. "In my office last month, you asked me to advise you when I thought it was time to exercise the durable power consistent with what we both understand to be your father's wishes. In my considered opinion the time is now."

As Greg cumbrously attempts to form an objection, Dr. Farrin shows a palm. "I know we had spoken about the possibility of another surgery, but I sent your father's file to three separate anesthesiologists the last several days. Each declined because they are all but certain he would never regain consciousness."

"But...," Greg tries to submit.

"Greg," the physician, without room for divergence, interrupts, "your father has endured chronic heart problems for the past twenty-four years. You've provided him with every form of treatment medicine has to offer. Science simply can't do more."

The purveyor of inexorable reality sets a comforting hand on Greg's shoulder. "In that room, the only thing functioning are machines. Your father has told us repeatedly and emphatically that is not his wish."

Greg chews on the doctor's words, then slowly lowers his head in recognition.

"Will you be the one to phone your sister?"

"She doesn't take my calls," Greg admits without shred of pretense.

Dr. Farrin studies his watch. "A little late in North Carolina, but it's more of a formality, really. She isn't named in the durable power of attorney. Let me try to contact her."

"Thanks, Doctor."

"I need to discuss procedure with administration here. You have your cell phone, I presume?"

"Yes."

"Why don't you take in some fresh air, and I'll call you."

"OK."

Before he returns down the hall, Dr. Farrin posts a final thought. "You gave your father quality life for an extended period he otherwise would not've experienced. You have my utmost respect for that."

Greg nods; his eyes droop.

With its Spanish-tile-and-white-stucco architecture, the nursing home looks from the exterior more like an expansive, well-maintained hacienda than acute care center for the elderly. As Greg plods in disarrayed steps along the front circular driveway, he is drawn to a huddle of oak trees across a spread of neatly manicured lawn. While heading in that direction, his feet find their own deliberation. Once he nears the oaks, he stops and stares into the trees. "Old man, I know you're there. It's time we talk."

Greg's stalking voice may have caused movement of a few night critters, but little else. Undeterred, he persists, "You can't lay what you did on us and just walk away. Come out here."

Outside of drawing brief attention of an attendant exiting a side door, Greg rouses no one. He gathers breath. "I want you to give my chance to my father. That's a great man in there. You let *him* live. You hear me. He's never taken a life. You give *him* the chance."

Coincident with his last word, sharp jolts shoot from Greg's chest to his fingertips, driving him to his knees. As he folds his arms in front of him and fights off searing pain, he struggles to continue. "You let him go on, old man. It's my chance. I use it the way I want." The burning spikes up the front of Greg's neck, choking his voice and contorting his face. He falls into a convulsing, sweaty mass.

On the other side of the trees, the aged man, plainly dressed, eyes sorrowful, slowly wanders from the nursing home.

Trina, in full uniform, right side of her face and left hand heavily scabbed, stands in front of a coffee vending machine in an alcove outside a police department briefing room. As she is reaching into her pocket, Captain Doolin, immersed in conversation with a muckety-muck on either side, walks down the hall. Seeing Trina, he motions for the two to go on.

Doolin, Johnny-on-the spot with a dollar bill, slips it into the machine before Trina can mine one of her own.

"How you having it, Officer?"

"Black," a somewhat startled Trina responds.

"What else would I expect?"

As the Captain pokes buttons for Trina's order, he informs her, "Read over O'Dowd's, Galton's, and Cronin's reports. We'd probably be down one patrolman if it wasn't for you, Lewis."

ACES AND ETERNITY

Incredulity momentarily pastes the Captain's face. "Damn miracle you didn't take a bullet when the bin top was caught in that pothole."

"Galton and I were both lucky to make it out of there." Trina pauses ever so slightly. "It was a good day for the women in blue," she can't resist appending.

The Captain's notoriously austere countenance turns kindly. "I know I'm a by-the-book pain-in-the-ass, Lewis, but that's the way I see my job shaking out. There's one thing, though, closer to me than any book: my officers. The commendation I've just signed won't say it, but," the Captain points towards her chest, "thank you for the honor you bring to that badge."

The sound of coffee splashing into the dispensed cup fills the spacious moment until a taken-back Trina fully processes the Captain's uncharacteristic compliment. "Thank you... thank you very much, sir."

The Captain starts to move on, but throws off one more endorsement. "If I could convince everyone around here to crank up their performance the way you have the past few months, I might actually have time for a goddamn vacation."

After what could be construed as a smile, the Captain marches off.

McManus sits in a middling government office, a house of worship to the phenomenon of print. Manuals, computer runs, reports, and reference books are crammed into surrounding shelves, giving the place the roomy elegance one normally associates with an undersized janitor's closet. As he is laboriously taking a yellow highlighter to contents of a prosperous folder, Allan and Greta, each bearing a lean file, appear at McManus's doorway. He motions to two chairs pinched in front of his desk. Once seated, the pair dutifully waits for McManus to finish his markings.

McManus caps the highlighter and turns his attention to his subordinates. "Whaddaya have?"

Greta removes from her file a photograph of House talking to Tully at Tailspin & Tonic and pushes it to McManus. She then arrays several pages of text around the photo. McManus studies the image and then quickly soaks up the remainder of the material. None too pleased, he tries Allan. "You're the one taking creative writing classes. Have anything," with a flick of his hand over his desktop, "better than this?"

"No, sir," Allan more or less gulps. He takes a stab at atonement. "We have a few more photos."

McManus has already changed lanes. "Is the Mick on both Arnett and his assistant?"

"Yes, sir," Greta confirms.

"Any searches outstanding?"

"No. You have what we were able to extract from all our available data bases."

"Absolutely nothing from open-source intelligence," Allan chimes in.

McManus directs a toxic gaze at Allan. "Now, there's a flash." Fester spreading in his voice, he asks of Greta, "When you say 'all our available data bases,' do you mean those the agency owns or all to which we have legitimate access?"

"All we have authority to access," Greta clarifies for her examiner.

McManus skeptically views his junior deputies. "Did this Stackhouse guy go on an extended Carnival Cruise for a decade or some fucking thing?"

"If he did, there were no ports of call in the known world. We've hit all our international sources, including major cobblers active at the time," Allan ponies up.

"What's with the police report?" McManus gruffly inquires.

"Bar fight in Santa Barbara. He disabled five bikers in a heart-beat. From the description of witnesses, sounds like at one time or another Stackhouse had extensive Krav training—very high level," Allan opines.

"Any transcripts yet?" McManus asks.

"No, Stackhouse uses a burner," Greta reports.

McManus drums his dissatisfaction. "From the material here, the guy has been in the stunt business for what—seven years? How in the hell does he function in the work world with pre-paids? Does he send out a flyer every thirty days with a new phone number? You're also telling me he has no email, Skype, or social network identity? Nothing like that *at all*? I find it hard to believe."

"Absolutely none, sir," Greta states with resolve.

McManus, finding the response as pleasing as a proctology probe, wheels in his chair and closely inspects a wall shelf particularly thick with reams of loose paper. After a prolonged inventory (during which time Greta and Allan conscientiously play the role of sphinx), McManus steps to the stacks, rifles though stapled pages, and soon comes upon the evident object of his search. He sits down and spends several moments digesting his find. Finished with his hopscotch reading, McManus eyeballs Greta and Allan. "A contact tree on this stuntman is essential. We need a tech on him that can source and track his communications."

"It'll take someone from the Bay Area for that," Greta crisply observes.

"We could switch the Mick over to Stackhouse."

"Don't want him reassigned from the TV clowns," McManus imperially responds. "Bring in Norcal for the stuntman."

Both Greta's and Allan's face display a level of surprise. "That kind of talent isn't cheap," Allan remarks.

"I'll draw contingency from a couple other cases," their superior replies. McManus then dispenses further direction. "As soon as we establish a line out from the stuntman to an identity, I want a full spec and tree on that individual as well. We're searching for the same black hole in their history." McManus taps his highlighter on the retrieved document. "Could be we find eight or nine off-the-grid types like this." McManus's voice then turns downright thorny. "Either of you have a feel as to how Arnett made a connection to Stackhouse?"

Discerning the mere mention of Arnett's name rankling the man in charge, Greta is short on the narrative. "So far nothing to indicate he had any lead other than we have." A politic Allan stays silent.

"OK, let's jump to it. We have people to fingerprint."

With that, Allan and Greta are out of the office. McManus uncaps his highlighter and begins to give color to the exhumed pages.

Greg exits Dr. Klein's office and, with a jeweler's precision, slowly turns closed a doorknob that closes automatically. He has in hand two prescription sheets, lab work results, and several other keepsakes from the diligent doctor. Entombed in reflection, he trudges to the elevator and stabs the down button. When the elevator arrives, Greg's steer sends him not into the empty cab, but rather to a nearby window, where his eyes and thoughts run pell-mell.

As Roland whizzes his nicked Lotus past shrouded residences of the Hollywood Hills, his cell phone rings. He checks the number and immediately answers.

"Hey Mitch, what's up?" After several moments of dividing his attention between the call and street signs camouflaged by drooping, leafy branches, Roland toots into his cell, "Have it handled. The two vehicles we I.D.ed from the hospital lot were the attorney and his wife. Must've come in separate cars. The third guy from the mountain drives a Jeep, Honda Element, something like that, but he parked too far out of range from security cameras to pin down a plate number. A woman who exited with him hopped onto a motorcycle. Nailed the plates, but since they're smaller than normal, had to put someone on blowing up the frames. Should have it in twenty-four hours, maybe less."

Roland raises his eyebrows, evidently enduring a due-course upbraiding of some moment. "All over the stuntman… all over him. He just turned in for the night." After a couple of protracted beats, "OK, OK, I'm on it." With that, he thankfully closes the call.

Roland parks near a house where lights, trendy music, exotic cars, and a glossy montage of too-too beautiful people on an outdoor patio confirm party de jour. He assays himself in the rearview mirror. After patting his hair, he tweaks his shirt collar to make certain it properly resonates his rank as high lama of media chic. He locks his ride, and, with a cocksure strut, heads to this particular evening's distillation of L.A. cool. Roland spots two hot young ladies alighting from a Maserati and, as would any other high-voltage man-about-town, nods invitingly at them. They pay him the mind one specially reserves for a recently swatted gnat.

Greg, bundled in reflection, sits alone on the patio, dusk throwing shadows onto hills behind his home. Diane comes out from the kitchen and steps gingerly to her husband. She takes a position just inside his field of vision. "Hung up with your sister. She's fine spreading your father's ashes next June in the lake near your parents' old cabin."

"Thanks," Greg remotely acknowledges. After a moment, he breaks from his engagement with lowering night. "How was she?"

"Distant."

"That would be a major step for me."

"Maybe when we're together at the lake things will thaw some."

"I lost her… a long time ago."

"You have ground to make up, don't you?" Diane responds with a gesture to equity. "You were undercover when your mother died, and how long was it before you found out about your father's first surgery?"

Greg motions to the chair next to him, on which Diane settles just enough to rest her rump.

"Am I losing you, too?" Greg asks in unfiltered earnest.

Diane clearly had set an architecture to a response. "Before we married, you promised that what happened on the other side of the world would never be a barrier between us, that it was in the past... buried. I've never asked a single question about it, because I believe our lives, House's, Hopper's, Trina's, the lives of the people in Northern California and ones they love all might suffer if certain things came to light. Have I ever betrayed my promise to you?"

"No, you haven't. You've been terrific."

"You and your friends have a tie I've never tried to break. That's true, isn't it?" Greg dips his head in agreement. "But now what's happening with them seems to be coming between us. Suddenly, they're taking strange risks. At the same time, you've retreated into a shell. Something is happening with all of you that's not normal... and it's making us not normal."

"I can't stop my friends from doing things I think are off the charts."

Diane nudges her chair closer to Greg. "I know how much the group means to you, but the bond you've all had for so long appears to be unraveling."

"I'd like to make that right, but the Streeter case is taking so much of my time," Greg the lawyer proffers in his defense.

"I heard you on the phone with Trina. You were awfully hard on her. She did an act so incredibly brave."

"If she had waited three minutes for a S.W.A.T. team, none of that risk would've been necessary."

"You know the raw treatment she and other women have sometimes received at the police department. Don't you think a lot of it was her wanting to cover another policewoman she saw as being left hanging out there?"

Greg considers the inviting coziness of deepening shadows. "I guess there's something to that."

"What's happened with House? He used to be here at least once a week for dinner. We haven't seen him at all since his accident."

"He's still recuperating... so he says."

"I can pick him up."

"I've offered, but he tells me he's uncomfortable on long rides."

Diane marginalizes the explanation. "It can't be just that, Greg."

"Sometimes friendships get out of sync."

"Is that what's making us out of sync?" Diane pebbles her husband, patience ebbing.

"I think maybe... after all these years... the four of us are growing apart. That's been weighing on me."

Diane hurdles past Greg's muddied explanation. "Every time I read the newspaper, there are articles about delayed traumas veterans suffer from battle."

Greg bristles at the military-speak. "I'm not a veteran."

"No, veterans serve tours of two or three years, then return home to a normal life. From what I understand, you were in black holes of hell for over a decade."

Greg can winnow no untruth in his wife's take; he chooses to circle it. "The life we had back then was complicated... very complicated. In a lot of ways, we're all probably still dealing with it. Don't know that it will ever really resolve itself. But I don't think House, Hopper, or Trina is experiencing any crises. Maybe a middle-age crisis, but I'm not seeing some kind of disorder."

"You're not experiencing trauma?"

"None."

"Then why are you becoming a regular at Dr. Klein's?"

"He wants to make sure we're taking every precaution so I don't go down my father's path."

Though swayed little by the spindly assurance, Diane chooses to displace enlightenment in favor of affection and feathers a hand atop that of her husband.

Inside the small shed in back of Our Lady of Perpetual Hope church, Hopper presses fine sandpaper to a freshly constructed cabinet. He is suddenly taken from his task by Honorio's distant voice. Hopper steps from the shed to see the boy, forehead swarming with full beads of panicky sweat, running feverishly toward him. "Brendan, Brendan, my mom! She's choking! Help her! *Please* help her!"

Hopper flies to Honorio.

In a sprawling amusement park that is a pastiche of rides, sports venues, concessions, arcade games, and veiled parental hazing, House, foot in walking boot, soft drink in hand, stands behind a batting cage where his nephew is taking swings.

After the young boy hits a couple of weak pop-ups, House instructs him, "Billy, take time."

The youngster backs away from the plate and shows his uncle a reluctant face.

"Where were your eyes after those last two cuts — clouds or straight at the barrel?"

"Clouds," Billy murmurs.

"What's there?"

"Directions to the dugout," Billy obligingly recites.

"Keep your head level until a one-count after you make contact, OK?"

"OK."

Billy steps in and waits for the next delivery from the machine. Noggin fixedly down, he raps the ball on a line into the far netting. House allows himself a satisfied smile before he culls a pill from a smoky prescription container and washes it down with his drink.

House sits across from his nephew while the youngster chomps on a hot dog. House's eyes wanders past Billy's shoulder to Cord's wife Marianne and his niece Darcy, who are banging golf balls around a miniature course dense with castles, moats, bridges, and folks fudging scorecards.

"What're the plans for the rest of the weekend?"

"Nothing much," Billy says as he reaches for a French fry.

"Not going to play video games all night, are you?" House inquires, somewhat parentally.

"No. Mom pulls the plug in my room at ten."

"What about your older friend Joshua Gregory? Are you still hanging with him? He seems like a good guy."

"He's on a Boy Scout trip."

"Interested in Scouts?"

"Wanna join when dad is back home."

"Why not now?"

"Mom doesn't have much time with her job, my sister, and everything."

"I could fill in until dad's back."

Billy finds a way to contain his ardor. "No, that's OK, Uncle Bill, I can wait for dad."

"Hey, I know I can be a pain in the ass, but only at the batting cages."

Billy's not buying the pitch; House recalibrates. "OK, a pain in the ass at the batting cages, library, lessons, and a couple of other places... but nowhere else." House smiles whimsically. "Scout's honor."

The boy breaks into a full smile, clearly pleasing his uncle.

As his nephew continues the demolition of delectables before him, House's eyes grow heavy, mind spacey from medication, dulling his highly honed antennae that otherwise might have sensed eyes upon him.

The front room of Our Lady of Perpetual Hope rectory displays few concessions to modernity, but a great many tributes to morality and frugality. Antiquated book shelves feature ecclesiastical tomes, tales of religious triumph, and instructional booklets for the spiritually perplexed and wayward. For cultivated, discriminating members of the good parish, several oil paintings of Messianic redemption grace the walls. Domiciled there also is a framed official photograph of an archbishop in mitre who apparently fine-tuned his smile at a party-poopers' academy. Thick matte velvet drapes ably seal off temptation lurking outside the windows... as well as any hint of natural light. Off the entryway in a sitting area, straight-backed chairs outflank the lone bastion of comfort—a couch imported from the set of *Father Knows Best*. There sits Hopper. Honorio, soundly asleep, is stretched out next to him, the boy's head resting against Hopper's leg.

Father Raymond trails in from the night. A tight smile does little to mask a tired, wan face. Making sure not to disturb Honorio, Hopper rises exactly and, out of the boy's earshot, joins the priest.

"How's Mrs. Fernandez doing?"

"It was a stroke... a severe one," a grimacing Father Raymond accounts for Hopper.

"How long will she be in the hospital?"

"Depends on the damage to her left leg. If she doesn't generate movement in the next few days, could be in therapy quite a while."

"Did you have a chance to talk with Honorio's aunt?" Hopper asks with scantly cloaked anticipation.

"I did. She agrees it's not a good idea to move Honorio to Pacoima in the middle of the school year and leave all his friends at Our Lady. They'll talk about it, but I think they'll be agreeable to Honorio staying here at the rectory during the week and going to their home on weekends... some arrangement like that." Father Raymond throws caution at Hopper's relieved look. "Brendan, I have only so much time to devote to Honorio. There's a whole parish to which I attend. You must play a big part in this for it to work. You'll have to be up to task."

"Most of my martial art classes are private, Father. I can move times to fit Honorio's schedule."

Father Raymond removes his collar and drops it into a coat pocket. "I'm concerned about a female influence in Honorio's life if he'll be here for an extended time. As much faith as I have in the good sisters at our school, they aren't the warmest bunch I've come across, I do admit."

"You met my friend Trina at the parish dinner. I think she could spend time with Honorio."

"The policewoman?"

"Yes."

The wary padre puts a stethoscope to the proposition. "She seemed like a bit of a loner."

"Taking her a while to come out of a long-term relationship," Hopper responds a mite defensively.

"Someone local?"

"No, actually British. Distance proved to be too much."

"How long have you and Trina been friends?"

"Over twenty years," Hopper answers deliberately, all too aware where the priest's line was leading.

"Was she with you while you were out of the country doing your soldiering, Brendan?" the priest tests Hopper.

"Yes, she was, Father."

Father Raymond lets a sober silence come between them before Hopper takes his friend's part... and his. "She dropped the hammer when it was the last resort... just like the rest of us. As I said before, no apologies then, none now. We weren't doing

God's work, but it was work that had to be done. If we're fallen angels, so be it."

"Let's sleep on it," Father Raymond says as he moves away to check on Honorio.

If one were to seek a haven of anonymity in the midst of a raging metropolis, he could do worse than donning a cardinal hat and shirt spangled with some USC logo or another and maundering through the banner-festooned campus of the University of Southern California the morning before a football game. Thusly attired, a partisan-for-a-day could likely go as unnoticed as shopping etiquette on Black Friday.

McManus, so decked out, eels his way through cliques of drunken, leather-lunged frat boys; a gaggle of teenage, would-be cheerleaders in the purview of their parents' watchful, albeit tipsy eyes; picnicking alums making high sport of cholesterol defiance; reunion honks serenading fleeing classmates with a jangly rendition of the school fight song; an undergraduate tart intriguingly wrapped in university colors; and a sea of fans anxiously waiting to join red-and-gold-clad lemmings following the school band in a march of destiny to the Los Angeles Memorial Coliseum. Spotting an opening in the menagerie of fans, McManus niftily buckets along to front steps of the university library where he joins a couple of hibernatic students headed inside.

McManus kills several minutes wandering around lobby displays. Certain he has not been followed, he veers to a stairwell and bounds up several flights past a descending bookish type whose pioneering beard is aspirational at best. There waiting on a landing, resplendent in USC attire, is the thewy motorcycle man with reddish blond hair and lumpy face who had House in his sights at Tailspin & Tonic. McManus stops a step below the Mick.

"This is a sign of real commitment," McManus saltily observes. "Your degree from Ulster doesn't revert to the university if a faculty member sees you gussied up like that, does it?"

"It's a risk," the Mick says in a voice with a trace of amusement and brogue.

"How are my people doing?"

"Both all business... clear on assignments. The guy has a chance to make it. Greta... she's a keeper. Has a long runway in front of her."

"Good to hear," a pleased McManus reacts.

"Should I fatten their package closer to what I feed you?"

"Not yet. Keep editing their dossiers so they're skinnier than mine. I need to see if they can connect the dots on their own... what kind of noses they have."

"OK," the Mick affirms his charge.

"How is that dickwad Arnett doing on his story?" McManus asks in a prickly tone.

Though there is a better chance of Achilles revisiting this particular venue of Troy than a snoop happening upon a library stairwell on S.C. game day, the Mick looks furtively around before responding. "He's not putting in much time. His assistant's doing all the legwork. They're trying to stitch something together, but until they get deeper pieces of intel, they don't have much of a chance. They'll need a birdwatcher to take it to the next level."

"We need to make that happen," McManus says with a settled stare.

In response to the Mick's decidedly unsure expression, McManus takes a systematically folded paper from his shirt pocket, opens it, and hands it to the Mick. After a slow read, the Mick returns the paper to McManus. "Positive about this?"

McManus nods.

"For that amount, I can do it," woodenly states the Mick, reservation riddling his brow.

"It's personal."

"OK," the Mick yields.

"You can place a dangle that Arnett will bite on… and I mean bite hard?"

"No doubt."

"Credibility of the leak?" McManus tests the Mick.

"Have someone at a local station that can sell it. Your mark will take the anchovy and dive with it. Bank on it."

"You're that positive?"

"Yeah. It's another local reporter. Have him totally hemmed in. Came across dirt on him… big-house-type stuff. In fact, I'll turn it over if you want. You can have him work for you. Consider it a return favor for that twisted fucking politico in the San Fernando Valley you clued me about."

"Great," McManus responds, a shimmer of revenge gladdening his eyes. "Just make sure you have one of your snoops ready when Arnett or his assistant comes calling… because I know that fucking rating-monger will be looking hard."

"I can, but from what I've tapped so far, Arnett already has a couple of resources that root G2 for him."

"Find out their names. I'll eliminate their interest in the assignment."

"OK. Your voucher, your show."

"Good enough." McManus steps to the landing, past the Mick, and up the stairs.

McManus emerges on a floor of library hinterlands where shelves are stacked with collections of musky maps and geography volumes, many of which appear to have been accessed last time Amerigo Vespucci toured the States. McManus cruises down a dim aisle and stops at a location where dog-eared atlases are spaced like teeth in a Halloween pumpkin. Momentarily, an upper body from the next aisle appears in one of the gaps. The man, attired in perfunctory red–and-gold USC paraphernalia, has closely cropped hair, sharply hewn chin, coffee-ground complexion, gimlet pupils, hard-boiled expression, and no-non-sense lean. If this guy wasn't military at some point in his life, then Patton made his bones as a milksop dairyman.

"Thanks for coming out," McManus opens. "How you doing?"

"Just fucking ducky. Does this square us?" this man of few embroideries grumbles.

"Yep."

"About goddamn time." The man shoves a thick, flat, legal-size envelope across the shelf to McManus.

"Have anything digital?"

The man unholsters a middle finger for display. McManus takes it in course. "Sources?" McManus queries.

"Few floaters; some ears into J.S.O.C., a Task Force or two, S.A.S. Boat Troop, and A.S.I.O.; and an old Brand X guy."

"Good enough." McManus taps the envelope. "Net it out for me."

"About twenty years ago, a multi-national, either mining or oil, recruited college students from the States with off-the-charts IQ and EQ, all from military backgrounds or locked into R.O.T.C. or some off-campus stars-and-stripes program. Physically superior... if not freaks. The multi-national wanted, in effect, their own tier-one special forces unit trained their way to have on call whenever any of their assets around the world were compromised or at risk."

"Where in the States did they come from?"

"Don't know. You want to tell the story?" the man, voice chill, needles his questioner.

McManus compliantly accepts the dole of animus; the man continues. "Depending on who you talk to, they trained under combat vets with ties to Shayetet 13, Spetsnaz, S.A.S., or G.R.O.M... maybe all of them... who the hell knows."

"Polish?" McManus asks with a dose of skepticism.

"Those boys are no hoot, McManus. They'd hand your nuts to you in a nanosecond."

"What else?"

"Pretty sure they did groundwork in either Central or South America before they launched. Arrangement didn't last long, though. After a year or two, they broke from the multi-national."

"Why?"

"Best I can figure is they lost their taste for being employed by a corporation that was running roughshod over undeveloped countries. For the next eight years or so, they were basically shadow, white-hat mercs."

McManus's eyes sharpen. "What kind of ops?"

"Took the guts out of extremist networks and sleeper cells. Threw down on fast-twitch counter-insurgents; rogue militias; cartel heavies in South America. Sent to sleep handy guns doing ethnic cleansing in the Middle East. Did bang and burn, evac in Burma. Handled black ops with serious scope time in North Africa, put an end to their music. Other than their own intel, always went in naked, jumped in deep."

"Proficient in wet work?"

"No doubt. Excelled in hand-to-hand, C.Q.C., but that was last resort. Specialty was planning. Maniacs about it. Closed missions with minimum casualties and clean E. and E. Experts at dry cleaning."

"Anyplace they wouldn't go?"

"Not that I've been able to tell."

"What was the makeup of the team?" a now unquenchable McManus grills the man.

"Seven to nine men, one to two women." In response to McManus's crumpled forehead, the man submits, "From what I hear, they never registered a casualty... very tight unit, so everyone on the team had to be slick."

"Why did they leave the business?"

The man shrugs. "Don't know. Last gig was either on the Thai-Burma border or the Sudan... some say ten years ago, some say sooner."

"If these people produced such a large body of work, how did they manage to create a black hole around themselves?"

"That's the way they crafted it. Not only are these fuckers a smart bunch, they have major cajones. Before they signed on with any government or took on a hire, they made sure there could never be any gray mail on them. No face-to-face meetings with employers. Communicated anonymously with one and one contact only... all remote... impossible to trace. Before they accepted an assignment, they made it flat-out clear that if they or their mission were ever exposed in any way, shape, or form, they'd load everything about the op onto the Internet in a snap. With the sensitive shit they handled, they could create a major diplomatic embarrassment—downright disaster in some cases—for very highly placed people around the world. It's worked so far. I couldn't come up with a single name, even a country in which one of them *might* be living. Whatever their mojo is, it's potent."

"Did they take assignments from any of our agencies?"

"They did... now and then."

"Is the profile I sent you a match for this team?"

The man further nears the file to McManus. "I heard a couple of years back there was an incident in Nevada... maybe Vegas. Might've involved one of this team. Word came down from the Pentagon no less to put the brakes on the investigation and bury it. Some local chowderhead assigned to the case decided he was going to be a hero, so he went offline and stayed on it. Way the story goes, when the powers-that-be found out, the next Monday this guy's new office was next to an outhouse in some Podunk government outpost near Carson City." The man, eyes grievous, tenders this counsel to McManus: "If I were you, I'd hang around here until they start the bonfire after the game and throw that envelope in it. You're too old to pitch your career into the shitter. These people are fierce. If you're onto them, let it go. You do not, I repeat, *do not* want to take up arms with them."

Books in a judge's chambers can tell much about the resident. Those of Jonathan Neuland are not long, idle rows of dusty case-books and esoteric jurisprudential discourses accessed the last Jim Crow laws were all the rage. Rather, his volumes are a care-fully arranged workbench of compact texts readily on hand for the steadfast judge to ratchet his way through cases.

The 70-year-old jurist, white hair thinning, face narrowed to skeletal essentials, reedy frame, and slight hunch crawling up his back, labors over a file on his desk. A knock on the door dislodges him from his reading. "Please," he says in an affable voice unre-lated to the wire-brush tone most often emanating from a court-room bench.

Greg, impeccable in a suit, demeanor sure, yet gaunt of face, opens the door and steps comfortably from a dimming hallway into chambers. "Thanks for making time, your honor."

The Judge points to one of the leather-backed chairs across from his desk. "Give your briefs a rest, counselor."

Greg takes a seat with both the ease and alert of a talk-show guest.

"How are you, sir?"

Neuland, showing a homey, nonetheless worn smile, looks to his desk clock. "Still wishing that damn thing had a quitting whistle. How are you, young man? Appears you might've lost a bit of weight."

"How did you describe it in class... pushing the iceberg? I bang on that thing day and night, and occasionally think I actu-ally get some forward movement in my cases."

"Not what I hear in the halls out there," says Neuland, flip-ping his eyes toward the corridor. "The judges you sit before give you the highest marks."

"Gracious of them to say, your honor."

"Wish I didn't have to recuse myself from your cases. I truly would like to see you in action. They say you're something when the stakes are big."

"That's because you had the patience to put up with an old guy like me for two semesters."

"Law school," the jurist reminisces as he spills back in his chair, a purifying look washing his face. "A more orderly world, wasn't it, where Justice Holmes was uncontestable scripture and I.R.A.C. was the one and only true path?"

"Yeah, way I explain it to our first-years is that law school is cotillion and the practice a demolition derby."

"Very apt."

Greg's purpose prods him forward. "Might I ask you somewhat of a personal question, sir?"

"By all means."

"Why did you leave your professorship to take a seat on the bench?"

"Usual question is why resigned a letterhead position at a national law firm to be a teacher."

"Was it the challenge of trying something new that led you to change?"

Neuland pushes his shoulder blades into the worn leather. His voice takes on a paternal grade. "I'll speak to you plainly, Greg. As few the number of truly exceptional trial lawyers and law professors, there are fewer still who can do this job... capably. I know that a county judgeship is viewed in legal circles as a largely pedestrian position, but, take my word for it, no ordinary attorney can do it well. You're juggling eighty, maybe ninety cases at any one time — for which you have ultimate and complete accountability. There are no partners or faculty to turn for counsel. I misstep, people can suffer... and suffer deeply, because many don't have money to appeal if I've not been up to snuff. Often justice comes from this desk and this desk alone. Each day is a new proving ground. At my age, that's a nice dose of adrenaline." The Judge scrutinizes Greg. "You considering giving the bench a go?"

"No sir, I'm not. Just thinking through things."

Detecting more layers to be peeled back from his former pupil, Neuland proposes, "I have another forty-five minutes on this motion. How about we meet at Jeffer's place in an hour? I'll let you buy me a Rob Roy, and we can haggle over who springs for steaks."

As Greg rises, a vial of pills rattles in his suit pocket. "That would be great, your honor," he confirms in an elevated voice. "See you then."

Vis-a-vis apartment complexes near the 210 Freeway east of Arcadia, this one is pretty spiff. While the parking lot isn't exactly electric with jazzy sports cars or recreational vehicles occupying more space than an offshore drilling platform, your average visitor can rather easily tell a nice class of folk is on the property. The common areas are well kept, potted plants with perky annuals ennoble a number of resident entries, and children dashing about are caringly clothed. As one scales stairs to the top of the complex's four stories, those windows whose curtains are drawn reveal pleasant, traditional living areas, perhaps even trending fogyish. A slit in the drapes in House's unit on the fourth floor, however, shows something quite different — barren carpet floor, elaborate poker table topped with fine black felt, and slight scattering of furniture possibly sourced from a frat house about to be exiled off campus. Bart Maverick gone grunge might reside here.

On a Friday evening when fall is clearly announcing its presence, Hopper raps on House's door. It takes several more knocks before a bedroom lamp backlights the front room. After a protracted minute or so, House, shaking off sleep, but firmly in the grasp of dazing medication, opens the door. His disheveled clothing and tousled hair appear to be the vision of a fashion consultant fixated on chaos.

"Hey Hop, what's going on?" House says in a voice that would ordinarily emanate more from a garbage disposal than a larynx.

"Grab a jacket," Hopper announces in a chipper tone. "We're headed to the All Souls football game."

House's face does not augur well for the home-team fan base. "Not feeling that great," he damply defers.

"Sure?"

House shows the expression of one prepared to league in no exploit beyond cracking open a refrigerator for a tub of rocky road. "I'm sure."

"That'll be a real disappointment to Billy," Hopper laments with a feigned frown.

As House is sorting this revelation through his diminished processes, Hopper throws a thumb over his shoulder. "Yeah, he's in the Our Lady van with Honorio and some other kids from my flag football team."

"How... "

Hopper puts the stopper to House's question. "Your sister-in-law is as tired as everyone else watching you turn into a slug. Let's hit it."

High school football games in Southern California don't quite match the spectacle of their counterparts in Texas, where some rivalries can make the Punic Wars look like a playground tiff. However, when two Southland Catholic football powerhouses square off with state rankings at stake, the game can take on a life of its own. This night in a small stadium west of Riverside, bands are blaring, stands are abuzz, and battle cries of school superiority, football supremacy, and Catholic ascendancy fill the air. At the very top of the bleachers on the blue-clad All Souls side of the field sit Hopper and House with Billy, Honorio, Ryan the altar boy, and a couple of other youngsters their age giddily soaking in the rivalry and catapulting catcalls to red-and-silver idolaters of St. Ignatius across the way.

While House, now seemingly part of the living, keeps one eye on the game and the other on Billy, Hopper laces an arm around a horizontal bleacher support just above House's head. "What's with the dark-side routine? Trying to work into character for the part of some troubled, sullen down-and-outer you're reading for at the lot, or are you just tweaked because the three of us still have our chance and you don't?"

Eyes markedly forward, House responds with a hint of pique. "Who's tweaked?"

"Since we've come back to the States, we've never gone this long without getting together. Greg says he hasn't heard from you in forever."

"Just taking a long time to heal."

Hopper is having none of the evasiveness. "You know, House, if you don't level with me, you'll be sitting at high school football games every weekend right to Christmas."

House observes his nephew laughing and jostling with the boys from Our Lady. He draws a melancholy breath, then emptily admits, "You saw me limping up those steps. I never thought something like this would happen to me."

"From what Trina tells me, the doctors say it eventually goes away."

"It does, but what doesn't go away," reveals House, his face reflecting a cruel sedition, "is the fact that we're not bulletproof."

"You actually thought we were?"

House scrapes lining from his soul. "Laid up in that goddamn apartment, I've run through it over and over. There's no explanation for all ten of us making it through those ops year in and out without someone being iced or, at the very least, seriously torn up. We were in the jungle in Burma for over three weeks straight, and we never tripped a land mine… not a single one. There are more of those fucking contraptions in that country than ping pong balls in Bangkok. How do we get a pass? How in the fuck does that happen? No other team I've ever heard of skated out of there without setting one off."

"We didn't take the kind of risk you did in the Valley. You tried it for all the right reasons, but you jumped in uncovered. You never took on anything like that before, and you tried your shot on what… two hours' notice? We sometimes took months mapping out strategy before we ever hopped a plane and put boots on the ground."

"I took a flyer because of the old man's chance."

"Yeah, but none of us knew the hooks that come with it. We said it at Primo's, didn't we? Shit, when it's cold like tonight, I can feel exactly where that bullet went it… probably always will."

House bends to Hopper's logic. After a moment, he asks in a wintry voice, "Think we'll ever see the old man again?"

"Only if we've earned it."

House chews on Hopper's reply before locking his hands behind his head and settling against the grandstand bars. "Why did that old man pick us?"

Hopper broaches a theory. "How do we know he hasn't done the same for thirty other people… three hundred… three thousand… if no one can talk about it?"

House's blank look speaks volumes. After a moment, he faintly replies, "We don't."

"Yep, we don't know. Since that day in the high desert, we don't know that and a whole lot of other things."

Newspaper and television reporters, their trusty camera operators in nearby waiting, mill around a side exit from a large, old-time courthouse of streaked whitish-gray stone. Mitch Arnett rests against his station's van, smoking a cigarette and jabbering on a cell phone. Roland, wearing a broad smile and toting a small satchel, laces his way through bodies to the big (limburger) cheese of the airwaves; he deferentially waits until Arnett finishes his call.

"When's the jury coming out?" Roland asks.

"Should be anytime."

"Picked your one?"

"Yep. Juror Six... dressed to the nines today. No doubt she can't wait to stand in front of a camera and blab." Arnett takes a drag from his smoke. "You look pretty fucking pleased with yourself. Get laid in the desert?"

Nodding to his satchel, Roland declares, "You'll like what I have here. Blew up the license plate of the woman who left the hospital with our mystery man from the mountain." As if exposing paired hole aces, Roland pulls out a department-issue headshot of Trina. "That's Trina Lewis — the policewoman who saved the other broad cop at the jewelry store heist." Roland taps the photo. "She just joined her buddy at superhero central. There's a major piece here. We have a great hook — spec ops bring their skills to the street."

"It's a bigger story, and *we* don't have it," Arnett says unsparingly.

"What are you talking about?"

"Leak from a source at Channel 8. Vertain's landed files on these people and their covert activities overseas." Arnett looks piercingly at Roland before hanging the rap on him. "Stuff we couldn't put our hands on."

"How could they have files!" implores Roland, now suddenly the dog's chew stick.

"They have 'em, and they're supposed to be dynamite. The stuntman, this cop, the attorney, and evidently six or seven others were deep into major global situations. We're talking international newswire if this hits."

"You're sure about Vertain?"

"He doesn't have enough yet to air, but his team is busting ass on it."

Nearly seizing, Roland blurts, "I swear... I swear I put the slam on every one of our contacts, and they all came up with absolutely blank fucking pages."

"Vertain still has holes," Arnett redemptively advises Roland.

"What does it matter? We don't have dough to do serious digging."

"Sure we do," Arnett slyly responds. "There's a check in your desk. Cash it at your bank, not one of the station's. Put Montrose or Palladian on these people. Neither one of those two has a conscience. They'll piece together what we need."

"How did you grind money out of the suits? Somebody else's story fall through?""

"It's my check."

"Your check? Shit, neither Montrose or Palladian is cheap."

"We're on the spot with market share as it is. If that lame-dick Vertain jumps ahead of us in ratings, we'll find ourselves in an afternoon time slot covering cakewalks and bocci ball tournaments at rest homes in Ventura County." Arnett brings an irrevocability to his eyes. "Not exactly the type of scintillating stories that'll propel you into production."

Roland is on board and on his way.

Just another day at a suburban Southern California mall — bands of gabbing housewives discharging a periodic social rite, shopaholics carrying out their sentences, bargain-hunters making tracks for sales, and those thin in the pocketbook luxuriating in an air-conditioned atrium. Trina and Diane sit at a table in a food court, a studied distance from a cluster of giggleful teenage girls.

"It's the first time since we've been together... even before we were married... that we're not communicating," Diane ponderously relates to Trina.

"Greg's practice seems to be really wearing on him," Trina replies, beginning a choreographed jig on the truth. "I could tell from a day I ran into him at the courthouse. His face was almost gray he was so drained. Maybe that's a lot of it."

"That I understand. But what's happening with the four of you? You're not spending nearly as much time together. House has fallen off the face of the earth. It's so different from the way you've been. Why is that? What's keeping everyone apart?"

Trina is shy a cookbook answer for all that. "Don't know how much of an explanation I have, Diane. There's a big part of each one of us that's private, so I really can only speak for myself. I had a couple of bang-bang choices to make on my job. If I didn't go the way I did, I wouldn't have felt good about the service I was doing to my badge. It threw me in the spotlight, and that's not what we all agreed a long time ago. We felt it best to keep our heads down and handle our business low-key to make sure our past stayed secure and people we care about aren't put in harm's way." Slightly thick-tongued, Trina concludes, "Sometimes things just don't work out the way you hope. I think that has kind of been a disappointment to Greg."

"You know how proud I am of you, what you're doing at the department. That policewoman wouldn't have made it from the jewelry store parking lot if you hadn't rescued her."

"Maybe, in time, Greg will mellow about it. Lord knows where he'd be as a lawyer if he spent even one percent of his time promoting himself."

Diane, face cluttering with emotion, combs a hand through her hair. "Trina, I'm worried about Greg... his health, his well-being. I'm seeing new prescriptions in the bathroom... when he comes home late and is too tired to do a good job hiding them. From what I can tell on the Internet, it's serious heart medication. And Dr. Klein is putting Greg through batteries of tests. I see paperwork from the insurance company."

"What kind of tests?" asks Trina, now clearly pulled into the gravity of Diane's concern.

"Hard to tell from the forms. I just don't know," Diane responds in a paltry voice.

"What does Greg say?"

"Nothing I don't drag out of him. And it's not enough to paint a solid picture."

The two sit silent for a moment, then Diane, visibly distraught over the condition of her champion, stares forlornly onto the mall. "Do you know how many veterans develop P.T.S.D., how many commit suicide every day?"

"You don't think for a minute… "

"Yes," Diane resolutely replies, "I think about it every waking hour."

"But we're not veterans."

"Where have I heard *that* before?" Diane's molten stare puts Trina in silent check.

Greta sits alone behind the instrument panel in the sepulchral room of wall screens. Extemporaneous headshots of House, Hopper, Greg, and Trina fill Screen One. Cropped photos of five men and a woman occupy space immediately across. Below on Screens Three and Four are collages of telephoto shots of House arriving at Tailspin & Tonic, House with his nephew at the amusement park, Hopper and House in the stands at a high school football game, and Hopper on the grounds of Our Lady of Perpetual Hope.

Allan, carting stacks of copied phone records and emails, gutting through mental dehydration, lunges into the room and unloads his paper ore onto the panel counter.

"'Nother all-nighter?" Greta perfunctorily asks.

"Yep," Allan croaks.

"That include everything from the law firm?"

"Yeah, it does."

"Positive we exited clean?"

"The law firm's electronic security is pretty tight, but no contest for Norcal's buddy Buzzard." Allan nods to the top left screen. "Hardisty's close to those other three... handled legal matters for them... the stuntman's scrape in Santa Barbara, ruckus the woman caused in Vegas, and a couple situations for Brendan Hopper. He put in a ton of time for the stuntman's brother on a manslaughter beef." Allan points to the photo of Hopper at Our Lady. "Hardisty's also done a fair amount of pro bono work for that church."

"Hardisty have contact with anyone on the right?" Greta inquires.

"Apostoli, but that was mostly when the guy was practicing law in the San Francisco Bay area. For some unknown reason, he retired from criminal defense work to open a restaurant in the East Bay; there hasn't been as much traffic since. Hardisty's in touch with Promardie and Lucci on and off. The others... it's mostly random."

"Mac's confirmed that the stuntman, Hopper, and Hardisty are the three from the mountain."

"What exactly is Mac wanting from us this afternoon?"

"Brief our findings, scheme resource utilization, give our recs."

"What's he really after?"

"Sure you want to know?" Greta asks with a jaundiced eye.

Allan, passing on the invite to a deep dive, chooses to massage the bridge of his nose. "How do you think we should deploy assets?"

Greta maps a plan. "Keeping the tech from up north on the stuntman's burner from here on is a waste. We have what we need from Stackhouse. What sent him to the hospital must've rocked his world... which now is bars, doctors' offices, and his brother's family. I just don't see him as a threat.

"In my mind, the attorney being in the mountains when the shooters were taken out isn't a match. Had to be a one-off thing. You have enough there on him to keep us busy a while. If there'll be fireworks or something unexpected, then it'll come from those two." Greta rotates a panel dial, highlighting Hopper's and Trina's headshots.

Allan studies Trina's image. "Lewis sure has taken her job to the next level the last few months. What do you think's happening with her?"

"If this *is* the team Mac suspects, that was in deep fighting those kinds of human atrocities, jumping into hotspots all over the world year after year after year, who the hell knows what makes her or any of them tick," Greta tautly replies.

Allan takes that as answer enough. "Do we switch the Mick from the TV guys to Brendan Hopper and assign someone to the policewoman?"

"Mac wants to keep the Mick on Arnett and his lackey."

"Why? Arnett and his assistant are both spread so thin there's no chance they'll root out anything before we can. We won't look real swift in our reports if a guy with the Mick's price tag is bringing in biscuits on his weeklies."

"There won't be reports on this," Greta dourly advises Allan.

"That come from Mac?"

"From above us."

Allan chooses to test the explanation not. "So we what... move Norcal from the stuntman to Hopper and bring in who for the policewoman? Iron Dave is back from Prague."

"Without a budget and with the voucher to the Mick every week, the kitty is thin."

"When will we have a budget?"

Yet another Greta pronunciamento: "There won't be one."

"OK," Allan swallows, "what's our rec then?"

"I say we split the tech between Hopper and the policewoman. If the tech taps out, we move his buddy Buzzard from spot backup into something more."

"Guess that makes sense," Allan acquiesces, stifling a yawn. "Norcal brings big apparatus. With Buzzard in the bullpen, he should be able to cover both streets... at least for a while."

"Let's bang this out. We're on with Mac at four."

Allan jumps into his heap of papers.

Hopper's Jeep is parked outside a small, well-kept, compact home with scarlet bougainvillea spidering onto stucco walls and over the tile roof. Much like other residences in this humble Hispanic neighborhood, pride of ownership is roundly evident. Hopper and Trina, both hauling cardboard boxes of Honorio's belongings, pass the boy as he whisks from the Jeep inside the house.

As Hopper and Trina stow boxes in the back of the vehicle, Trina remarks, "He's such a polite boy... so easy to be around."

"His mother has done a great job raising him... especially with no dad in the house."

"He sure seems to have a skip in his step when you're around."

"Like spending time with him?" Hopper asks somewhat searchingly.

"I do."

"Appears his mother will be in physical therapy longer than we thought. Father Raymond keeps bringing up the need for a female presence when Honorio's staying at the rectory... during dinner... things like that."

Trina hesitates, carefully laundering her response. "Not sure I'm the one for that."

"Why? Honorio's really himself around you."

Trina gazes to the house, then away from Hopper before responding, "It's just that he... boys his age remind me of... "

Hopper's voice swiftly takes on voltage. "Your needle's still not stuck on Sudan is it?"

"Honorio isn't all that much younger than that boy."

"How many times does it have to be laid out? He wasn't a boy. He was a shooter. If you hadn't dropped the hammer, he would've dusted Lance or me... maybe both of us. You didn't put the rifle in his hand. It was one of those fucking maniac tin generals that conscripted him from his family. You want to feel good about something instead of feeling bad? Feel good about the number of those motherfucking butchering warlords and their lieutenants we took out of commission so they couldn't march anymore kids to the grave."

As Trina wrestles with Hopper's reply, Honorio springs out of the house, but then suddenly freezes in his tracks. When Hopper notices Honorio still struck, he inspects the street. Parked at the far end of the block is the black SUV he had seen at Our Lady. In an instant, Hopper bounds down the walkway and is on his knees in front of Honorio. He puts arms to the boy's shoulders. "What is it?"

Clearly out of plumb, Honorio sinks his head.

"What does Father Raymond tell us?" Hopper says firmly, but not overbearingly. "To be family, we have to be honest with family. Who's in that black SUV?"

"Men that want me to play soccer," Honorio replies with a thick tongue.

His conversation with the boy's mother spinning in his mind, Hopper asks, "Have they ever tried to give you drugs?"

Honorio's head sags further in confirmation.

"Stay here with Trina, OK?"

"OK."

Hopper stands and turns. Eyes magnetized on the Jeep, he walks directly to it. As he passes Trina, he says in monotone, "Think there's a situation with that SUV. It's the one we talked about. Need you to stay here with the boy in case there's another vehicle."

"Sure," Trina responds without the slightest rise. She ambles toward Honorio, and, as Hopper starts his Jeep, turns back and smilingly waves to him as if all is hunky-dory.

Hopper drives at normal speed toward the SUV, which is occupied by the two Hispanics who had earlier approached Honorio. The instant the driver descries Hopper's size and singeing stare, he quickly calculates trouble squared, starts the SUV, and zooms in the opposite direction. Hopper makes a nifty U-turn and trails the SUV, giving it distance. Once the speeding SUV has cleared family neighborhoods into a sparse area of vacant lots and small industrial buildings, Hopper jams his foot to the pedal. He soon is on the bumper of the SUV. He bashes into its back, nearly sending it into a spin. The SUV squares itself and accelerates around a corner. Hopper jumps a curb, zips through a near-empty parking lot past the intersection, and vaults onto the street in front of the SUV. He slams on his brakes, snags a revolver from under the seat, and rolls onto the pavement. The SUV, unable to either swerve or stop in time, crashes into the Jeep. The jolt sends the Hispanic passenger through the windshield and driver violently against the steering wheel, compressing his lungs.

Hopper, arms and neck showing deep strawberry scrapes from hitting the asphalt, comes out of his tumble, and, with pointed pistol, advances on the SUV. As the gasping driver struggles to gain his senses, Hopper takes a handful of shirt and drags him to his vehicle.

"See that!" Hopper bellows, his voice rabid with rage. "You see that Jeep? I've had it nine years. I like it. I'm attached to it. If I were a fucking creep like you, I'd probably have a name for it. But I gave it up pronto so you and whoever in the fuck you work for know one thing... I don't give a shit." Hopper yanks the woozy Hispanic's face within a micrometer of his. "Tell your boss this: You or anyone else comes near that kid, and..." Hopper snarls as, in a spasm of furor, he jams the pistol up the Hispanic's nostril. "...You'll deal with the business end of this."

Hopper tosses the Hispanic to the ground. After receiving final benediction from Hopper—a bellicose kick to the groin, the driver finds the welcome company of unconsciousness. As Hopper clears his cell phone and enters numbers, a small device set into his smashed taillight catches his attention.

One thing you can safely say about a bowling alley on League Night: There typically is no dearth of avenues for folks to unleash the inner titan, overwhelm the order of pins with the chaos of might, and crow to the heavens about luck as if it were a birthright. As a general proposition, it takes some scouring to find a league bowler who doesn't get his money's worth... and then some. The postulate is certainly proving out on two rackety middle lanes in an everyman alley where opponents are letting balls and spirited cajoling fly with equal abandon. Greta, bedecked in jubilant team colors, is squarely in the middle of the mix. In this assemblage of outsized personalities, she suffers no wilt, goes at it with both barrels, giving as good (if not better) than she receives.

Behind the lanes is a long counter where sumptuously shirted contingents eagerly await their time on the hardwood stage. [This particular evening the top of general choice is a retro, panel type favored by Charlie Sheen in *Two and a Half Men* and Ray Liotta in *Goodfellas* (when he wasn't muscling some schmuck)]. Wedged into this prismatic throng is McManus. Wearing slate corduroy pants, button-down shirt, tweedy sweater, and plaintive expression, he stands out like an Amish on Ipanema.

After Greta's team caps the evening with a rousing comeback, she makes her way to the counter and shoulders herself into a sliver of a space next to McManus. Greeting her with a shallow, coaxed smile, he murmurs, "Exactly what happened today?"

"The rear device our man from up north spotted in the Jeep was exposed," Greta responds in a subdued tone.

"How badly?"

"The target extracted it, evidently searched all the lights, found the one in front, and removed it as well."

"Are they identifiable?"

"No. Our man makes his own gear."

McManus's tongue grows slightly abrupt. "What's the read on this mountain man?"

"Nothing outside the box... spends his work hours as a martial arts instructor and, beyond that, a whole helluva lotta time at that church."

"The woman in blue?"

"Just a bust-ass broad who puts in long hours... couple of casual dates."

McManus watches a baroquely outfitted, exotically coiffed man samba toward the foul line, rear back, fire a ball down the lane that buzzes through all the pins, and, in celebration, put on the gyrating dog for his team, opposition, and some subgod of gaucheries. McManus refocuses on Greta and snips at her, "We've been compromised. What's your rec?"

"Odds are that, starting today, all four will be looking for a presence. We have about everything we're going to from the stuntman and attorney for now, so no problem being distant there. We'll be clear of the woman in blue's and mountain man's apartment complexes by 3:00 a.m. tonight. Our going-forward plan is to spot static devices near locations the mountain man and woman frequent. If we see any break from their usual pattern or positive indicators that they might be gearing up for something, then we jump back in live."

McManus gazes onto the ribbons of glassy, varnished pine and maple and valiantly suppresses the urge to preach. He slides off his stool and closes the powwow. "OK. Keep me posted," he blurbs before disappearing into the shuttle of bowlers.

Primo leads Greg up moaning stairs to his office, which, in essence, is a loft walled in with plywood stained a color largely unknown in nature. Inside sits a small wooden desk whose sole concession to organization is a beer mug filled with writing implements. A pace from the desk is the conference area, i.e. a cardboard table surrounded by folding chairs, where Hopper, House, and Trina, all with pensive faces of a hastily convened war counsel, are gathered. At this moment, Hopper fiddles with two small lenses, Trina knocks out text messages, and House amply displays a mopey mood. Greg, in full business attire, whisks into the room. After the counselor's brief apology for tardiness and a subdued go-around absent usual badinage, Hopper bores in on the heart of the agenda as Primo returns downstairs.

"I found these," he says with a somewhat operatic sweep of his hand over the lenses, "in the headlight and taillight of my Jeep. They're from remote cams on a signal range—somewhere in the neighborhood of two to three miles."

"Origin?" Greg clinically inquires.

"Not traceable... custom-made... advanced."

"Run it by the Pro?" Trina asks.

"Yeah, he took them to two different shops. They both said it's off-market, high-end assembly." Hopper rotates his eyes around the table. "Any of you had a sense of surveillance, electronic intrusion?"

Trina tries to float some humor. "If there are snoops on me and they come up with something interesting about my life, hope they clue me in."

Hopper issues a crabby stare. "That's a load of fucking help."

Trina spells it out for Hopper. "I live in a low-security apartment. I share a garage with two other guys in the complex that have bikes. If someone with large reserves like the company is on me, they could put together a reality series and I'd be the last to know. But even if they did, what would they find? My sensitive stuff was cleared out to Florida a long time ago."

Hopper's eyes bounce to Greg who needs no more prompt. "Anything, and I mean anything, I have locally that even remotely relates to our ops is on a hard drive locked in a floor safe in my basement that's state of the art and then some. No one's breaching that there unless they blow up the goddamn house. I have my immediate work area at the law firm dry-cleaned once a month. The firm has the best security for email you can buy. That being said, the system is no match for some all-world hacker from cyberspace who cracks government data bases for a living. I checked on our stashes in the Keys and Caribbean last week. Our guys say status quo—not a hint of activity." Greg throws fingers toward the devices. "How did you come onto those?"

"Found one in a rear light when I was in an accident," Hopper explains, leaving the heart of the story on the cutting-room floor. "Took apart the other lamps. Found the second in a headlight." Hopper circles to House. "What about you?"

"If anyone's surveilling me, his camera better be on super slow-mo. I haven't been doing shit since the accident. As far as my comm with anyone, it's like it's always been: burner only— both text and voice. Can't take more precautions than that." House solders his eyes to the lenses. "Any idea how long they've been there?"

"The Pro says that, based on the electronic array, could be anywhere from two weeks to two years... intentionally very difficult to decipher."

Screening off his snarky side, Greg asks in a balanced tone, "Surprised you're in the crosshairs?"

Hopper has clearly prepped himself for the line of questioning. "Like I told you all, I tricked out the plates on the Jeep before I hit the mountains. With my gear, no one could've made me while I was on the targets. I was in the clearing with you and House for only a few minutes, and that was away from ground cameras. A helo shot of the three of us then couldn't have turned anything positive."

Hopper's logic is hardly catching with Greg. "You did fantastic work there, Hop. From what I read, those kids might've been goners had you not stepped in. But you did leave something— nothing, which is the mark of a very high-value asset. And you showed up uniforms on the ground. My guess is one of them has found a way to you."

"How?" asks Trina, taking Hopper's part.

Hardly a stumper for House. "What did we say when someone came to us with an assignment that seemed impossible. We said, 'Then we'll just find a way to make it possible.' Who says we have a stranglehold on that?"

No one at the table has issue with House's able take. Hopper, momentarily dry of words, rocks in his chair.

"Greg, maybe you or Apostoli could contact one of the people in D.C. to see if they can find out anything," Trina proposes. "They stepped right up for my situation in Vegas."

"The reason they got behind us in Vegas, for House's deal in Santa Barbara, and Hopper's jams is because, in the total picture, they were small potatoes, kind of shit that can happen to anyone in the mainstream. If I make the call, they'll want to know the back story. I tell them what happened with those hostages, and all of a sudden, in their eyes, we become wild cards. You want to be in that position with them?" Trina shrinks her neck ever so slightly and passes. Greg finishes his thoughts. "The other thing is that we only have so many chips with these folks. Do we use one here?"

"Let's see how things play out for a while," Trina replies, backing away from her suggestion. "You OK with that Hop?"

"Yeah."

Trina checks her cell, then stands to absent herself. "Start my shift in forty-five minutes."

"Anything we should be doing in the meantime?" House asks the group.

"Keep your antenna up and an eye around the corner," Hopper submits as he too rises. "Have to head to Our Lady."

"How's it going with the boy?" House inquires.

"Pretty good. You know, it's funny. One of his subjects is geography. I was looking over maps in his textbook after we finished homework the other night. We've covered a lot of damn ground, didn't we?"

"That we did," House agrees, remembrance lightening his expression.

"What are your plans for the evening, House? Gonna have Primo call you a taxi or 9-1-1?" Greg jests.

"Well, I do have a couple of scheduled magazine interviews about my much anticipated return to the entertainment business, but I suppose I could push them back," House responds in kind.

"Why don't we slip downstairs for a liquid refreshment or two?"

"That I could do."

Greg and House kick back at one of Primo's side tables, away from the bar (where folks are vigorously unloosening their ties, pocketbooks, and tongues); a couple groups of chatty, peppermint-personality secretaries; dartboards (where an elephantine reincarnation of Robin Hood is having his way with a boisterous, well-liquored field); and a folk-guitar player (island buddy of Primo's) who is enjoying the reception of an alpine yodeler opening for the Jimi Hendrix Experience. Greg nurses a beer while House drills down a stiff see-through cocktail (which, on the tavern's drink menu, is the entry immediately below "Anesthesia").

"Trina says you might be moving to the East Bay, working with Judson."

"Thinking about it. Would be nice to spend time back there. But nothing will happen until Cord's out of the clink."

"How's he doing?"

"All right. He's an arm for some inmates with serious bank, so he's pocketing cash for the family."

"I thought Cord was in low security."

"He is... thanks to you, but there are predators even in that kind of place."

Greg knocks suds off his beer. "When are you coming over for dinner?"

"Diane been asking?"

"She has." Greg permits the invitation to simmer, then adds, "But I gotta tell you, it would be great to have you at the table. Probably make it seem less like a Doctor Phil session."

"Things still a little rocky?"

"Sort of... in some ways better since my dad's gone. He was in so much pain the last few months we were all stressed. Now he finally has peace." Greg bides a moment before uncorking the question he was sitting to ask. "How much peace are you having, buddy?"

With frail conviction, House reveals, "Some... I guess."

"Trina thinks you might be down because you lost your chance."

"Something special went by the boards, didn't it?"

"Did it really if it made you realize you'd be happier with Judson and Lucci in the East Bay, working with regular people every day, not entertainment types? Isn't that a good thing?"

"Yeah, I guess it is."

"I mean, we haven't represented a whole lot of movie people, but the ones I've come across... man, are they going to be surprised when three days after they die the rock doesn't roll away from their tomb."

"Kinda like that Sutter Nance guy?"

"Kinda," Greg ruefully acknowledges.

Arnett and Roland alight from Roland's Lotus at the base of a rocky hill topped by a massive electrical transmission tower. Arnett disseminates a fair portion of sour mood. "Neither Montrose or Palladian has ever turned down an assignment from me. Those money-grubbing fuckers should be goddamn jitterbugging at the dough I'm willing to lay out if they deliver the goods."

"You've never asked them to pull papers on people that might be black ops. Get sideways with a troop like that, and you could find yourself with a third nostril... in the middle of your forehead."

"I thought those two pricks had balls," Arnett bridles.

"I think their keeping them might be a big part of it."

"Read that to me again when I have a fat assignment to dish out."

As they trudge up the hill, Arnett woofs, "So this is the name both Montrose and Palladian gave us? I didn't know those two guys could agree on anything. Where's he from? Never heard of him."

"Just moved here from D.C."

"Why?"

"There he is. Ask him."

A husky man with thick, bristly, light-brown hair and dressed in a baggy, gray athletic suit has stepped from cover of the tower base. A furry eyebrow bisected by a telltale scar, deep facial creases, craggy forehead, and unforgiving twist to the corners of his mouth evidence a man of little mirth and gentility.

"That Kiefer?"

"That's him."

When they reach the top, Arnett and Roland find Kiefer has stepped down to a shallow gulch running between the bottom of the tower supports, where he stands like the last surviving member of a defiant plains tribe. They make their way to him.

After Roland does the introduction, Arnett frostily opens, "Roland tells me you're here from D.C. Why the move?"

In a barely discernible Charlestown accent, Kiefer issues a canned response: "Some people thought a change of scenery would do me good."

"You hot?"

"No more than usual."

Arnett's arm refers to the towers. "Why are we meeting here?"

"Best practices."

"Why did you want to see me personally?"

"To know the money."

"In case I don't pay in full?"

"That... and a couple other things."

As Kiefer re-surveys the area for a specter of intrusion, Roland tries to lower tension. "Have I given you everything you need to move ahead?" he asks Kiefer.

"I'm set."

"How will you source data?" Arnett gruffly inquires.

"Records can be locked away forty feet underground, but the people who created them in the first place can't. Just a case of finding that one person who will leak ... at the right price."

"Don't have an unlimited budget," Arnett cautions.

"Once I have a way clear, that's your choice. If you decide not to step up, I'm still paid full boat on my end. Understood?"

"I understand."

"One other thing," Kiefer rules, "name of the source stays with me."

"How do we judge credibility?" Roland asks in a mannerly voice.

"You already have... or we wouldn't be meeting."

Arnett scrutinizes Kiefer a deep moment before relenting. "OK."

"Good." Closure achieved, Kiefer starts to drift away.

"Staying here?" Roland asks.

"Until you leave."

As Arnett and Roland trek down the hill, Arnett grouses, "I thought Montrose and Palladian were weird ducks. That guy makes them look like Welcome Wagon hosts."

"They say he's good."

"Better be. Vertain's staff is looking to knock out a multi-segment piece. We have serious ground to make up."

"Vertain still have holes?"

"Fewer."

"Shit."

This evening the only sounds in the dimly lighted law office corridor are humming vacuum cleaners and muffled voices of an industrious cleaning crew. In the law library, Greg and Paul Thornberg, both looking frayed, sit at computers across from one another. Surrounding them is a depot of files, reports, transcripts, memoranda, legal digests, and other manifest opportunities for prolific billing.

Sutter Nance, face braided in anxiety, hastens in to announce, "Proctor just read the deposition of Streeter's E.V.P. He thinks we have a clear cause for punitives."

"Just read the Streeter E.V.P.'s deposition!" Greg exclaims. "It's been sitting on his desk for over two goddamn months."

"He's been busy on the North Africa trade agreements."

Greg skims a hand over the conference table. "We've been busy here."

"No matter," Nance snipes at Greg.

Greg, voice daggering, counters, "It's a pretty goddamn big matter to me. First, we have to make a motion to amend the complaint this close to trial, which will be a bitch to win. If we *are* successful, then everyone in this room will have violated the code of professional ethics."

"Nonsense," Nance scolds Greg. "There's a colorable claim for punitive damages."

"Have you actually read the E.V.P.'s deposition?"

"Not in excruciating detail."

Greg signals to his right. "There it is—the one with all the paper clips. I tell you this point blank: There is absolutely *nothing* in that document or any other discovery justifying a good-faith claim for punitives. That being the case, the State Bar of California sets forth in no ambiguous detail we cannot prosecute the allegation."

"I disagree," Nance briskly contends. His eyes dart across the table where Greg's colleague has been earnestly harboring hope the *Starship Enterprise* or other intergalactic vessel would beam him up to avoid the impaling question about to drop. "What's your view, Paul?"

A dark insularity overtakes the world of Paul Thornberg. He knows Greg to be correct. However, he more compellingly understands that every second he does not emphatically endorse Nance's cause, his chances at partnership might well wane. Thornberg posts his position, "I can reasonably make a case for punitives."

Greg glares at Thornberg with an expression both scolding and scornful. "You can't be serious."

While Thornberg locks on Greg, his focal point is clearly Nance. "I am. I can state cause in a motion."

"Then I have a flash for you. *You* can argue it."

Greg, a glaze of disgust across his face, abruptly rises and stalks out of the law library.

Cronin walks from the Senor Salsa fast-food counter bearing a tray of chorizo burritos, chicken taquitos, chips, flour tortillas, a healthy (or not-so-healthy) offering of guacamole, and sufficient quantity of hot sauce to fuel an entry in the Firecracker 400. Trina is in tow with two super-sized cups of coffee stout enough to float manhole covers. This plainly is a lunch for those with polyurethane innards.

The uniformed partners settle onto a bench immediately off the parking lot, close to their patrol car. After a brief taste-testing to make sure the smorgasbord before him is F.D.A.-worthy, Cronin asks Trina, "How's it goin' with that boy at the church? Seems like you really enjoy your time with him."

"Yeah, he's such a genuine kid. It's not easy living most of the month at a church rectory, but he doesn't let it bother him."

"Make you rethink being a mom?"

"Need a relationship first."

"Looking for one?"

"I'll let one find me."

"The guy you brought to Dimokopoulos's wedding was nice enough."

"We'll see."

Cronin takes a slug of coffee, then tries to boost the low-yield conversation. "With all the good things happening for you at the precinct and the Captain in your court, I woulda thought you'd be more upbeat."

Trina's excuse bin is bare. "Just in a different space for a while, I suppose."

Cronin lets his food-friendly rest. "Look Trina, there are as many stories going around the precinct about what you did before you joined the force as guys in uniform. I've seen you in action enough to know there can't be many people anywhere in the world with your trade. Whatever your prior life was — and, believe me, I truly do not want to know," Cronin charily underscores, "this much I can guess — the final score everyday was pretty easy to register, because somebody usually didn't walk away." Cronin directs his vision to the black-and-white. "In this job, the score isn't always so easy to settle... or even figure. Sometimes guys in the same uniform can be a bigger problem than the ones on the street, which isn't exactly an ideal team concept. None of that's gonna change... on your shift, my shift, or anyone else's that I can see."

Trina's response is dashed by a cackling from the car radio. Cronin swings off the bench. "I'll get it."

Cronin steps quickly to the patrol car and ducks his head in the passenger side. Instantly, he is hustling around to the steering wheel and impelling Trina, "Let's roll, partner. 207 at Prescott and Ashton."

"207 or 207M?"

"No attempt. Straight-up 207."

"Shit, that's Our Lady."

Trina rockets to the patrol car.

Diane and House sit at a patio table outside French doors to the Hardisty dining room, where remnants of Diane's veal piccata dinner and fixings are in evidence. The two have their backs to a large masonry barbecue pit where cool evening air is hastening the coals' retreat into chalky soot. Diane has both hands around a cup of tea, while House is taking the top and then some from a big boy's glass of brandy. A few feet away, Greg, coffee mug in one hand and cell phone in the other, is deep into a conversation with an evidently grim progression.

"Did the other witness have any new information?" Diane asks House, scraping for a toehold of optimism.

"No. Pretty much the same story as the groundskeeper at Our Lady. Honorio was coming out of the church when all the teachers were rounding up kids into classrooms after lunch. A dark-colored station wagon, probably domestic, drove in front of the church just as Honorio was walking down the steps. Two Hispanics jumped from the car, bagged him, and threw him into the back. Whole thing couldn't have taken more than ten, fifteen seconds."

"The old lady on her way to church didn't see the license plate?"

"She's eighty-nine and has glaucoma."

"So no license for the station wagon from anybody at all?"

"Nope, but I'm not sure how much it would help. The plates were probably bogus, stolen, or untraceable."

"When Trina called this afternoon, she sounded just beat."

"She's up against it, Diane. She has a license number from the prior incident with Hopper," House says with little expansiveness, "but that paperwork hit a dead-end in Belize — even with all the extra people the department has involved. You don't realize how many kids go missing until you are thrown into the system.

There are a lot of parents, agencies, and support groups competing for a limited amount of law enforcement horsepower. Trina's Captain has a lot of stroke, but it only goes so far."

Greg closes the call. Lips mum, face mealy, he dumps into a seat at the table. After House and Diane exchange unsure glances, House ventures, "Is Hopper coming over?"

"Yeah, talked him into stopping by. Be here in an hour or so."

"Does he have anything more?"

"Not really. He took me through what happened when he chased the two Hispanic guys shadowing Honorio and what Mrs. Fernandez had told him about drug dealers trying to recruit the boy to play soccer." Cribbing his annoyance, Greg observes, "Just wish Hopper had filled me in earlier... or made a call to Judson and Lucci. They would've jumped into the situation without anyone the wiser. That's what the hell they do up there."

"Hopper has a real emotional tie to the kid," Houses notes.

"All the more reason to step away. Emotion and attachment breed mistake in conflict. Isn't that the Pro's mantra?" Greg leashes himself lest he become preachy.

House shruggingly agrees; Diane dutifully sips her tea.

Greg, pecking a message on his cell, and House, having at another brandy, sit on sofas in the spacious, subtly coordinated living room. The only sound is the drone of a dishwasher in the freshly scrubbed kitchen. The doorbell rings. Almost before Greg can push off the couch, Diane is around a corner and opening the front door. Hopper, who appears as though he just had his bodily fluids drained at the corner radiator shop, clumps into the entryway. Diane, an ambassadress of the highest order, welcomes him with eyes of empathy and arms of warmth. She leads him to the living room. "Have you had dinner?"

"Had a bite earlier," Hopper wearily replies.

"How 'bout I fix you something?"

"That'd be great."

"A little spirit for the soul to go with it?"

"Not unless you want me passed out under your coffee table. I'm wiped."

"OK. I'll leave a plate on the counter. It'll be there for you when you're ready."

"Thanks."

As Diane moves to the kitchen to re-open shop, Hopper flops on the sofa next to House.

"Pretty tough go with the mother, huh?" House asks in a voice of comradely compassion.

"Yeah," Hopper confirms. "Father Raymond was still with her when I left."

"Did she remember anything else that would help?"

"She was pretty heavily sedated. We didn't talk all that much. I told her I'd do everything I could to bring her son back."

House tries to make sail on the positive. "Trina said that either Honorio or his mother mentioned that the dealers who had approached him were trying to convince him to play in soccer tournaments in the San Gabriel Valley. Any leads there?"

"I've been all over that the last day and a half. Problem is the paperwork for most of those tournaments is so shoddy. All the organizers really care about is that there's valid proof of insurance so they aren't sued if one of the kids is hurt during a game. Saw a couple of applications I thought might be live, but they went nowhere. Still working on it, though."

"So the only solid lead in hand is the tag number from that SUV and it died offshore?" Greg asks.

If possible, Hopper blanches further. "That's it, I'm afraid."

Greg allows himself no chastisement. "Where do you want to take this, Hop?"

"No doubt the kidnapping is payback for my roughing up those handlers who were on Honorio. This whole fucking mess is my fault." Hopper penitentially admits. "I'm thinking that if these people are moving enough merch to drive hundred-thousand-dollar SUVs and underwrite a youth soccer team, my guess is some agency has a beat on them."

"Trina's tried all of them... so has her Captain," House reminds Hopper.

"How about the people in D.C. you and Apostoli have dealt with?"

"They're military, Hop," Greg responds.

"All part of the same system."

"If we approach them, something might shake out, something might not. Remember, we didn't always do what *they* wanted in the day. There were some very honked-off folks back east when we passed on the situation with the ex-K.S.K. team and that close-protection assignment in the Gaza Strip. They've helped so far when Judson and I have reached out, but no guarantee, you know."

"Don't have another way to go," Hopper prods Greg.

"I'll make the call."

Hopper droops back into the couch. "Jesus, I put that boy in harm's way."

House has his own take. "That damn gift from the old man put *us* in harm's way."

"It's no gift," Greg posits without equivocation.

"What is it then?" Hopper quizzes the host.

"It's what Trina said: a test."

"Of?"

"Friendship, priorities, how we'd change our lives if we could."

"If it's a test," House conjectures, "the old man may have just handed out the final exam."

Greta sits at the long console, readying to shut down wall screens before her. A weary McManus, garment bag in hand, enters from a corridor claimed by stillness and night. He lumbers into the room and flops into a chair near the door. His drawn face is a visage of a musher who has endured one too many Iditarods.

"Just in?" Greta solicitously inquires.

"Yeah. Had a delay on a connection at O'Hare."

"How did it go?"

McManus curtly abstracts a trip most obviously he'd like to put behind him. "Got my ass handed to me on a plate, along with a stale dog biscuit and fresh turd, for that fucking debacle in the mountains."

"Able to raise anything about the bunch you think it might be?"

"Had to really pick my spots, because the team I have in mind packs major, major air cover way up top. They evidently turned around extremely touchy situations overseas, so they've stored a ton of chips," McManus reports as he creaks out of the wall chair and shambles to one next to Greta. "From what I was able to piece together, my gut tells me we're onto them… but I can't be sure. We'll have to handle this even more delicately than I thought."

Though there are likely more Clem Kadiddlehoppers or Bird Beboppers about than eavesdroppers, McManus nonetheless scans the room before he takes the forward-leaning posture of a confidence-trader. "Where are you keeping your files on this?"

"My laptop only. Download everything at the end of the day onto a Thunderbolt. Once files are copied, I wipe the drive on the laptop and overwrite it. Store the Thunderbolts at the offsite location with the rest of our sensitive materials."

"What about Allan?"

"Follows the same protocol. Brings me his Seagates before he leaves."

Satisfied treasonous parlays are not imminent, McManus relaxes slightly. "Whaddya have?"

Greta activates the console. With a couple of jabs to buttons, she has on top screens opaque images of the black SUV that trailed Honorio. "These are from the implant camera in

ROBERT RICHMOND FARRELL

Brendan Hopper's Jeep. I copied the SUV license number and tracked it."

"None of our regular channels, right?" McManus frets.

"No, everything was outside the reservation," Greta assures him, "but that's the problem. Without going deep into our data bases, the plates aren't traceable. The vehicle is held by a series of interlocking trusts using local offshore agents. I was doing OK until I hit Cyprus. I couldn't crack trust beneficiaries there. If I drill any deeper, it may have repercussions."

On bottom Screen Three Greta throws a shot of Hopper working over the Hispanic driver. "When I saw this and other frames, I made a call to a friend from the academy who's been in our San Diego office the last couple of years. Figured there may be some drug connection, so I took a flyer. Hit a winner. That vehicle has been recorded on tape by an agency contractor at operations of Domingo Covarrubias."

This sends no small amount of current through McManus. "Domingo Covarrubias! Are you fucking shitting me?"

"The ante goes up," Greta says with a modicum of relish. She shows on Screen Four fuzzy serial photos of two Hispanics abducting Honorio from the front steps of Our Lady of Perpetual Hope and spiriting him away in a deep green station wagon.

"When Brendan Hopper discovered our devices in the lights of his Jeep, we went to remote surveillance... the way we talked about. We spotted equipment in a light pole across from the church where he spends most his time. From some of the policewoman's cell activity Norcal piped into a while back, apparently Hopper has assumed a guardianship role for the boy who was hijacked. We weren't able to gather much more... other than the kid's evidently a soccer phenom."

Greta fills the top two screens with a series of new images. "This is from my San Diego guy. These are surveillance shots of the same two Hispanics who lifted the kid... exiting a different car...

must've ditched the station wagon... and loading the boy into a Covarrubias plane near Otay Mesa the night of the kidnapping."

"Retribution for Hopper jacking up that driver?" McManus surmises.

"That... and Covarrubias is a soccer fanatic. He sponsors a premier team in Mexico. He also funnels players to soccer-obsessed cartels in Columbia and Guatemala that he services. Could be he's importing the kid into his academy to either play for his team down the road or, at some point, ship to South America to make a client very happy."

"Where's the academy?"

"At his compound outside Campo Chana."

As McManus's curiosity flames, Greta throws yet another morsel into the pot. "When I pieced this together, I put Norcal back live on Brendan Hopper and the policewoman... figuring that's what you would've wanted. Norcal just nabbed a slice of conversation between her and Hardisty. They might try to call in a favor to find the boy. All they have is that SUV tag number I tracked, and they hit a dead-end before I did."

"A favor from Washington?" McManus asks in avid anticipation.

"That's what it seems."

"It's imperative to know if that call is placed," McManus ordains.

"I already have Norcal on alert. Besides Buzzard, we're bringing in Iron Dave. My San Diego contact has his periscope up. We're covering the entire waterfront."

"Good... good." In revived fettle, buoyed by prospects, McManus imagines, "This could really be that team. We can make up a lot of ground here if we play a smart hand."

It is one of those buzzy, archetypal watering holes with a stool for just about every delegate of the Beverly Hills bar scene: high-born corporate executives in their popinjay best; celebrities with egos caroming off exotic wall panels; surgery-sculpted women displaying ample wares; unblushing, rubbernecking wannabes angling for connections; prolific cocktailers making yet another stop on the Rodeo Drive crawl; young babes on whiff trolling for more; show business networkers conducting subtle-as-a-starter's-gun client-campaigning; attention-deprived closet comedians raiding the limelight of anyone who couldn't out-decibel them; a caboodle of hangers-on in outfits crusading for a collective audition as a TV test pattern; and paparazzi hovering outside like so many pirate hummingbirds. On this particular evening, a sniff of exclusivity cordons off a section of the bar for media types. Mitch Arnett, Undersecretary of Investigative Snooping, is in the midst of other local television reporter noteworthies, larking from one conversation to the next with an unapologetic disdain for decorum, tact, or basic civility. A nattily attired, tall, dark-complexioned man with a crop of wavy, black hair and sense of subterfuge about him, who appears quietly dialed into several media Brahmans holding court, watches Arnett with some amusement. Before exiting, he shakes Arnett's hand, leans into his ear, and whispers a dispatch that leaves Arnett talking, for once in the evening, not at somebody else, but to himself.

Soon the tall man is hastening up a nearby street where the Mick sits in a plain white car, subdued enough for even the most image-conscious actuary. The man and the Mick exchange deliberate nods when the man passes.

Moments later, Kiefer knocks on the passenger's window. The Mick switches open the lock; Kiefer eases inside.

"Is that Cary Vertain who just walked by?" Kiefer inquires in a much more Irish voice than the one displayed for Arnett and Roland.

"Looked like him" is the reply. The Mick takes from beneath his seat a paper file, which he hands to Kiefer.

Kiefer opens it and quickly leafs through its contents. "You want me to give the TV guys *all* this?"

"That I do."

"I have absolutely no exposure?"

"None we can't mitigate... eventually," the Mick muddily replies.

"I'd feel a lot better about this if it's a dead drop."

"Has to be a live transfer. No deviation."

"Brush contact?"

"Need you with him longer."

"You'll be there with a long lens?"

The Mick nods.

Kiefer rolls over in his mind the Mick's response. "Why do I have the feeling your plans for me in L.A. are short-lived?"

"Because you're a most astute mole."

As Sutter Nance enters Greg's office, Greg is not sure if he is wearing the gravitas of the moment on the shoulders of his exquisitely tailored suit, solemn face, or calculated hand that closes the door behind him. Whatever the sign may be, it is abundantly clear no glut of glad tidings accompany Nance.

Greg disengages from his computer, faces the senior partner, and prepares for the magisterial lowdown.

"Proctor and I had a long conversation over dinner last evening," Nance inhospitably opens. "He's extremely concerned about your commitment to the Streeter case and his company. He, quite frankly, is dismayed over your position relative to prosecuting a punitive-damages cause."

"He's the client. He has the latitude to be dismayed and whatever else he wishes. But I'll tell you this, he'd contemplate an action against the weatherman if it rained on his son's birthday," Greg tersely remarks.

"The point is larger than that, Greg. I'm disturbed about your loyalty to our firm."

"I'm disloyal because we differ on interpretation of a legal issue with serious ethical ramifications?"

"The last few months, your focus has been off," Nance censures Greg.

"My work product or focus as you see it? The level of my practice has never been higher. Any of my clients... other than Proctor... will recite you chapter and verse."

"You seem preoccupied with something outside this office. I know your father's death has been a large burden, but it really started before that. Are you weighing an offer from another firm?"

No courtier to duplicity, Greg directly responds, "Honestly, I'm approached regularly for positions with other firms... ones we know quite well. To date, I haven't given them serious consideration."

Sensing a threshold moment, Nance boxes aggression with reason and poses a query of some design. "Let me ask you a question. If our client is intent on prosecuting a punitive-damages claim and you refuse to assert it, where do you believe that leaves us in terms of trial strategy?"

"Might elevate Thornberg to first chair, but he's not ready... may never be," Greg detachedly replies. "You or one of the other senior partners... maybe Jenkins or Perault... could take lead, though it would be a struggle to get fully up to speed by the time of trial. Whatever team you cobble together at this late hour, I seriously doubt they'd be able to argue the case I would, punitive damages issue notwithstanding."

Having been hosed down by Greg's abrupt forthrightness, Nance replies in kind, "There absolutely will be no appeasing Proctor on this matter."

"Well then, Sutter, the Rubicon runs outside your office door, because I'll not contest an issue that, in my view, ethics imposed by the State Bar proscribe."

The divide between the two men is much wider than any slab of mahogany.

Trina stands on the rim of a reservoir converted into myriad soccer fields. She is observing the pageantry of young boys in colorful uniforms with enough patches, emblems, and inscriptions to do justice to an Indy 500 pit crew. As she takes a reading of various elite travel teams displaying their immense skills, on a far field she spots an object of her search: a group of sky-blue-outfitted Hispanic youngsters playing the game with such fluidity, artistry, and deftness that they make the opposing team look like a bunch of poky grape-stompers. Trina scours the incline and parking area above that game. She settles on a black limo hosting four to five swankily dressed Hispanics in their twenties reveling in the play of the young blades so fleetly cutting through their rattled and overwhelmed opposition. The men have the carriage of banana republic impunity.

Trina makes her way past claques of doting parents, cater-wauling spectators with soccer epiphanies, and drooling high-school coaches to an area within earshot of the limo. Her working knowledge of Spanish is left at the gate by the lippy Hispanics who evidently attach to profanities novel meanings understood only within a very unselect circle. As Trina brushes the side of the limo away from the men, she slips an unnoticed object underneath a tire well and moves on. Before she is out of range, though, she catches the eye of one of the men—an overweight, mouthy sort with a sizeable front bay, pompadour, designer sunglasses, and tailored silk threads. (But, then again, how much fine silk men's wear comes off the rack to snugly fit a lardy phone booth?) "Hey, pretty lady, you a soccer fan or you just like little boys?" he jaws, drawing cackles and homage from the others.

Trina is all too ready to cross swords. She passes around the front of the limo and walks squarely up to the tubby one. "Little boys, eh. Tough to imagine a hunk of blubber like you was once a little boy."

A short Hispanic seizes his crotch and hoots, "I got something for you to imagine."

Churlish comedy central is now open for business. "Got a fucking lame kid playing down there?" another scoffs.

"Yeah, but he's no match for those boys in blue. They sure can play."

"Yeah, they can play, but not as good as we can play," the short Hispanic sneers as he pokes a hand toward Trina's breast. She catches it with one hand, twists it, forcing the thumb outward, and jerks down. In an instant, the man's on his knees, howling for release. Trina rocks his jaw with a knee thrust.

The large Hispanic lunges toward her. Before he can plant a foot, Trina sweeps it away, bars her left arm underneath his armpit, locks it onto his chest, and, as he tips backward, launches a furious right punch to his mouth, ripping open his lip. Seeing scurrying, she drops the big man, rolls to the ground, and comes up with a revolver from an ankle holster before any others can free pistols from the limo.

"Bring anything out of that vehicle," Trina dares in a biting voice, "and you better be ready to lube it, because it's going straight up your ass."

"Who the hell are you!" one of the Hispanics gnarls at her.

"A soccer mom with attitude."

Gun outstretched, Trina backs away until she is behind the cover of a recreational vehicle. She quickly disappears before surrounding spectators can fully absorb the incident. The passenger from the black SUV Hopper had waylaid, his face a practice patch for needlepoint, peers out from inside the limousine.

Moments later, as Trina barrels out on her motorcycle from a soccer-field parking lot, a showy silver SUV with oversized wheels and chariot-apropos rims speeds up behind her and bashes into her back wheel, sending her and the cycle flying into a roadside berm.

An elderly lady in a front pew clutches rosary beads as she silently cycles through a progression of Hail Marys and Our

Fathers. Another a few rows back, hands spiraled beneath her chin, looks on high, seeking divine intervention that apparently has not been previously forthcoming. To the side, a middle-aged prodigal, engulfed in a lumberman's jacket and moral malaise, spades his soul to unearth religion lost. At the back a tattered, homeless wanderer tries to work through his default condition of confusion. Hopper, posture tight with distress, is camped at a middle pew, transfixed on a Station of the Cross, The Third Fall. When Father Raymond enters the church, House is rising from a rear row next to the holy water font to shake his mending leg.

"Hi, Father. How are you?" House asks with a smile reflecting little merriment.

"Fine, William. How's Trina?"

"Outside the concussion, she's OK. If she had been thrown into a parked car or concrete instead of that berm groundcover, it woulda been a whole 'nother story. Meant a lot that you came by to see her at the hospital."

"One of my second homes." The priest gestures to Hopper, appearing to bear the yoke of looming earthly doom. "What's his state?"

"Not one of his better days. We're not really making progress locating Honorio on the track we're on, so he'll have to make some hard choices."

"Has he talked to you about his intentions?" Father Raymond cautiously inquires.

"On that subject, he's not really accepting visitors."

"I see." With that, Father takes his leave from House, advances to Hopper's aisle, genuflects, sidles down the row, and sits. He waits for Hopper to break from his thoughts.

"How's Mrs. Fernandez?" Hopper asks.

"Better."

"Did you tell her we're doing all we can to bring Honorio home?"

"Yes, but she already knows that. I talk to her sister every night to relay whatever news we might have."

"Yeah, that's right. Forgot."

"Do you have a firm sense where Honorio might be?"

"Nothing concrete. Indicators are Mexico... maybe points south."

"Do you believe Honorio will be returned through normal law enforcement channels?"

Diplomacy falls to the onslaught of honesty always brought on in the priest's presence. "I don't, Father." Hopper casts his bleary, empty eyes to the altar. "I can't imagine how scared that young boy is... and I don't have a plan to bring him back."

"I want to help, Brendan. One of my children, God's children, was taken from this sanctuary. I am responsible to our Lord and his mother for his return." Father Raymond gives a needed voice to hope. "If Honorio is in Mexico or Central America, perhaps there's something we can do. Many of the parishes in the archdiocese have sister parishes in those countries. Priests there know the local landscape very, very well."

"Father, with all due respect, if Honorio's anywhere, my guess is he's in a cartel fortress that's isolated and basically impenetrable."

"Exactly where some of the most opulent Catholic churches in that part of the world are located."

"Priests conduct Mass there?"

"They do." In response to a scrupulous look Hopper cannot hide, Father Raymond makes his record. "Our lot is not to rebuff sinners, Brendan, but to point them to the Lord's path. Was not much of your work in dens of lawlessness and inhumanity?"

Hopper defers to the priest's logic. "Maybe you can help us find a way." He raises his head to a lofty stained-glass window. "Lord knows I don't have one."

In the megalopolis that extends from Ventura to the Mexican border, a welcome respite is the stretch of seaside highway from San Clemente to Oceanside that passes through Camp Pendleton. On this fall night, the sun has just forsaken a rich salmon horizon and Byzantium clouds threatening rain are in a holding pattern. Gouging lights of commute traffic are surprisingly sparse, leaving twilight to weave between the water and hills a last muted splendor of the day.

As Greta motors her beige sedan, a model all the rage in Des Moines, north to Orange County, her cell rings. She checks the number and, chop-chop, clicks on her headset. "Hey there."

Greta ingests a good bit from the caller before responding, "Yes, indeed, the attorney from the mountain made contact. That's confirmed." After a much briefer interim, she says, "The brass the attorney phoned is way high on the food chain. When that general steps into a room, a lot of people are saluting."

She listens for a moment and then replies, "We have that well underway. We have more work to do, but from what I learned today from my friend in San Diego, I believe we can re-route any inquiries from the Potomac, maybe even quash them."

After the next installment of conversation from the other end, she continues, "I spent an hour at a safe place near the Gaslamp with him. He's extremely piped in... dialogue was very productive. He likes our concept. They definitely have something to trade."

After Greta jumps onto a slower lane to make way for an impatient trucker with blowtorch high beams, she tumbles to a close of the elliptical conversation. "That small package taken from the church was delivered where we thought it might be south of the border. But it's such a special package, the receiving party may be under pressure to forward it a continent down."

As Greta approaches the immigration checkpoint south of San Onofre, she signs off. "Makes sense. See you first thing in the morning. You'll like what's on your desk, sir."

Greg, toting a large briefcase, walks down imperial court-house steps along with a bustling ensemble of those who ply their trade within: lawyers, clerks, bailiffs, sheriffs, administra-tors, expert witnesses, and case reporters. He pauses to take a call on his cell, the dim subject of which clearly dispirits him. Shortly, he powers off the phone and indignantly stuffs it into his pocket. As he moves into the boil of sidewalk pedestrians making their way home, the Mick, in a gray suit and white, open-collar dress shirt loosely fitting his burly fame, falls in limp rhythm behind Greg. He threads his way through foot traffic, keeping several paces off his target's rear. At an intersection where Greg waits for a green crossing light, the Mick moves up and drafts him into conversation.

"Understand you're looking for a boy," the Mick says in a slow, measured tone bereft of brogue.

Greg deliberately turns to the Mick. Rather than immedi-ately questioning or answering him, the trial lawyer, eyes tight with scrutiny, studies the man, locking first onto his shoes, then watch, clothing, and finally a face dominated by a scarred nose as crooked as a swindler's heart. He searches for clues of the identity on the other side of this one-eyed jack. The Mick, a veteran of many errands of intrigue, impassively endures the once-over.

Greg tilts his head toward clanky, chugging traffic. "Couldn't have done much better had you piped in white noise."

The Mick, not to be beguiled from his sheet music, waits for a reply. Greg straightens his tie and tie tack before he advances, "Might be looking."

"There may be information as to his whereabouts."

"If it's the boy I'm thinking of and you have a lead on him, you're committing the crime of withholding evidence, which is a felony in this state."

The Mick's grounding is far from disturbed. "So might you if I pass it along and *you* hold it."

The knot of end-of-the-day workers surrounding Greg and the Mick quickly disperses upon changing traffic lights. Seeing nothing more to be gained in further sparring with this shadowy man, the counselor submits, "What if I *am* interested?"

"There's an envelope at the front desk of your office. Don't bother with the name of the law firm or return address. It's a dummy. If you want in, call the number inside."

The Mick beats a hobbled path across the intersection before the light turns red. Greg wastes no time firing up his cell.

Roland leans from the second story of a LAX parking structure, watching an exuberant Mitch Arnett and fawning cameraman exit the passenger terminal across the street. After Arnett obligingly recognizes a couple of appropriately impressed weedy travelers waiting curbside and accepts a final bit of homage from the cameraman, he skips across the street to the parking structure. Roland, large manila envelope in hand, buzzes to an elevator to wait for his boss. When Arnett arrives, they hoof it to a recessed area of lesser sunlight and find a couple of adjacent parked vans that shield them from unwelcome eyes.

"How did it go?" Roland mechanically asks.

"Caught the fucker totally by surprise," Arnett froths. "Our source was right on the money."

"Were we the only ones there?"

"Hell, yes. Since that prick whale couldn't get back into the terminal without having to pass through security again, I had him until one of his flunkeys rescued him. Made him stutter and spit like a school kid."

Arnett takes a moment to fully absorb the magnificence of his exploit before directing Roland, "When you check in at the station, I want you all over those desk jockeys on the second floor. As soon as our piece airs tonight, they saturate social media."

"Consider it done."

Arnett motions to the manila envelope. "How did Kiefer do?"

Roland slips out a thick packet of paper and hands it to Arnett. "See what you think."

As Arnett pages though the documents, satisfaction spreads across his face like hyperkinetic coral. "They were involved in this much shit?"

"Wait 'til you hit reports on the Philippines."

Arnett flicks a finger on the pages. "This is fucking dynamite."

"That it is."

"How can we be sure the people from the mountain are part of this group? All the names are redacted."

"We have to rely on Kiefer."

"There must be a clean version somewhere."

"Kiefer's almost certain there is."

"And?" Arnett impatiently calls upon Roland.

"It's outside his channel."

"Which translates into how much?"

"Ninety grand."

"Ninety grand on top of what he's already being paid!" Arnett fumes. "Why doesn't the cocksucker just round it up to an even hundred?"

Roland removes a single slip of folded paper from his coat pocket and hands it to Arnett, who snaps it away for a quick once-over. Ace Reporter confers no props. "He wants us to believe this is actually an email from Vertain? When did you tell him Vertain had the story?"

"Mentioned it last week. Figured he might help us get a leg up."

"How the hell did Kiefer crack a television station's electronic mail? Broadcasting companies are absolutely loading up on security with all the hacking from overseas."

Roland turns analogist. "Don't know what to say other than Palladian's take: If an anaconda is a serious snake, Kiefer is serious snoop."

"So Vertain doesn't have in hand anything not redacted?"

"Looks that way."

"If we pass on forking out ninety grand and Kiefer lands the virgin document, you think he'd offer it to Vertain?"

"Any doubt? He's in the cash-and-carry business, isn't he?"

"I could give this guy Kiefer ninety grand and never see him again."

"You could hand him ninety grand and have multiple pieces on network for a month if he can deliver that package clean." Roland peels to the golden kernel of ratings. "International coverage would be a lock. No one else in our time slot has ever had that."

Arnett dials down his war cry. Odd how the prospect of dateline fame can quickly pulp prudence.

Greg steps into the night from one of a pack of small, tilt-up, wind-whipped warehouses aligned along alligatoring concrete of a ruler-thin, aging airstrip dropped onto a prairie of scrub and sand. Next to him is a tall middle-aged man, cheeks hollowed by the same regimen that had cut his wiry frame to bones, sinew, and mechanisms of efficiency. If jokes are to be played, Quinn Promardie does not appear a particularly fertile playground.

Promardie holds forth a grainy front facial photo of the Mick in the suit from the courthouse. He studies it before flipping it toward Greg. "You shot this with that tie-tack camera I gave you Christmas before last?"

"Yep."

"Ever used it before?"

"Nope."

"When did you start wearing it?"

"Right after Hopper found those cam lenses in his car lights."

"Not bad given where technology was then."

"You seem to have a knack for timeless gifts," Greg says with a suggestion of a smile. "Think you can make him?"

"You're positive he was trying to mask an accent?"

"You know what the Brits taught us about dialects and cants. If you're practiced on them and can't place one, maybe that's because it doesn't exist, it's a construct. From his walk to the way he delivered the message to how he sized up people around us, the guy was all economy. But he had this slow, deliberate cadence you'd expect of a brain-drained surfer dude from Leo Carrillo. Just didn't match everything else about him."

"His limp?"

"Don't know. Might've been to throw me off. But his face was rough, scarred. Could've been dinged in combat, maybe some contact sport. Had real size across the shoulders."

After a moment of reflection, Promardie settles on an appraisement. "Our friends in Manchester still have an open line to S.A.S. and beyond. If this guy is as Irish as he looks and works for consumers... here or anywhere off the island... the Brits will have him on their radar. They view an Irishman with tradecraft as a potential threat. If this guy is operating on any scale whatsoever... even if he's a cleanskin, my guess is our friends can find out about him... no matter how good a dry cleaner he is."

"The way it ended with Trina and Aidan didn't screw things up for us with them, did it?"

"No. They all know that's just Trina."

Greg takes this as gospel. "Good enough. I can catch up with you tomorrow?"

"Yep."

"All right. Gotta go back in there and hash this shit out."

"When is Judson coming down?"

"Soon as we decide which way we're going."

"Nello coming with him?"

"Depends."

"OK. Let's talk tomorrow."

The two lock hands in a firm shake. The man whose face had adorned one of Greta's screens hops into a ho-hum white Volvo that, except for an odd circular plug in the back window, could be found in queue outside just about any suburban grammar school at final bell. Greg steps back inside.

The only light in the warehouse of extreme clear height is above a long metal table around which Hopper, Trina, and House sit. Barely discernible in long shadows are the plane Greg had flown with his flight instructor Marek, another its like, long shelves of parts and tools, an extended workbench, and a wide roll-up door. As Greg makes his way to the table, Hopper and Trina are fixated on a white board overrun with a jumble of symbols, lines, arrows, and acronyms that would have been an absolute delight to Rube Goldberg. House closes a call on his cell. "Marek will be here in forty minutes," he trumpets. "Bringing Chinese." The announcement goes altogether unnoticed.

"Let's dope it out one more time to make sure we've tracked everything," Greg says as he plants an index finger at the top of the board. "Hop takes out the sentries. Two scenarios: he's made or he's not. In either event, some honchos with seniority at the site undoubtedly take heat for the intervention... especially with the play in the press." Greg drops down his hand. "Next milestone: Hop finds his car lights bugged. Given our history, could be random domestic security trying to keep tabs on us. The Pro just confirmed that he couldn't put a date on the technology; so theoretically, the cam lenses may've been there for a couple of years. If Hop was I.D.ed on the mountain... "

"Or if you or House was I.D.ed and a connection was made to Hop," Trina says, tacking on yet another permutation.

"Right. Either case, an agency from the mountain with egg on its face might be on Hop... or everyone. They could be monitoring us, trying to gather intel, looking to take us down a notch as payback, or...," Greg starkly adds "take us out."

"Gonna be awfully tough for anyone to crack the radio you and Apostoli put in place back east and overseas," House remarks.

"Depends on how motivated we may've made someone," Greg responds.

"Fair enough," House cedes.

"Next, we make the call for help on Honorio. Inside a... "

"There's one thing the Pro said when we were getting air outside that I hadn't really thought through," Hopper interjects. "Thanks to Trina burying the report, I walked away from working over that slime-rodent I dragged out of the SUV. But on the chance that the device in the rear brake light was still live after the SUV slammed into it, that's damning evidence for an aggravated-assault beef given my martial arts training. If the Mountie that ordered the cam plant was out to burn me for tromping on his turf, he could've anonymously turned over that evidence to the D.A. and I'd be looking at serious charges."

"Which could mean somebody has a notion, but wants to nail everyone, not just Hop," Trina suggests.

"Or may be looking to compromise us when they have something bigger in hand," House adds.

"Possible," Greg allows. "Back to Honorio. We reached out to D.C., made the call for an assist. Inside two days, I'm hit up outside the courthouse. Could be my contact passed it down the line and that's the way it's shaking out, but no one we've gone to in the past or their adjutant general has worked off that kind of M.O... or anything remotely like it."

"Confirmed it with Judson?" Trina asks Greg.

"That I did. Let's say the Pro verifies this guy from the courthouse is a legitimate asset. Assuming he's not connected with the hierarchy we're tapped into, then he could be working on a voucher or as a lone wolf for an agency that now has us as persons of high interest because of the mountain event. That be the case, then they somehow had to plug a line into my call to D.C. brass. So all of us could being hit with taps, intercepts, complete electronic surveillance... what Hop suggested at Primo's."

"You really don't think you should just phone your man to find out if it's coming from his chain of command?"

Greg gestures to the lower part of the board. "We didn't give our contact a lot to go on — tag numbers from the black SUV Hop tied up and two vehicles from the soccer field. Even if our man or his four-star goes to bat for us... which is no guarantee... they could come up empty. Military usually don't have their bayonets into drug trafficking. I mean, how many times were we issued packages that were supposed to be complete, only to find one arm of a government didn't know jack shit about what another was doing... with our asses caught in the crossfire?" Heedful nods.

Greg's finger bounces back and forth between two blocks of writing. "Let's say this guy from the courthouse is a resource doing fetching for an agency we are crossways with. Maybe they *do* have real-time intel about Honorio that our military guys can't dig out. If we press up through our channels about the courthouse asset and put heat on whoever's behind him, they could fold their tents and head for hills. Endgame is we might find ourselves with zilch about the kid."

"But assuming that's true and we have people pissed off enough to put a hunting pack on our asses, how do we know they're not setting us up for a big-time fall? They could be baiting us into a black hole so deep we don't have a way out," House conjectures, splicing in yet another variable.

"You've just about quoted ex-public-defender Judson Apostoli verbatim from our conversation last night," Greg relates to the group. "His view: risk is out there, type and degree... we simply won't know until we jump in. We bite, and we're taking our chances. In the case that an agency does pipe intel our way, they could be sending us into a zipped-in position. Or maybe they're setting the table for a quid pro quo — they provide G2 on Honorio and our side is to take on a messy situation for them no one else has been able... or wants to handle. That *was* our calling card, wasn't it?"

"Ten years ago," House editorializes.

Hopper rises, circles behind the board, and stands next to Greg. "Say we are in the bull's-eye of an agency that has a hard-on for us and they're paying black-bag operators to tail us. Then they must have an idea about our capabilities... especially after those sentries went to sleep so quickly. Outside chance they've even made a connection to one of our missions. Assuming they've gotten that far, then they have to understand that there will be severe collateral damage for them should they throw down the gauntlet on us just to settle a score. If they really have high-level intel about Honorio, my bet is they're looking to trade. And," Hopper concludes in upper casing, "odds are, whatever party they want us to crash, they'll be expecting us to bring a lot more than a pocketful of Primo's darts."

"Which means we trust them how much?" Greg squeezes in.

"Just like the past — absolute zero."

The three sit in somber appraisal. Greg eyes them intently. "Do I make the call to the guy from the courthouse?"

"Make the call," Trina replies without flinch.

"OK. I'll put in the order for our usual dossier. When we see what comes back, we'll know a lot more about how real this is."

Trina and Anita Galton stand behind Paula, a squat uniformed policewoman with professorial glasses; bun of erratic, wiry, black hair; and passing acknowledgment of cosmetics. She is stationed in front of a terminal in a server room chaotic with computer equipment, racks, trays, and cables. Paula pushes readers up on the bridge of her nose, squints at the screen, and taps a plain fingernail at a line of data. "OK. That's the tag number of the black SUV involved in the 11-83 with your friend Brendan Hopper. The vehicle was cited three-and-half months ago for blowing a red on a left at the location in the San Gabriel Valley you see here." She inches down her finger. "That's the tag of the limo at the soccer fields... *also owned by an offshore trust*. Nothing on it going back as far as when it was shipped into the U.S. Here's the reported number of the silver SUV that damn near sent you into orbit." Paula turns to Trina. "How in the world did you walk away from that, lady friend?"

Galton smiles at Trina. "She has someone watching over her… and me. No way we should've made it out of that jewelry store inferno."

"Just living right," Trina says with a snapshot smile.

"Well, whatever spin classes you're taking at the club, I need to sign up," Paula jests.

"Haven't I been telling you?"

Paula reverses to the screen. "All right. According to D.M.V. records, the tag number turned in for that last vehicle is assigned to a '98 Honda. I pulled the report from the soccer field. There was only one witness who spotted the plates of the silver SUV, and she was a mother with a car full of kids going the other way. Is that right?"

"Yep," Trina confirms.

"If you change the second-to-last-number on the reported tag from a six to an eight, then we have a silver SUV… *registered to an O.S.T.*… with a mover," Paula puffily points, "at the same intersection in the Valley where the black SUV was cited."

"We don't have direct access to a program for that kind of cross-checking, do we?" Trina asks.

"No," Paula responds jauntily, "but I owe Anita here a favor or two." She pecks her keyboard; a screen of arcane diagrams and data pops up.

Trina and Galton bend down to make some sense of it. "Basically," Paula translates for them, "this tracks the number of movers during a given period of time for that location. After I assembled these fields, I made some calls and found out it's one of those intersections where if the east-west traffic on the main artery drops way down, green goes to red incredibly quickly. Local cops feast there… particularly late night, early morning.

But almost all vehicles written up are commercial, because this is a warehouse district." Paula spins around in her chair. "What are two high-end SUVs doing on a trucking route in the Valley well after midnight?"

"Headed to a warehouse where they're staging something more than produce," Trina submits.

"Yep," Paula concurs.

Trina and Galton let the revelation sink in.

"How are you doing with the printouts I gave you?" Paula asks Trina.

"OK. Have a couple of friends working on them," Trina tells her. "If they have questions, can they call you directly?"

"Sure. The Hopper fellow is one, right?"

"Yeah. Bill Stackhouse is the other, but you'll likely hear from Hopper."

"Great. Anything else?" Paula inquires.

Trina points to the screen. "Maybe you could I.D. a friendly property owner at that intersection."

"No problem."

Greg sits at his office desk, editing a document on his computer screen. Jimmy, an office clerk in his mid-twenties with cherubic face; mop of chestnut hair; white, short-sleeved, polyester shirt grayed to a remarkable drabness; and amateurly knotted tie of indeterminate pattern, loads documents from the floor onto a cart.

"Are there any more Streeter files besides the ones here, Mr. Hardisty?" Jimmy asks in a dragging voice.

"No, that's it. Laid them all out for you earlier this morning. Where are they headed... Mr. Nance's or Mr. Thornberg's office?"

"Mr. Nance."

After Jimmy has stacked the last of the files on the cart, he grips its edges, dips his head in hard reflection, then unfurls his discontent. "Mr. Hardisty, people are saying you're leaving the firm. Is that so?"

Greg rolls away from the terminal to address the question head on. "Have no offers, so there's nothing to leave for, Jimmy."

"When I told Johnny about it, he was bummed."

"Tell Johnny to save his energies for finding a new girlfriend," Greg, tone beneficent, advises the young man.

"He will. He's feeling really good about himself since you got him out from under that boss who was bad to him."

"Your brother didn't deserve it. Nobody does."

"You're right there." Having said his piece, Jimmy directs the cart toward the door as Greg pushes back to his keyboard. Before stepping outside, Jimmy has a last item to clear. "Mr. Hardisty?"

Greg, swiveling his head to the door, answers, "Yes, Jimmy."

"Guess how many partners know my name?"

"Really have no idea."

"Six. That's not too many after being here over four years, do you think?"

"The rest are missing out. You have a great soul. So does your brother. I'm pleased you share them with me."

Words from the heart are of great fledge: they erect Jimmy to a posture fit for the front gates of Buckingham Palace.

Rain screaming off the Pacific Ocean had largely driven downtown San Diego residents from bistros, street-side cafes, and toney bars into their lofts and high-rise condos. Greta, swathed in a floppy knit cap, two layers of scarves, and long wool coat, waits under an overhang on Broadway for the red trolley line traversing east. When it arrives, she takes to the inside with a sure will.

She passes seats occupied by a huffy businessman (he with the body of a mishap prune) put out by the stop; bundled, spacey couple palsied in some form of social exile; woman of apparent moral turpitude poured into an unseasonably scarce outfit; grimy version of Amarillo Slim in a discount-store slicker, flashing cutting, observant, though thoroughly sotted eyes; and, comforted by a down coat, an octogenarian, whose facial brag is that he occupies a trolley seat, not a rest-home recliner.

At the very back, a distance from others, is a man in his midtwenties, shrouded in a hoodie of dogmatic simplicity, pupils locked onto a laptop where, one might imagine, alien commandos are suffering the worse of digital warfare. Greta slips into the seat next to him. "Jesus, Paulson, picked a damn fine night, didn't we?"

"What's up, Berggren? Take you long to drive down?" Paulson asks in a rock-ribbed voice belying his schlep appearance.

"About an hour forty-five."

"Not bad with the rain."

After opening top buttons of her coat and unwinding the outer scarf, Greta is ready to talk shop. "What were you able to put together?"

"Crew you're looking to enlist asked for a lot of data points."

"We intend to ask a lot from them, don't we?"

"That we do."

Paulson works the keyboard, producing headshots of Hispanic men in their forties and fifties, each projecting indelible ill will. "These are the main operatives in the Covarrubias hierarchy. Domingo and his top three lieutenants run things from a compound outside of Campo Chana. These other lieutenants and handlers are in the field in Texas, New Mexico, and Arizona… mainly the Tucson area, but most are in L.A."

"Covarrubias people never take a stake in product? Is that their deal?"

"Right. Covarrubias will have absolutely nothing to do with ownership of goods. His clients are cartels. He doesn't want to compete with them in any way, shape, or form. Plus, he needs to keep certain politicos in the States happy, so he can't take a slice of the drugs."

With a knock of the keys, Paulson produces a map of the greater Los Angeles area with large arterials, particularly in the San Gabriel Valley, highlighted in red, producing seven or eight distinct zones. "These are Covarrubias's strongholds in L.A. He provides financing and transpo for goods once they land in the States. He offers staging, storage, ground rigs... whole host of options for cartels to move their merch to the streets as quickly as possible. They say a load's never been lost once it's in his network."

"Where are their hubs?"

"No set pattern... which is intentional. Could be a small warehouse; plain, single-family home, insides blown out, in a regular neighborhood; back storage area of a strip retail shop; you name it."

After studying the map a moment, Greta is prepared to turn the page. "What do you have on the Covarrubias headquarters?"

Paulson brings up a satellite shot of a sprawling complex of tiled buildings cut into a hillside of tropical vegetation. He pegs a point on the screen. "That's the main house. Next to it is an operations center. You can see all that equipment on top the roof. Over there are chopper pads." Paulson lowers his pen to the bottom of the screen. "There are soccer fields in the flat area. To the right... off by itself... is a big living area... dormitory or something like that. Across is what we think is a school. If the boy we have a shot of being taken into that plane in Otay Mesa is in the compound, that's the area he'll likely be."

Greta focuses on a large structure to the far side of the soccer fields. "What's that?"

"Huge damn church."

"There at the other end of the fields?"

"Hard to tell with the overgrowth. Could be storage."

Greta squints into the screen. "Looks like bars on top."

"Don't know. Ventilation grates, you think?"

"Cells?"

"Maybe… to keep people in line."

Greta circles a finger around images. "You have plans for how much of this?"

"Whole shebang. We hacked into the system of the architect in Mexico City who designed it and did all the construction drawings. We have C.A.D. files, complete mechanical and electrical plans, and specs for every single building system. They're all tabbed in the flash drive I have for you."

Greta, somewhat perplexed, asks, "With all that, you can't find a way in?"

Paulson zooms out the screen to show the surrounding area. "Inland roads are impenetrable. The operations center has a sophisticated radar system that catches any inbound and outbound air traffic within a forty-mile radius. Only air route that can't be detected is skimming in above the ocean. Problem there is that between the compound and water… well, look for yourself. It's nothing but dense jungle. Covarrubias has installed surveillance cameras, infrared scopes, lasers, carbon fiber telescopes, motion sensors, and a whole bunch of other shit in just about every square foot of it." Paulson brushes a hand over irregular, rugged terrain. "See this mountain area above the jungle? Some locals say there's a way from the ocean inland through caves, up cliffs, over real nasty ledges."

Greta pores over highland topography. "Think it's possible?"

"Hard to say. If there's a route, none of the villagers will give it up. They're scared to death of Covarrubias… and they should be."

"No signals intelligence?"

Paulson shakes off the possibility. "We've tried everything to penetrate electronic data in motion. We can't crack Covarrubias's air. He's put together a balls-to-the-wall cyber-counter-espionage team from Eastern Europe, China, the Netherlands, and who the hell knows where else. Their firewalls are immense; Souffletrough, Jetplow, all that stuff was useless. They're constantly rotating two sets of servers around the world. While one's up, they're moving the other. Soon as that's in place, they disassemble the first and ship it somewhere else. On top of that, they're fanatic about upgrading security and retooling equipment. We brought in ex-T.A.O. people, and even they didn't come close to cracking Covarrubias's encryptions. That's why we need to break into their landline." Paulson releases his attention from the computer. "You really think these people you've I.D.ed have the horsepower to plant the device we need? We're cutting loose a whole lot of secure files here."

Greta issues her caveat emptor. "We think so, but, fact of the matter is, no guarantees. We'll all have a lot of skin in this game if the team bites."

Paulson's eyes rinse the trolley before he wades into harsh, cold essentials. "If these people jump, they go in naked, completely unattached. They understand that?"

"They will."

"We could have real exposure if the op goes sideways. Covarrubias is one savvy operator. He funnels big dollars to pols in the Southwest who dump his money into P.A.C.s. There's a lot more than Texas billionaires funding those goddamn things, you know. Covarrubias's P.A.C.s have placed important people in D.C., some piped directly into drug enforcement. We're basically under a directive to focus on organizations generating product and moving it across the border and lay off the space Covarrubias is in."

"But the head of the agency still wants to get to Covarrubias? You're absolutely certain of that?" Greta probes.

"Covarrubias is very well insulated. Can't take him down. That would cost the Chief his job. He wants, though, Covarrubias's data bases badly... very badly. Covarrubias, at one time or another, has worked for all major cartels who deal in the U.S. He probably has records of every significant drug grid in the Southwest and California from San Diego north to Ventura."

Greta digs for the depth of the quicksand. "How large a risk of us getting sideways with big dogs on the hill in D.C. if we're exposed?" Greta asks.

"Very large risk, very large reward… especially for your boss if he can pull this off with no one the wiser."

Paulson takes a flash drive from his pocket and hands it to Greta.

"Can this be sourced?" she asks.

"Absolutely not. Our wonks scrubbed the shit out of it."

Greta takes to tightening her scarf around her neck. "Anything more on the call from the military?"

"It's been completely deflected… won't go anywhere."

"Could it've gone someplace else as well?"

"Doubtful. We're the clearing house for all drug movement from El Salvador to Tijuana. Even if another office had live intel on Covarrubias that connects his organization to those plate numbers, they probably wouldn't give it up. They want everyone thinking their hands are off him… just the way we want everyone thinking ours are… to keep goddamn pols off our asses."

Greta rises from her seat. "I owe you, Paulson."

"Not if you place the device."

Armed with her deliverable and homely truth, Greta moves to the trolley door.

House, rolled magazine in hand, and Cord amble along the prison boundary fence near the metal tables where loved ones are trying to lift the spirits of their fallen angels. The brothers both appear brightened.

"Darcy was here last weekend. Treatment is really helpin'. You can see the improvement," Cord enthuses.

"Once you're back home, it'll be even better," House inspirits his brother.

"Billy says he wants to start Scouts. You have time for that?"

"Nothing but." House glances about before slipping the magazine to his brother. "Take this. Have something serious to talk about."

Expression and gait unchanged, Cord accepts the magazine and raps it lightly against his thigh as he walks along. After several steps, he inquires, "Whaddya have?"

"Check out the bottom of page forty-seven."

Cord opens the magazine to the designated page and scans it. Showing not a ripple in his cool countenance, he closes the magazine and again drums it against his leg as he saunters on. "Have troubles, Willie Buck?" Cord asks.

"No, someone else does."

"Exfil? Extract? Smash-and-grab?"

"Along those lines."

"Weapons free?"

"Yep," House ping-pongs to his brother.

"Where?"

"Somewhere south of the border."

"How far?"

"Don't know yet."

"Couple of guys I look out for in here can definitely bring what you need to that party."

"On short order?"

Cord is unequivocal. "Very short order."

"Price."

"I'll make sure it's highly negotiable."

"Good."

The Stackhouses take a turn toward the tables.

Promardie is led into the broadcast studio by a white-hot woman with fluttering, feather-duster eyelashes, ironed-on pants, strappy high heels, and enough curves to dizzy a parson's sense of propriety. She clicks over to Clarkson, a rotund man with body flab for a couple of winters. He is packed into a seat in front of several computer terminals displaying data shooting across like tracer fire.

"Well, here you are, Mr. Promardie. So very nice to meet you," the siren coos in a smoky voice before turning back.

"You as well."

As the shapely woman par excellence rhapsodically ankles to the studio door (favoring Promardie with a racy smile before she exits), Clarkson takes off his headset, making sure not to ruffle strands of dyed reddish-black hair strewn over his bald plate like so much dark, wet cabbage. "Some dish, eh?"

Promardie nods.

"Her name's Yvette," Clarkson clues Promardie.

"Her name's whatever she wants it to be." Promardie's eyes do a quick tour of the studio. "When did you go Hollywood, Clarks?"

Clarkson points to a preoccupied, gawky man wearing jeans (evidently impervious to detergent) and a Laker warm-up jersey with number "22" gloriously stitched onto the back. His oily hair curlicues to his shoulders in a fashion all the 70s rage on Shattuck Avenue. The man nimbly works on server innards as masterfully as an L.A. floozy on a rube tourist from Tucumcari.

"See that guy? Fucking computer genius. Can turn a paperclip into the gateway to the electronic universe." Clarkson circumscribes the studio with a proud hand. "Made all this happen. Key to the equity raise from offshore investors. He's just tying together loose ends for me."

"Looks like some folks ponied up big time."

"That they did. So what brings the Pro north of Sunset?"

"Have a minute?"

"Sure." Clarkson rolls a nearby chair to Promardie, who settles in. "What can I do for you?" Clarkson amiably inquires.

"How many feeds you have going out Saturday for the Ireland-All Blacks game?"

"In the L.A. area?"

"Yeah."

"Three... maybe four. I'd have to check."

"Need to know locations as soon as I can." Promardie removes from his pocket the photo of the Mick given him by Greg. "If this guy makes an appearance at one of your spots, can you have your man there ring me?"

Clarkson grows immediately wary. "You're not putting me in the middle of one of your situations, are you? Who is this guy?"

"No, I'm not. His name is Michael Lowry... from Derry."

"You mean Londonderry... IRA Londonderry!" Clarkson skittishly inquires.

"He ran with some of them, but never had rank."

"What's he doing here?"

"That's what I'm trying to find out."

"The guy likes rugby, I take it." Clarkson holds the picture to thick wayfarer glasses. "Looks like he took the short end of his share of scrums."

"Yeah. Contacts in England tell me he and his mates played club in Derry and Belfast. There's five or six of them over here — all supposed to be nuts for the Union team."

Clarkson returns the photo. "Sure, I'll handle that. Least I can do after that problem you cleaned up for me. Have Yvette make a copy on the way out; I'll send it to my people. They'll call you if the guy shows."

"Thanks, Clarks. What time do the Blacks start the haka on Saturday? Figure seats will be filled by then."

"Yvette has the schedule."

"Couldn't have a better keeper. Take care, Clarks."

"That I'll do. Stay in touch. Still owe you."

Clarkson turns to his screens, Promardie to the scent of Yvette.

Greg and Trina, restless from a car-bound night of surveillance, sit in his BMW, sardined in between storage bins at the perimeter of a corner warehouse lot in a dismal industrial area. On this rainy early morning, the intersection is hosting as much traffic as a Hollywood fast track to humility.

Trina takes a sip of coffee from a thermos cup. Greg focuses on the intersection where cycling traffic lights modulate little more than wind, rain, and gloom fit for a Wes Craven movie shoot.

"What time will House and Hop be out?"

Trina unsheathes a watch from beneath her jacket. "Little over an hour. Could be just House."

"Hop whipped?"

"Yeah. I'm feeding him every lead we're turning up. He's running himself into the ground."

"Anything come of your plant on that limo?"

"No. Went dead in Chula Vista. Likely swept there," Trina reports. She adds grudgingly, "Smart operators."

"Probably better if Hop doesn't come out. If he did get a sniff of one of those high-end SUVs passing through here, not sure what he'd do."

"He's amped… no doubt."

Greg tugs down his pilot's cap and sluggishly pores out verses of U2's *Beautiful Day* on one that is anything but with the nagging downpour.

Trina dares trespassing on Greg's crooning. "You can't keep pulling all-night stakeouts like this and expect to be sharp for your practice, can you? Aren't you scheduled for trial on that big case soon?"

"Nance is trying it," Greg reports with little adornment.

"That the way you wanted it?"

"Way it had to be."

"Nothing to do with your health?" Trina, eyebrow arched, drops into the mix.

"No." Greg shoots Trina an eagle eye. "You and Diane been running out of things to chat about?"

The smothering intensity of Greg's voice momentarily stills conversation; Trina redirects it. "Think the Irishman will deliver the intel we need?"

"Depends on what they want from us... and how badly. My guess is that we'll have enough for an extract."

"What if we're the only ones who can bring home the boy?"

"Been ten years since we were in the kill zone."

"Except for House, none of us has lost more than a half-step."

"You, Hop, Lucci, the Pro, and maybe Lance are still in the routine. The rest of us... face it, we're civilians now."

Trina lets Greg's response waft a moment before commenting, "You know, there'll be no holding back Hopper if there's a way to Honorio."

"Exactly the reason he needs to stay here—emotional attachment. For me, I promised Diane that life's past. It's nothing you'd consider, is it?"

"I've grown real fond of that boy. Think I owe the world a good turn for a kid or two. Besides, those motherfuckers could've killed me at the soccer fields."

Greg confronts Trina with her tottery circumstance. "If I'm not mistaken, you're in the field of law enforcement. You dive into a rogue extract and the department gets wind of it, your career is cashiered. Given the fact that you have a ten-year hole in your resume and strings Apostoli had to pull to enlist you onto the force in the first place, that's not a great situation, is it?"

"I'm out a few days, and who's the wiser? I have vacation on the books. Everyone at the station knows the time I'm spending on this."

"Did that flight into the berm at the soccer fields make you spongy behind the eyes? Compared to the way we operated, this mission is totally off the cuff. What if the op goes sideways and you have to claw your way back to the States? You have that much vacation time?"

While Trina examines moisture puddling on the windshield wipers, she does likewise to her psychology. "You know what's great about the old man's gift, Greg? I've been going after it on the job exactly like we used to—just make things right and forget about the rest of the shit. I've gotten more fresh air in my lungs from that alone than anything else since we've come home."

"How does it play out when you no longer have your chance?"

"Guess I'll figure that out when I'm there."

"Sure you're not already there?"

Trina turns disputatious. "What do you mean?"

"That SUV could've thrown you into a parked car."

"It didn't."

"One of those bullets at the jewelry store could've just as easily hit the mark."

"But one didn't."

"Why was that?"

Trina scrutinizes the provocateur. "Are you saying that if I didn't have my chance, I would've bought it one of those two times?"

Greg, without blandishment, notes, "The old man never said how the gift would materialize. He said we would *pass* death."

"He also said we would die and come back to life. I remember that specifically."

"When House asked if we would resurrect, he didn't say we *would*, he said *sort of*. If Hop takes a bullet that should've finished him and doesn't, that's one way to pass death. If a bullet misses that would've otherwise iced you, that's another, isn't it?"

Trina is not fancying the concept. "Over and over and over again for ten damn years you and I… we all survived worse fire and a helluva lot more bullets than were flying at that jewelry store."

Greg responds with eyes that are, at once, ethereal, enlightened, and problematic. Trina grapples with his enigmatic expression before incredulously sputtering, "Are you actually thinking the old man was there for us overseas... and we didn't know it?"

"We were close to what... three or four other units who were maybe near our level? How long were they together? The most I remember was Ilya and his ex-Spetsnaz. For them, it was two and a half, three years tops. That unit and the rest, and I mean every last one of them, had casualties... if not multiple casualties. In ten years, we didn't have a single K.I.A... not even a serious disability. How does that compute?"

"We had a plan. You and Apostoli always had a plan."

"Maybe somebody else had a plan."

Fan blades inset behind an imposing circular grill in the cavernous, subterranean parking-garage basement appear to have capacity to propel Captain Nemo to Hades or points further south. Roland and Arnett, doing his best to save his comb-over from the blowback, wait impatiently near an empty loading zone beneath flickering, outworn fluorescent lighting. An eeriness creeps throughout the bowels of the cold, sunken concrete structure.

Kiefer, in dark, bulky athletic wear, steps out of a door several feet from the grill. He checks scattered parked cars, a catwalk, and ill-lighted corners for spectral figures. Finding none, he shuttles to Roland and Arnett, where greetings consist of nods, fleeting eye contact, and enunciations somewhere between grunts and grumbles.

"Have the files?" Arnett sounds off above competition from the commanding blades.

"Yep."

Arnett motions to Roland, who removes a small nylon bag from underneath his overcoat. "Forty-five here. Rest when we confirm that the files are clean and complete."

"They're complete and clean... and encrypted."

"What's with the fucking encryption?" a spleenful Arnett jabs Kiefer.

"You give me half the money, I fork over keys for half the files. When I'm paid my final forty-five, I release keys for the rest."

Arnett takes this news as well as a chunky gallstone announcing its charted course. "No one else has these files?" he huffs.

"No one that'll steal your story."

After a reluctant moment, Arnett motions to Roland who hands Kiefer the nylon bag. Kiefer opens it, inspects the contents, and zips it shut. He takes a flash drive from one pocket and delivers it to Roland. He roots another pocket for a piece of paper, which he also hands over. "Call that number. You'll be told keys for half the files," Kiefer instructs Roland.

"Sure that nails down coordinates and puts names to players all the way up the line?" Arnett crustily questions Kiefer.

"Enough that the lawyer and broad cop will have to find new lines of work, and every one of the four will be searching for very deep holes for themselves and their families. My guess is that troublesome people will be calling on them soon after this shit hits the air." Kiefer looks around one last time, slips to the side door, and is gone.

Roland shows uptight eyes; Arnett tosses aside Kiefer's fateful portend. "Fuck those people. That's the line they chose. They're in the stealth business. I just one-upped them."

McManus and the Mick are crouched in a cramped, faintly-lighted area behind a large vent shaft looking onto the concluded meeting of Arnett, Roland, and Kiefer. The Mick ropes in a lens at the end of a tube extending from his camera to the vent opening.

"Captured video of it all?" McManus thirstily inquires.

"Whole performance."

McManus, satisfaction smearing his face, gushes, "I'm gonna have that prick Arnett dangling so high he'll be looking up Peter's Pan's flitty ass." His cell phone buzzes. "Yes." He carefully listens, then says, "OK, great. Stay there for five." McManus concludes the call. "Greta's upstairs in the mall… at the planter near the bottom of the escalator. She has a zip drive with all the intel the attorney wants and the gizmo from the agency that needs to be planted at Campo Chana."

"I'll take care of it."

"Can you deliver it to the attorney this afternoon?"

"No choice. Have to be in San Pedro tonight. Shamrocks are playing the Blacks."

"Tough assignment for your boys." McManus gestures toward the garage below. "O'Keefe going with you?"

"Oh, yeah. He'd be there right now with the rest of the lads holding down front seats if we didn't have to take care of this."

"Keep your time with the attorney as tight as possible… in and out… just like the courthouse. Don't show him a fucking thing."

"Understood."

McManus and the Mick make their way out of the tight space.

On this late afternoon, a winter sun on the lam is layering its last light through the open roll-up door of the airstrip warehouse. On one side of the meeting table sits Trina, iPad nestled on her lap, and Hopper, etching notes onto a long tablet of yellow, ruled paper. Across is Judson Apostoli, ruggedly handsome man in his forties with stern Latin features; swept-back, wooly brown hair; stump of a neck spiked into a wrestler's body; and eyes without a microbe of frolic. He appears a bit stockier than in Greta's feature-player photo. From a laptop, Apostoli operates a large screen at the end of the table. Next to him, House noshes on a candy bar while reviewing a handwritten menu of Italian dishes. Greg sits at the end opposite the screen. Behind him stands Marek, wiping freshly scrubbed hands with a towel.

At a workbench crammed with multiple laptops, circuit boards, computer chips and parts, whizzy electronic equipment, and strands of wire in county-fair colors sits Laker man from Clarkson's studio, wearing the same purple-and-gold top and grungy jeans. He is going to town on complex instrumentation inside a cobalt case about the size of an ambitious Popsicle.

Apostoli manipulates the large screen so it bifurcates into a satellite shot of the Covarrubias compound and next to it mechanical plans of a state-of-the-art air-conditioning system. Apostoli dances a red arrow around the drawings, pinpointing a juncture. "The vial with the virus needs to inserted somewhere in this vicinity in order to have maximum distribution." Apostoli sends the arrow further down the drawings. "This is the other side of the main quarters. Separate ducts to the church, school, and dormitory, so the virus won't blow there."

"When do the vials arrive?" Trina asks.

"Being driven from outside of Cambridge to Logan, Logan to an airstrip near Tucson, Tucson by ground here no later than noon tomorrow," Apostoli rattles off.

"They come from Banner's shop?" House queries Apostoli.

"Banner's retired, out of the business. It's Patel's show now."

"How far from where we inject the vials to the location the Irishman's people want that device on the work table planted?" Hopper probes.

Apostoli flips the arrow to the compound satellite shot. "Right here. About fifty yards away."

"Sure the Irishman's device will be a fit?" Trina, face penned in gravity, inquires.

Apostoli tilts his head toward the workbench where Laker man is working his digital magic. "Reviewed schematics with the poor man's Elgin Baylor about an hour ago. If the electrical plans of the compound we were given are accurate, then it's simply unplugging one piece for another. The Irishman's device is a precise match to detail drawings. It'll be nothing more than a blip at most on the screens in the Covarrubias operations center."

"And genius Odd Al Stankovic over there is doing nothing to the device that will queer the fit?"

"Nope."

"Looks like a three-man op to me," House swerves the discussion.

Having none of House's electioneering, Greg precludes the option. "Like Judson said earlier, it's a two-man mission."

"I don't know," House mutters contentiously. "From where I sit... "

Never the parliamentarian, Trina interdicts, "You're in no shape to take on the loops at Magic Mountain, let alone sign onto this, House. Passage through the Campo Chana mountains will be fucking brutal. If we could find someone else with legs to do it in the window we have, Hop and I would be staying home. It'll take everything we have to make it through the high route inland."

Hopper eases himself into the discord. "Look House, I appreciate that you're willing to go the distance for Honorio, just like we'd all do if Billy was the one down there. But we have bases to cover here. Someone has to shadow the Irishman and his rugby buddy O'Keefe."

"Thought the douchebag's name was Kiefer," House testily puts forth.

Greg logs into the exchange. "O'Keefe, Kiefer, Keenan... he's used those names and ten others according to the Pro... just the way any hard target does. We *have to* connect him and the Irishman to the agency that has us doing their bidding or they'll have us on a string for who knows how long. We're pulling big exposure here... for good reason. But we don't want to have to do it again and again because we've been compromised. And," Greg resolutely adds, "we must stay on that location in the San Gabriel Valley to see if we can spy a Covarrubias warehouse and find a way in."

Apostoli hitches onto Greg's point. "Could need that as insurance, House, to bring Hop, Trina, and the boy out of Dodge and back home."

"Thought the Pro has that covered," House retorts.

"If the intersection goes live, House," Trina adds, "no telling what the Pro will have on his hands."

"Right. The guy who put those Kaddafi guns out of commission almost by himself needs help locking down some drug mules. Give me a fucking break."

Greg dilutes House's jarring by roping Marek into the flap. "Where are you with your pilot friend?"

"Here Friday, 3:00 a.m."

Greg glances at Apostoli who zooms out the satellite shot to show a stretch of shore ensconced between jungle west of the Covarrubias compound and the Pacific Ocean. Marek steps to the screen and points to a long strip of darkish sand close to the break. A large cove looms to the south. "Either an inbound or outbound can use that middle part of beach as a landing or takeoff strip for about an hour and a half either side of low tide. There's enough room north of those cliffs at the cove."

"Which means that if we don't hit our window, we're stuck inland for what… ten hours?" Hopper sounds up.

"About right," Marek confirms.

Hopper: "Is that the best res of the beach we have, Jud?"

Apostoli nods.

Trina, a smidgen skeptical, asks, "Marek, will your flyer have to hang the moon to bring us in and out?"

"No, sand in that location is compact."

"Has he put down wheels there before?"

"Not there, but same condition, similar layout twenty miles or so north. He's done it a couple times without a hang-up. Shouldn't be a problem… as long as the beach is clean. "

"How will we know that?"

"Can fly sixty feet above shore for miles... below the floor of any radar. Easy visual."

Greg spools the conversation down-table to House. "Plane be here tonight?"

"Yep. Marianne confirmed with Cord this afternoon."

"Untraceable?"

"Sure is. Cord's guy in the joint guarantees it."

"With what?" an exacting Apostoli inquires.

"Well, since Cord is looking out for the dealer while he's inside, I guess you'd have to say his life," House deduces.

Greg's eyes rotate to Hopper. "Everything set with Father Raymond?"

"Yeah. An acolyte to the village priest will meet us at the ocean. He'll lead us across the mountains."

"How far from the compound?"

"Quarter mile... maybe less."

"On the way over, better do some serious recce of that jungle below," Apostoli forewarns Hopper, "or you and Trina could be orphans down one deep rabbit hole... no matter what number twenty-two over there drops into that black box for us."

Somberness descends over the situation table.

As deepening of night encapsulates the warehouse building, Marek takes wrenches to an airplane engine, Mr. Laker tinkers with circuitry at the workbench, and Apostoli and Greg, butts against the end of the table, burn eyes on airplane schematics displayed on the large screen.

Apostoli circles a knotted neck. "How do you read Hop's state of mind? The Pro's worried he's too wound up in the circumstance, not the outcome. That Covarrubias compound is a major hard point. It'll take all he and Trina have to stay chilly, crack it, extract the boy, and make it back."

"I think once he's down there and digs in, he'll be OK. But realistically, we're dry of options. Ten years ago, we had on speed-dial the names of what... six or seven samurai who could be in that jungle in a heartbeat wreaking havoc? Guys the Pro and Marek said they could turn out this week... we really don't know anything about them, at least firsthand... and they don't come cheap. With what you and I are laying out for the plane up and back, bringing those chemicals here, and paying Laker man, not sure it's in the budget to commission anyone from outside... even if we thought they could handle the territory."

This rings true enough to Apostoli. His eyes stroll the yawning ceiling. "You know, from the original time we were really all together — when those First Intifada vets put us through that goddamn course that almost had me on a plane back home — it was clear Hop and Trina... maybe also Lance... had it physically on the rest of us... had it on us all by a ways. They've both stayed in top shape. Even if we had issued a call, not sure we could do better on something like this with all the hair on it."

"Think you're right."

Greg's cell rings; he checks the number and answers. Instantly, the message from the other end dumbs him. Eyes vessels of misgiving, he finishes the call simply with "I understand... I understand."

"What's up?" Apostoli asks in a deadened voice.

"That was Hop. Father Raymond received a message from the priest in the village near Campo Chana. They're flying Honorio to Columbia Friday morning."

"Sure it's the package?"

"No mistake. Only one of the boys spends his spare time kicking around a football."

"But Marek's pilot doesn't arrive until Friday."

Greg throws back his head. "I know… I know."

"Marek," Apostoli calls out.

"Yo."

"Got a minute?"

Marek, sponging oil from his hands with a well-travelled rag, makes it over to the table.

"Any way your guy can be here earlier than Friday?" Apostoli asks.

"Not a chance. He has work for an Odessa crew. When you're on with them, no timeouts, no early departures. Not a fun bunch. He's paid in advance through Thursday midnight there, so he's locked in until then." It takes little for Marek to suspicion something astray. "What is it?"

"The package will be moving Friday," Greg says in a morose, freighted tone.

"I'll take the flight."

"No, you won't," Greg rigidly responds.

"Why's that?" Marek, affronted, shoots back.

"Because flying's your livelihood. This thing goes sideways, you could lose your license… "

"And a lot more," Apostoli tacks on.

"I've flown in and out of a lot worse than what you have mapped out."

"Can't let you," Greg resists. "If you're going to be left hanging on a cross, won't be one of our making."

"Can you bring anyone else in earlier than Friday that's up for this kind of mission?" Apostoli, face brittle with qualm, inquires.

Marek rolls through options in his mind, then submits, "There's a guy in Bosnia I could scramble. Earliest I could get him here would be Thursday afternoon. When do you have to leave?"

"Thursday at oh-five-hundred."

"That I can't do," Marek flatly states.

Greg stands, posing the question that now cannot be deferred. "Marek, all the hours I have are with you, so you're the only one to answer this: Can I take a plane in and out of that beach? Yes or no."

"Yes."

"I think so, too."

Before either Apostoli or Marek can utter exception, Greg outs himself from the discussion and heads to the door.

Greg sits atop one of a series of large bollards between the warehouses and narrow airstrip. He takes deep breaths, hoping cool night air will simmer blood boiling in his chest and stem a worm of apprehension banqueting in his stomach. As pains flash up the front of his neck, Greg feels his body start to short. He drops to his knees and wraps arms around the bollard. His leadened feet are suddenly a distant appendage to his legs. Hissing shadows close in.

Suddenly and remarkably, an analgesic coats his body, calm eases reaming stress. Greg slowly unwires himself from the bollard... to find the aged man, in bland dress, seated on an adjacent bollard a few feet away. Greg beseechingly beholds him, expecting, no, hoping for some form of communion. Alas, the caller offers only a thin smile.

Greg wades into the many questions percolating in his mind. "Did I use my chance at the rest home?"

"No, you did not," the aged man evenly replies.

"What happened?"

"What your doctor advised you: You developed so many auxiliary arteries to your heart during your training and combat, you survived a heart event many would not."

"Were you there?"

"Yes, I was."

"Why?"`

The aged man replies not.

"Why didn't you give my chance to my father?"

"It's neither yours nor mine to delegate."

Though doubting, Greg marches on. "Did I use the chance just now?"

"No."

"Why did you allow Hopper a second chance and not Bill?"

"I'm here but a short time."

Realizing teachable moments would be few, Greg pivots his thoughts. "Does Trina still have her chance?"

"That's a matter I can share with her only."

Greg continues to burn through his examination. "If I have a fatal heart attack, use my chance, and return, do I come back with the same physical impairment that could kill me again an instant later?"

"It's possible."

"That's not much help."

"How much help would it be if you didn't have your chance?"

The lawyer in Greg would not be railroaded into the defensive. "When we were in situations overseas, we didn't suffer casualties when reason now tells me we should have. Were we given chances during combat without our knowing? "

The old man hesitates the slightest before presenting Greg a discomfiting revelation. "Yes."

"How in the holy hell," Greg salts the conversation, "could you save lives of those who were taking others?"

"It wasn't me."

"*Please.*"

The old man relents. "Had you not intervened, many, many more innocents would have been slaughtered."

"Why didn't you tell us then? Why did you choose now? If we've had it, why will it end? What about the people in Northern California?"

Before Greg can proceed with his interrogation, the aged man rises from the bollard and sets unyielding eyes on him. "The choice you make tonight will impact the significance the chance brings to your life."

"How do you expect me to process that?"

"You've been granted new life because of right you've done. If what you have been doing these past years is in furtherance of that right, why are you discontent? Why is your heart bringing you to your knees... rebelling against you?"

Feeling his soul disemboweled, Greg fumbles for a response, but doesn't find one before the aged man is part of the darkness.

Allan and Greta walk out of a complex of four unimaginative, low-rise office buildings into chill, bleak winter night already dining on their ears. As they head to a sprawling front parking area nearly divested of cars, Allan hands Greta a disk drive she squirrels into her purse.

"How was training?" she asks.

"OK. Two days too long. People trying to justify their budget, you know."

"Where did you stay?

"Rosslyn."

"Any fun?"

"Little difficult to roll into a bar and come off as suave and debonair when it's so damn cold outside you can't tell if you have snot running down your nose," rightly reasons Allan the cosmopolitan.

"Freezing cold... exactly why I've passed on assignments back there." Greta tightens her coat around her neck. "This is bad enough."

"When does the op south of the border go live?"

"Waiting on word from the attorney Hardisty. Sometime in the next few days. They'll provide twelve-hour notice."

"Mac believe they're actually real on this?" Allan asks a bit cloddishly.

"They didn't make a move until we proved up. Good thing we had those shots of the boy being loaded onto the plane in Otay Mesa. Anything else we offered would've given up our SIG. INT. and COM.INT. on them... which really raises the stakes for us. Once they had photos, they became serious very quickly."

"Intel package from our San Diego office enough for them?"

"No, they came back three fucking times," Greta spices the discussion.

"For what?"

"More detailed building plans, system diagrams, air-conditioning specs. Ended up handing over just about every C.A.D. file San Diego had on the Campo Chana compound."

"What will they do with all that? Blow the place?"

"That's what Mac's thinking. With the number of hostiles at the Covarrubias compound and barriers encircling it, our San Diego people give a clean extract a six percent chance at best."

"Even with the tradecraft of this team?"

"Have to come in over the water. Only hope. They might be able to find a circuitous route from the beach through mountains into the compound, but they can't return on it. No amount of skill changes the realistic way out. Best guess is that if the team nabs the boy, they have two, two and a half hours max before someone discovers he's gone. If they return via the mountains... assuming that's possible, it's at least three hours to the ocean... maybe more lugging the kid. By then Covarrubias will have choppers all over the Pacific. They can beat three hours with a straight shot through the jungle, but Covarrubias has thermographic cameras, lasers, footfall detectors, and high-tech gear you can't imagine covering that ground. Unless these ops have capes and can fly... which they might if they're the ones Mac thinks... they wouldn't move twenty feet through the jungle without kicking a can. "

"Unless they blow the operations center," Allan tags onto the scenario.

"Exactly, and maybe, *just maybe*, then they have a chance of making it out of there with the boy alive."

"What does that do for San Diego's capturing data?"

"Paulson and his guys threw everything they had into the plant device. It's a work of art. His techs need no more than an hour's landline access to Covarrubias's systems to extract everything they'll ever want. So that's our only rule of engagement with the lawyer and his people. They have to wait one hour after they activate the device, then it's open season. They can burn the place to the ground for all we care."

"What will the Mexican government say about that?"

"They won't have an inkling. The San Diego office has connections to a special section of *Direccion General* for Northern Mexico air space. They secured a twenty-four window for the team's plane. No one in Mexico City will ever know rogues from the U.S. breached their air."

"What happens after safe passage ends... assuming the unit can make it out?"

"Since the plane won't have a flight plan, best guess is *Fuerza Aerea Mexicana* scrambles jets and blows it out of the sky," Greta guiltlessly replies.

"Do they know how tight their window is?"

"Maybe we took some license there."

"You're kidding, right? What about the boy? He's no risk to anybody."

Greta catechizes her disillusioned colleague. "There's no midway with people like this, Allan. Right now, they can't be sure how or who put them onto the kid, but they're willing to take the risk and make a stretch for him. If they do bring him back, no doubt their first order of business will be closing the door we've opened to them. You saw what they did in the San Berdoo Mountains under the noses of every agency that has an office in this state... including us. You want them running up your ass? Mac doesn't want them up his. He's minimizing our exposure."

"If three or four of theirs are killed down there, you think the ones here will just figure that's game, set, match, and let it go? From what I can tell, these people are about one thing: covering each other," Allan kicks back.

"If some of them buy it in Mexico, the others in the States won't know how. From the time they go over the border until they cross back, the unit doing the extract can't have comm to the U.S. or else they risk giving away their position. If the plane is vaporized, who the hell will be the wiser? The rest of them here will think real hard about trying to get to the bottom of what happened at Campo Chana. Any hint they were tied to the mission, and they'll have people in Washington, the Mexican government, South American drug cartels, and who knows who else crawling all over them." Greta drifts a finger toward her colleague. "You didn't sign up for an officers' club, Allan."

"That's just not right," he observes as he turns a collar to the biting air.

"Nice concept. Never saw anything about it in our job description," Greta tidily responds.

House is parked in a nondescript sedan, pawing at a fake, though applaudably applied beard, while wiggling under several layers of padding that have given his upper body generous, marshmallowish proportions. It appears an air hose has been taken to his thighs. But overall, as far as fat-guy rigs go, this one isn't too darn bad. (Indeed, the jelly-roll neck is a dilly.) House peers down through the dark at a transportation facility where a fleet of shuttle vans are being parked, serviced, and cycled through electronically controlled, camera-patrolled gates. He trains binoculars on a back corner of barbwire-rimmed chain-link fence surrounding the facility. Impatient, he pounds a number on his cell.

Also on an aching late-night vigil, Promardie is camped in his Volvo in the warehouse district where Greg and Trina had been on watch. Evidently inoculated for boredom, he has rapt, caffeinated eyes on an intersection, abysmally lacking in traffic, but barbaric with ripping winds. He grabs his buzzing cell. "Hey, House, what's goin' on?"

"At the van station," House responds, maintaining fixity on the distant perimeter. "Can't see a way through the fence in the far corner."

"It's there," Promardie verifies. "Lance trailed a shuttle the Irishman caught in San Pedro to that location and saw him exit. He picked him up two days later at the same spot, hopping a van to WeHo."

"Must've cut links and wired ends to the corner pole."

"Don't know. It's not a passenger hub, so the Irishman has to be dishing cash to someone there to turn the other way when he comes in and out."

"OK."

"Did the gals at the studio doll you up the way you want?" Promardie razzes House.

"Yeah. Remember that old wrester Haystacks Calhoun?"

"No, I only go back circa Jumpin' Jim Brunzell and B. Brian Blair."

"Who?"

"The Killer Bees."

"Whatever. Well, I could pass for Haystacks' cousin."

"Make sure you snap a couple of shots of yourself. I'll work it into my Christmas-card collage."

"'Only for you, Pro."

"Your boys ready?"

"Yeah. Tully and his crew have a light schedule this week," House relays to Promardie. "Anything on your end?"

"No signs of flash mobs ready to storm this particular warehouse district for my autograph."

"Call if you need me."

"Shall do." As Promardie signs off, a gaudy, metal-flake steel-blue truck with alloy wheels oversized enough to fit out the Batmobile rolls through the intersection.

Greg sits in his living room, envisioning the Christmas tree that would soon blossom next to the fireplace. This, though, would not be a night of bijou, bows, cheer, or twinkly lights. Nope, this is an hour of numbing verity, coarse reality, fractured covenants, a crisis point where a marriage could teeter, fall, or irreparably fracture. He holds a glass of bourbon that offers little calm and no bearing. It tastes only of bitterness from loyalty corroded... by his own hand. Lamentably for Greg, neither alcohol nor time would provide further buffer to his condition.

Diane, in a robe and hold of a rattling anxiety, comes downstairs into the living room. She takes a place on the floor at Greg's feet and reaches for his hand. His wistful face tells her what she had dreaded. This conversation would be no box of yuletide chocolates.

Greg begins in a lumbering voice, "Honey, we need to talk... "

Diane presses her husband's fingers. "You have to bring that boy back home, don't you?"

Compassion flooding his wife's expression makes Greg feel all the more the beard and mutinous to his marriage. "Yes, we do."

"Do you honestly feel you're the only ones who can?"

"We think if he isn't extracted by Friday, he'll be sent to South America, and then we may never find him. We can't bring in anybody else quickly enough. Even if we could, I'm not sure they would have the stuff to find a way in, grab the boy, and make it out safe."

"Where is he?"

"Mexico."

"Bad part?"

Greg leaves filigree for the holidays. "Very bad part."

His lady bites hard on her emotion, then tries to settle herself with the psychology of the situation. "Does this have anything to do with your dad?"

"His values, I suspect."

Diane rests her head against Greg's leg. "What about your heart?"

Greg slips a hand under Diane's chin and brings her eyes to his. "I'm trying to do something good for my heart."

"Am I still in your heart, really in it?" Uncertainty in his wife's eyes nearly crushing him, Greg answers with all the bona fides he can muster. "You're the love of my life, honey. Until you came along, my nights were ghosts, bayonets, and cold sweats. You brought me back to the living."

"What does Dr. Klein say? Tell me honestly."

The fact of the matter could be pawned off no more. "If I don't make a change, the office will kill me."

Diane, tears pooling her eyes, hops onto the couch and ropes her arms around Greg's neck. "Quit the firm. Those aren't your kind of people. They never have been."

"I'm resigning when I get back. Clients I want will go with me. I'm sure of it. That's more than enough to start."

Forcing a bubble to her voice, Diane says, "If that's best for you, then terrific. Will anyone from the firm leave with you?"

"Just Jimmy Teague."

"Who?"

"Clerk in the office."

"Why him?"

"He's our kind of guy," Greg says with a warm sense of communion.

Diane savors a bond recaptured for but a moment before being tugged into the murky wild before them. "When will you leave?"

"Late tonight."

"Who's going with you?"

"Best possible people."

"Do they know about your condition?"

"They will before we lift off." Greg kisses Diane lightly on the lips. "I wouldn't go if I thought I was putting anyone at risk."

Diane finds in that the solace she can. Greg finds little solace in withholding that he will be piloting a plane.

A fidgety Roland paces Mitch Arnett's office. His face bears the excruciation of a gossipy secretary panting for her water-cooler fix. He stops in restive tracks when Arnett, dapper in broadcast attire, blows in. "We're in the money," Arnett beams.

"When?" Roland hungrily inquires.

"First piece runs network Saturday — prime time news." A lobbyist stocked with pocketsful of votes could not have been prouder.

The sum of Roland's next available verbiage: "Credits?"

"You trail as Assistant Producer."

Roland's face shouts glorification. "That's *so* great."

Saturated with self-accomplishment, Arnett steps behind his desk. "These fuckers have lived in the dark for two decades. Saturday night klieg lights go on them. Let's see how snooty that prick attorney is then."

In that triumph, Roland does not so easily share.

The shimmering white, single-engine, four-seat plane cuts low through misty air off pristine, uninhabited Mexican beaches. Accoutrements of conflict fill the cabin. Greg, in fatigue bottoms and sleeveless T-shirt, pilots with singleness of purpose. Hopper more than fills out the front passenger seat. With ballistic vest of overlapping circular ceramic discs and body armor covering his shoulders and thighs, he appears equal parts hulking middle linebacker with a lizard fixation and tricked-out soldier. Trina, in Kevlar vest and camouflaged military pants, is asleep in the rear.

Hopper tests an olive-black camouflage cream to his face. "Who mixed that?" Greg asks after a quick swivel of the head.

"Jud. He checked foliage in the Campo Chana area on the Internet. There'll be close to a full moon. He thinks this will be the color of the leaves."

Greg's slight smile is shaped with praise. "Judson Apostoli... my man."

"Yeah, he's something," Hopper concurs.

"Which camos you wearing tonight?"

"Slate gray and F.G. 502."

"B.D.U.s from Burma?"

"No. Bought these yesterday. N.I.R." Hopper checks the watch on his rubber wristband; he reaches to stir Trina. "Time," he succinctly announces.

Trina instantly shakes off sleep, views the glassy sea, and then surveys above. "Clean air?" she asks.

"Yep," Greg confirms. "The Irishman did his part. No Mexican military. No ripples in the sky. His people gave us the path they promised."

"Good enough."

"We'll be at drop-off in three mikes," Greg advises the two. "Need you both to spy the landing point for rocks, debris, anything that might give us trouble."

Hopper and Trina nudge closer to side windows.

Soon enough the plane is skimming above a break slapping onto clear, white shore open to the north, but bordered on the south by a cove of formidable rock face carpeted with mossy vegetation. Greg, Hopper, and Trina view below what Marek had described: a long swatch of level, damp sand without obtrusion, between waves flopping off a turquoise ocean and deep brush spilling from the jungle onto the beach. Greg banks the plane through salty air for his approach. He completes the turn, rights the wings, and drops over the cove. Face bundled in concentration, he lowers wheels to ground. The tires hit squarely, leaving shallow ruts in the sand—a flawless landing. The plane surely decelerating, Greg slowly disgorges tension from his torso.

Suddenly, a back tire catches an object beneath the surface, tilting the left wing into foaming waves. As water recedes, it drafts the wing with it. Greg battles to keep the tail from sliding and being sucked out to sea. Surf splattering the wing and spraying the back of the plane, he strains to maintain wheels parallel to shore. Hopper and Trina, composure unshakable, push their weight against the land side of the cabin. Just as the plane is about to lose its traction, the tires find a long sand bar parallel to the break, jutting onto the shore. It provides enough lift for the wing to rise out of the sea. Ground secured, Greg throttles up until the nose is due north and tail clear of sudsy water. When he safely comes to rest in the caked midway between the sea and loose sand at the jungle's edge, he kills the engine and lets his senses settle.

As Hopper unbuckles his seat belt, he quips, "So, Trina, how would you rate Sky King here on style points?"

"Terrific. Best ride I've had since the Matterhorn at Disneyland with House and Billy."

Paulson, shoulders rounded, swaddled in a familiar hoodie, sits on the side of a small fountain outside a cheerless office building whose windows are covered with drawn, inhospitable blinds. He downs a cup of mid-morning coffee from a local San Diego java shop. Arneston, a spare fellow in corporate techy ensemble, tiredly plunks next to Paulson and sparks a cigarette. "What time do we go live, Pauly?" he asks in spent voice.

"If all goes according to Hoyle, sometime around dawn," Paulson, tone bare, responds.

"How long do you really think we have to be in their lines?"

"With the job your team did to bypass circuitry once the device is set, we shouldn't need more than an hour... but we'll be busy."

"How do we know when the assets have made the plant?"

"Our screens go live."

"That's it?"

"Yep. No comm from the assets. Too much risk of interception for them." Paulson finishes the last of his coffee. "How we doing on the download interface?"

"Locked and loaded by midnight," Arneston warrants.

"Great." Paulson stands, stretches his spine, shakes dullness from his legs, manfully spits a loogie into looping fountain waters, grubs his pants pocket, comes up with a coupon, and hands it to his colleague. "Here, Arn. Double espresso on me."

"Thanks, Pauly."

Paulson straggles to the office building.

As one shift is returning to the East Bethune police department precinct, another is belching out of a briefing room where an animated sergeant waves his arms (as might any peppy, self-respecting symphony conductor) about a recent spate of heinous, nighttime crimes against unsuspecting mailboxes in high-rent districts. Outside the room, Cronin catches Anita Galton as she is slipping on a motorcycle helmet.

"Used to the two-wheeler yet, Galton?"

"Yeah, have it under control," she replies, not seeming particularly stirred to chat.

"When are you back in the cruiser?"

"Pressey is out of rehab this week, so we should be good to go by the first of the year."

"Hear from Trina?" Cronin asks with a largely failed casualness.

"Yeah, caught up with her early this morning," Galton replies, wading into the flow of cops nearing the exit to the vehicle lot.

"Any news on the boy?"

"No, but she's hoping that if she throws all her energy into it for a few days, something might break."

"She barely made it through that 246 with you and then was sent flying from her bike. I was kinda hoping if she took time off, she'd rest a little."

"If it was your boy that was nabbed, Cronin, you know she wouldn't waste a minute until he was back home."

"That's true... so very true," he wholly agrees. "Anything to do for her?"

"Think she's at the stage where she's doing for herself." Galton shoves out of the door, leaving Cronin to facts he believes have been reloomed for him.

Greg crawls from underneath the dry-docked plane. As Trina unloads rifles and sets them on a tarp, Hopper stumps back from the strip of beach on which they landed.

"What did we catch?" Greg asks Hopper.

"Part of a plane wing buried just below the surface."

"Lot of rust?"

"Not much."

"Nice omen," Trina skimpily observes.

As Hopper kneels next to Greg, he asks, "Where are we?"

"M.L.G. strut has been compromised."

"For the foot soldier, *mi capitan*."

"Landing gear has a problem."

"How bad?"

"Can't say. I'd have to open the strut."

This draws Trina into the tepee. "What's the fix?" she soberly asks.

Greg is short on elaborate prescriptions. "Judson and I figured it could be a problem landing on a porous surface, so we reviewed the flight manual and diagrams for struts and wheels.

Since there's no wobble to the outer casing, we probably have at least one more landing."

"What *kind* of landing?"

"Can't be sure," Greg fesses.

Trina cements eyes on Greg. "You're not giving me a great feeling here."

"We have to scuttle my waiting north on the coast during the op. We can only risk one more landing—back home. This assembly gets worse, and we might not be able to lift off."

"We can't leave the craft exposed here for twenty-four hours," Hopper pastes onto the problem.

Greg scopes the dense growth beyond the shore. "We can strip bark from those trees, lay it over the beach, and tug the plane into that cover. We have about an hour before RV with Father Raymond's guide. That should give us enough time. While you're humping it over the mountains, I'll chop down palm branches and throw them over the fuselage and wings."

Hopper, concern clouding his face, fixes on the plane. "Wish that damn thing weren't so bright."

"Composite body, glossy white paint—secondary transport of choice for today's drug dealer when his G650 is in the shop. For such a short turnaround, we did OK by Cord, no?"

"Yeah, we did," Hopper allows.

Greg steps to the arrayed rifles. "What are you taking?"

"Mk-11 with suppressor," Hopper responds.

Trina: "Chopped 4."

"That covers sniper and C.Q. Leaves me with the 60 and the rest, right?"

"Yep," Hopper confirms.

"That should do if I have company."

Greg pulls two machetes from the plane and hands one to Hopper. "Let's cut away some bark."

"You up to that?" Hopper asks.

Greg lets the machete dangle from a discordant hand. "I told you last night: Dr. Klein gave me enough medication before I left to pump blood through a pinhole. I'll get you through this and back home... unless you think you'll run across a temp pilot agency on the way over to your meet-and-greet with that happy bunch at the compound."

With that, Hopper and Greg take to the work at hand.

Promardie is stretched atop an interior, whirring, vibrating air-handling unit above mezzanine storage space inside a large, archaic industrial facility where machinery on the floor below blows out a continuous thunderclap. Concentration unpunctured despite turbulence below, he focuses through a vent opening on a slumberous warehouse across a lot, dusted by strong winds, occupied only by parking stripes. He perks up when the electronic entry gate to the lot opens, allowing in a tow truck with a battered, rusted van on the flatbed. As it motors past a bevy of security cameras perched atop the warehouse roof and then into the building, Promardie scrunches his eyes, locking on license plates of the truck and van. After registering strings of numbers and letters into his cell memory, he places a call.

Inside Marek's airstrip building, there is no Marek, one plane, Laker man asleep on a cot next to the workbench, and Judson Apostoli at the conference table, banging away with industry on his laptop. Apostoli's phone buzzes; he answers. "Where the hell are you?" he bellows. "Inside a goddamn turbine?"

"Close to it," Promardie replies above the furor of clangorous equipment. "Gonna text you an address, plus tag numbers of three vehicles—high-end truck, old van, and tow truck. See what you can track down. If the owners come up offshore trusts, we may have hit pay dirt."

"Did you spot a vehicle last night at that intersection?"

"Yeah. Followed it to a warehouse about a mile away. It's been inside since before dawn. Just saw my first mover."

"What is it?"

"Beat-up van on a flatbed. There's no oil anywhere around the building, so it's no repair shop. My guess is the van's a packer: drugs stuffed into hollowed-out engine block, rolled inside axles, tucked under rocker plates, something like that... maybe all of that."

"What's the plan?"

"Depends what you find," Promardie volleys back to Apostoli.

"Have exposure?"

"No. Made my way into a machine shop behind the warehouse before the place opened. On a H.V.A.C. unit above storage space. From the dirt on this thing, people haven't inspected it in years. Couldn't hear me down there if I did a Ginger Baker on the ducts."

"Need House?"

"What's happening with him?"

"Still sitting."

"I'll let you know. Be back to you inside an hour."

"OK." Apostoli ends the call and instantly raises another.

Greg has shimmied up a palm tree and is hacking leaves to cover the plane, now sitting in high brush off the sand. Hopper hails him. "Rally-point time, kemosabe."

Greg slides down the tree, snags a Beretta 92FS from the plane, and tucks it inside his waistband. With painted faces, body armor, camouflage pants, black ball caps, web vests of brimming modular pockets and magazine pouches, and pistols and machetes strapped to their legs, Hopper and Trina are fully equipped for their errand of redemption. Hopper loads an Mk-11, tranquilizer gun, and archery case over his shoulder; Trina, short-barreled M-4 over hers. She carefully slips the carbon tube on which Laker man had ardently labored into a padded pack on her back.

Greg fingers a dab of camouflage cream from Trina's cheek. "Butched yourself up pretty good, Miss Trina," he banters.

"You know, if you made an appearance at Primo's like that, might attract a live sort of guy," Hopper joins in.

"Understand Revlon's coming out with this in a rose/hot pink swirl next spring," Trina ripostes. "Think I'll give it a shot."

The three share what would be their last smile for a long while.

Hopper, humor instantaneously siphoned from his face, snaps a GPS navigator to his wrist. "OK, let's hit it."

The three decamp south.

As Hopper, Trina, and Greg are hiking down the beach, a rangy Hispanic in his late teens emerges with terrier intensity from thick green growth at the fringe of the sand. Greg flashes the gun from his waistband. Hopper and Trina stop and wait for the boy to weigh in. He does not immediately speak, most probably because the last time he saw people so outfitted was when he took in a performance of the Three Martian Tenors. Greg steers the gun at the boy's head. The teenager furiously spits out his message in rubbery English. "I am Arturo... Arturo from the mission... here for you."

"Who's your parish priest?" Trina hotly quizzes him.

"Father Montejano."

"Who's his friend in America?"

"Father Raymond."

"You mean Monsignor Raymond?"

"No, no," the Hispanic excitedly responds. "*Father* Raymond... *Father...* "

"Why are you here?"

"I am your guide."

"Where?"

The teenager turns to clay mountains beyond the trees. "There... *montanas*... to Campo Chana."

Trina keeps firing testing questions. "What's our name?"

"You are the *peacocks*."

The magic word having dropped, Greg releases the boy from his gun-sight. Hopper steps toward him. "You are Arturo?"

"Yes, yes... Arturo. I am *Arturo*," the teenager ringingly confirms.

"Are you ready to lead us, Arturo?"

"Yes."

"Then let's go."

Hopper and Trina look to Greg, who broadcasts, "Zero-eight-hundred tomorrow... ocean won't wait."

"Be here. Party of three," Hopper responds in a quick, firm clip.

Trina points inland. "Arturo... *montanas*."

Greg watches the three forge off the sand.

House, in his doughboy padding and bogus Burl Ives beard, sits in the sedan, squinting into a midday sun at the shuttle facility below, ruminating about the inexact science of a stakeout. As chagrin is infecting House's stolid features, the Mick suddenly appears behind the back corner of the perimeter chain-link fence. With an untwisting of a few wires, he's inside the lot. After re-securing his access point, he is on his way to the dispatch office.

House immediately raps digits on his cell phone and waits a tick before issuing an elementary call to arms: "We're live." He summarily clicks off and watches the Mick skip to a shuttle van and hop in. House turns over his engine and waits for the vehicle to steam out of the facility.

As the Mick's shuttle minnows south through modest traffic on La Brea, House keeps a tactical distance. A stoplight from Melrose, the Mick pops out of the shuttle and into a convenience store. No novice to the artifice of escape, House slips onto a narrow adjoining street. True to evasive form, the Mick puts a foot out a side door of the store, scopes the street, then darts into a dated, beat-up Peugeot, auto nonpareil for any self-respecting Bohemian.

About 15 minutes later, House is tailing the Mick on Pico heading toward the 110 Freeway when he notices a service van without markings lurking a couple cars behind. He recognizes the driver Kiefer as one of the Mick's companions from the San Pedro rugby-night photos. House instantly lights up his cell. "Where are you?"

Tully, behind the wheel of a low-slung Camaro, glances down at a tracking device in his console as he broadcasts into his head-set, "Running parallel to you on Venice, half-block back."

"Need you to take over at Vermont. There's a trailer on the Peugeot... blue service van."

"OK," Tully rogers.

"Where can I pick up fresh wheels?"

"Mario and Jake are riding boundary. I'll have 'em meet you four blocks south of Venice on Hoover."

"Won't that put a whole in the coverage?"

"Nah, Mario'll jump back in without a hitch. He can handle both sides. He's the best I have."

"OK. If one of 'em has a cap, that'd help."

"Let me see."

As Tully swings down to track the Mick and Kiefer, House veers off to a side street. He guns his car several blocks until he spots a buff guy, 30-so with Mediterranean features and prob-able penchant for punches, standing outside a worn Chevy El Camino, rumbling engine running. Another equally redoubtable man sits in the passenger's seat of an idling, vintage Oldsmobile muscle car in an adjacent parking space. House pulls over and shuts down the sedan. He clunkily waddles to the El Camino, exchanges passing acknowledgements with the standing man named Mario, offers the passenger an abbreviated wave, crams himself behind the wheel of the El Camino, swipes a hat from the dash, and is quickly on the prowl toward the 110.

House, big country bumpkin outfit intact and Def Leppard cap low on his forehead, and Tully stand behind fuel pumps at a service station, chatting as they ostensibly fill their tanks. While eyeing a poker parlor across the street spotted in the middle of a parking lot flush with cars, House slips a cell phone to Tully. "Use this when you see the Irish guy you tailed here. Put it to your ear, point it in his direction, and keep hitting the pound button. Don't worry 'bout focus or any of that shit. Need shots of anyone he comes into contact with."

Tully acknowledges the charge. "OK. You gonna stay outside?"

"Yeah. Wanna see if anything happens with the guy in the blue van. I'll drift over in a bit."

"OK."

Trying to type-cast the crowd at a Southeast Los Angeles poker parlor is much like attempting to impose a thematic overlay on piñata innards — chances, not so good. At any given table, one might find an industrialist sporting Saville Row across the felt from a down-and-outer who's mortgaged his last gold filling to stay in the pot; housewives with attitude, their true home the nearest deck, taking their bluff and stuff to retirees pensioned off to chance; slick semi-pros facing down fresh-off-the-road, stubble-chinned semi-drivers. Varied though they are, one trait all these players do share: total immersion in the game. There are no chairs here for the bet-and-giggle crowd. Whatever their job, position, penance, or levy in life, these people most definitely have a career in gambling. If the Flying Walendas were doing a routine above a table, doubtful any of those seated would spare a moment for the show.

Certainly no one takes heed of two blah guys like McManus and the Mick, drably dressed for a PTA encounter session. Ostensibly idly kibitzing near a high-stakes game, the two are having a conversation with heft of its own.

"Did Arnett's Boy Friday bite on the fake email from Vertain?" McManus, greedy with anticipation, queries the Mick.

"Oh yeah. Couldn't wait to gloat to O'Keefe that when Arnett's first segment hits network Saturday night, they'd bury Vertain in their dust."

"Keeping Saturday afternoon open, right?"

"Wouldn't miss it for the world," the Mick carols.

So consumed are the two with their mutual triumph that they take no heed of a boxy, dark-complexioned man of rowdy face and ferrous physique circling the casino perimeter, eyes on different tables, yet cell phone pasted to his ear always directed at them. But, then again, Tully Simkins' occupation in film is remaining undiscovered.

As House waddles in his overgrown-farm-boy getup through the parking lot to the front of the casino, he takes a call from Tully exiting the rear.

"Have enough shots for a documentary," Tully reports as he legs it toward the gas station.

"He meet somebody?" House asks in a voice flagging from lugging his newfound figure.

"Yep. White guy, buttoned up, corporate or government."

"Can you follow him until I can catch you later?"

"Sure. Shoot doesn't start until dark."

"Mario available if we have to tail a second car?"

"Absolutely. He's on the same shoot. He and Jake are waiting 'round the corner."

"Thanks, Tull."

"Always for you, brother."

House stashes his cell, makes his way to the front of the casino, and plumps down on a planter. He unpockets a breathalyzer and takes several hits of... nothing... to convince any watchful eyes that he is a dumpy, wheezing geezer a stagger away from collapse. As he arches back to presumably suck in air, he takes stock of the idle cars. Near a front row, he spots Kiefer in the blue service van a couple of vehicles away from the parked Peugeot, intently viewing the premises. His eyes gloss over House.

Inside the casino, McManus and the Mick close their conversation.

"Did you mark the tapes of the wire with Arnett?" McManus inquires.

"Sure did. All teed up for you. This fucker has no idea how deep he's in," the Mick larks.

"You have the tapes, right?"

"As you wished, your majesty," the Mick lightly replies. "O'Keefe has them outside… in his van."

"Have him lay them on the ground underneath the back of the van."

"Will do." The Mick zips out his cell; McManus does likewise.

House has tottered inside the front entryway where he's cornered a Philippine attendant and is vigorously petitioning for wider table seats to accommodate gamblers with generous girth. In truth, the diminutive man, pinned and perplexed by the big man's blarney, is simply a stationary foil for House's subtly keeping an eye on the service van. He watches Kiefer step from his vehicle, stoop beneath its rear, and lickety-split get back inside. Shortly, a sauntering Greta, twirling car keys on her finger, appears in the row behind Kiefer. When she reaches the van, the car keys… surprise… fly off her finger and, by gosh, just happen to land underneath the back of Kiefer's ride. When Greta straightens, she has her keys in hand and is closing the flap of her oversized purse.

House releases the glassy-eyed attendant from his ruse, steps away, and whips his cell into action. "Tull, have a leggy blonde in black pants in the parking lot. As soon as she hops into her auto and drives out, I'll peg the make and color for Mario and

Jake to follow." After a couple of seconds, he closes with "Great. Thanks."

The clay face of the craggy mountain, punctured by the mouth of a cave near the crest, presents a climber with nature's tyranny of randomness. Protruding rocks, crevices, thin lines of shelf, and fingerholds are offering a tenuous, zigzag course to the top. The nimble Arturo skillfully cobbles his way up the cliff, quickly gaining altitude. Hopper and Trina, though saddled with gear and weapons, exhibit strong limbs and exquisite athleticism to propel themselves upward, lagging little behind. They will their way into the hollow below the summit where Arturo is catching his breath.

As she is uncoiling her hand muscles, Trina points a flashlight down a tight spiral of darkness. "Where does this take us?"

"This cave is the only way to a ridge and long path on the other side that leads to Campo Chana," Arturo replies in labored breath.

"Is there cover along the path?" inquires Hopper.

"Yes. We will hear a helicopter before it can see us."

Trina extends an arm. "Show us the way." Arturo gathers himself and, on hand and knees, leads them ahead through the narrow opening for 20 feet or so until he abruptly stops. Hopper squeezes next to him and asks in dampened tone, "What is it?"

"Wind is from the east today. There should be more air coming in."

"Could part of the tunnel have crumbled?"

"That has happened, but I came this way this morning, and it was clear."

"Then probably either man or large animal between us and the ridge, no?"

Arturo purposely nods.

"Animal," ventures Trina.

Hopper motions for Arturo to move back; Trina crawls beside Hopper, who taps his pistol. "We fire, and the echo could give away our position."

"Might also cause some of this tunnel to collapse," Trina adds.

Hopper takes off his archery case, removes the bow, and hands arrows to Trina. He pulls from a pouch a small canister, opens it, and places it on the dirt. While Hopper strings his bow, Trina dips four arrowheads into the gummy substance inside the tin.

Trina scooches down, Hopper readies the first arrow, and Arturo drops lids over doomsday eyes. Trina blinks the flashlight at long intervals. Shortly enough, they can make out what indeed Trina suspicioned: an approaching animal, and a pip of an animal it is: a lion, not a mountain one, but a real, from-the-plains-of-Africa lion, that, from blood stained around its mouth, appears to be in the midst of a four-ridge eating spree.

Trina aims the flashlight at the big cat's face that broadcasts it is primed to pounce; Hopper cuts loose an arrow. It whistles down the tunnel and splits one of the lion's eyes. With an incensed, snarling roar, the animal charges. Hopper pulls back a second arrow and lets fly, skewering the other eye, which lessens not the lion's ferocity nor its rush. Hopper launches a third, this time into its gaping, raging jaws. The frenzied creature only gains steam. Trina readies her Glock 17. Hopper, short of treated arrows and ground, stents the cat's throat with his last shot. As Hopper clears his machete, the lion suddenly convulses. Its charging legs skid out from underneath it. A few precarious feet from its assailant, the animal lapses into spasmodic fits before its growling, foaming mouth and body shut down. Hopper moves forward to see what life it has left, but finds he is impeded by the clasp of Arturo's quivering hands around his ankle.

Having feathered palm leaves completely over the plane and sprinkled brush branches atop, Greg places around its perimeter dark green canisters with black fan tops. When finished, he moves to a covey of rifles, pistols, and machine guns clustered against the trunk of a nearby palm and begins loading ammunition.

Hopper, pores spigots of sweat, kneels on a ledge over the jungle, removing arrows from the lion carcass. Trina, planted on a nearby boulder, sops perspiration from her face with a small towel. Arturo kicks dirt over the trail of animal blood from the back portal of the tunnel to the ledge.

Hopper motions for Arturo to join him.

"What in the world is a lion doing up here?" Hopper asks with no little exasperation.

Arturo opens a hand to the overgrowth of trees, plants, and vines below. "The Covarrubias has a zoo. Last year, animals escaped…," Arturo gloomily points down. "… There."

"What kind of animals?"

"What you saw and big gorillas, *tigres, guepardo.*"

"Cheetahs," Trina interprets the last.

"Did they escape or were they released?"

Arturo tilts his head in uncertainty. After a moment, he reveals, "*Camaras* down there are so many, they see every bird fly, every snake crawl. None but the Covarrubias can pass through *la jungla*. No one. No animals are needed to keep people away."

"Well, I guess it's a good thing we cleaned up that cave so we won't have *guepardo* chowing on dinner when we come back through," Hopper jauntily concludes.

"Yes, this is a good thing," Arturo agrees.

"Find as many rocks as you can. We need to cover this animal."

"I will do that."

As Arturo goes gathering, Hopper stands to study through a narrow view corridor the lay of the densely vegetated land below.

To say this configuration of computers and electronics is a data operations center would be to conclude Dylan Thomas had a remote appreciation of liquor. Four distinct, self-contained pods with near garrison separation occupy 10,000 square feet of floor space. Partitioned groups of computer brainiacs, each toggling between five to six screens, communicate in a mix of languages as diverse as found on an Ibiza summer dance floor in full cry. On a platform above the main floor are four supervisors, each overseeing through multiple terminals a quadrant immediately below. Suspended above all at the highest level is a bald-headed, pasty-faced, lean man with a miniature Salvador Dali moustache, piercing eyes, and algorithms boiling out his ears. (One could safely estimate this puppeteer suffers few reversals.) He sits alone in a swivel chair on a deck where no one dare step heavily. In constant rotation, he keenly analyzes supervisors' screens below. Whether Domingo Covarrubias and his tech chieftains had elicited this configuration from a Las Vegas pit or Spielberg set is uncertain, but this much is most evident: it's one shrewd, crackerjack I.T. setup.

Off the main floor, seated young Hispanics sharply study a battery of camera feeds from in and around the compound, throughout the jungle, and at multiple buildings in metropolitan areas where drugs are being received, broken out, processed, re-packaged, and shipped. One such screen shows workers extracting packs of white powder from bodies of a junk van and older hearse. Drugs are carted from the vehicles to a long table partitioned by floor-to-ceiling sheets of Visqueen, wherein clean-room processors open packs, scrape every bit of precious powder, mix drugs with baking soda and cornstarch, measure portions into small plastic packets, insert packets into hand-size ice-cream-bar boxes, and seal them. The most efficient Detroit assembly lines had nothing on this crew.

It's well-neigh noon and Promardie has moved not an iota from his roost atop the air-conditioning duct inside the antiquated industrial building. He answers a call from Apostoli who is camped in front of his computer, photos of McManus at the poker parlor populating part of his busy screen and reduced copies of grant deeds and vehicle records the rest.

"Hey," Promardie answers, "any luck?"

"All kinds. You might be sitting on the mother lode. The tow truck, that old van, truck you I.D.ed at the intersection, building you're spying, *and* one next to it are all owned by off-shore trusts."

"One next to it? North or south?"

"South."

"It's vacant." Promardie zeroes in on an idle, adjacent distribution facility with a lineup of bolted, dock-high loading doors. "Some roll-up doors have rust."

"Don't know what to tell you, brother. Can't imagine they're saving it for a Cinco de Mayo margarita blend-off. Something must be cooking there."

"Sure haven't seen anything."

"Any new movers?"

"Yeah. Hearse came in about an hour ago on another tow."

"What's your guess?"

"Probably unloading goods, cutting them for the street, and bagging for distribution," Promardie reckons.

"What's the plan?"

"Call you when I have one."

"House is on the move with the Irishman. Do you have Lance in the hole?"

"Depends which head he has on his shoulders when he wakes up. If he doesn't answer the bell, I'll need a case… and probably a lot of tools."

"All right. Let me know as soon as you can."

"That I'll do."

Promardie stashes his cell and closely inspects the still distribution facility. He slowly scans roof-top equipment, stopping at a large air-handling unit overlooking the object warehouse. Damned if cigarette smoke isn't drifting out a side vent.

As Ryan and two other altar boys broom the communion area of Our Lady church, Father Raymond, face sapped, eyes shy of sleep, trundles from the sacristy to check on his charges. In a back row, behind several elderly parishioners wrestling with vagaries of looming eternity, kneels Diane, face bloodless, head bowed, hands clasped, trying to manage a dark tempest of suspense within. Father walks down the aisle to offer her an assuagement sorely escaping him.

Arturo leads Hopper and Trina over a slim belt of dirt near the top of the mountain range. Vaulting boulders and a relentless, glaring sun obscure terrain below. The boy stops and points to a chasm in the rocks. "There," he says, a bug of fear biting his voice.

"What is it?" asks a leery Trina.

"Through there you can see below."

"What will we see?"

Apprehension sewing his face, Arturo replies, "The Covarrubias."

"Their compound? This is it?"

Arturo nods.

Hopper stretches an arm around Arturo's shoulder and convoys him several steps back down the path. "You're a brave young man. You've done all you can. Now you must return to your village. Please thank Father Montejano many times."

Face coloring, Arturo proclaims, albeit somewhat flimsily, "I am not afraid."

"We know, but you can't wait here. There may be gunfire when we return. We promised Father Raymond that you wouldn't be hurt. You don't want us to break our word to a priest, do you?"

"No," Arturo permits in deference to the cleric and his own sketchy resolve.

"Go now, please. Be safe."

As Arturo departs, Trina brightens her face to show thanks. The boy offers a trace of a smile and then disappears among boulders.

As Hopper and Trina are stripping gear so they can shimmy through the fissure, Trina asks, "Think he's convinced we're returning this way?"

"Yep. He'll be waiting. He knows he showed fear. He'll want to make that right."

"Good. Safer for everyone."

After Hopper extracts binoculars from a pouch, he and Trina press through the thin opening in the rocks. Below is the Covarrubias complex. Hopper takes the first survey, pressing the camouflaged field glasses tight to his eyes. It lays out precisely as the Mick's site plans had detailed: sizeable electrical and mechanical equipment at the base of the mountain and, in undulating terrain below, sumptuous, sprawling residences across a courtyard from a citadel of an operations center with more antennae, satellite, and radar equipment sprouting from its roof than mushrooms in the Black Forest. In the flat are two Russian Mil Mi-28 Havoc attack helicopters poised on pads; soccer fields; dormitory; conspicuous church; and indeed, veiled by trees, many zoo cages... but few animals. Hopper registers military-efficient tower security stations spotted throughout. The entire place is repellent with an all-too-familiar air of dictatorship, notes he.

Hopper fixes on generators and mechanical equipment in the foothills and three interspersed platforms occupied by guards armed with German HK PSG1s and Soviet Dragunov SVDs. Two of the lookouts are grizzled sorts, likely not on temporary assignment from positions as kitchen ice-cream stewards. The other is young, late teens, standing as correctly as a country squire behind his rifle. Worry webs Hopper's face. He hands the binoculars to Trina. "Check the mechanical supply house."

Trina scopes the area, then sags against the stone, knowing what's coming.

"See the guard on the east side?"

Trina looks away. "Yes."

"We may have to throw down on him or someone like him."

"I know."

"There can't be any hesitation like outside of Primo's," Hopper admonishes Trina with the tough side of his tongue.

She takes umbrage. "That was the streets of East Bethune, Hopper, not Culiacan, the Middle East, or playground of some goddamn, heathen Somalian pirates where we made our own rules of engagement. The Department has policies on discharging a gun. As long as I wear a badge, I follow those policies. They're not paying me to be fucking Annie Oakley."

"All right, but I can't have your mind on Sudan if we have to take out a shooter that's short in the tooth."

"Like I said to you and Greg on the way down, if I thought it was a problem, I would've stayed home."

"OK. Let's go through H.V.A.C. plans one more time."

In a designer kitchen area of an office building, Roland pours a cup of brewed coffee. He eschews regular cream and sugar for a shot from a bottle of sweetened hazelnut creamer and drip from a vanilla one. He clanks the bottles back amongst those of caramel and almond. As he sips his gentrified caffeine elixir, Jordan, a dishy brunette with ice-blue eyes and bonny smile, sashays in.

"Hey, Roland," she opens in a honeyed tone. "Hear your piece is going network tomorrow night."

"Yep, prime time."

"That's *so* very cool."

"It's Mitch's story, you know. I'm just receiving A.P. credits," Roland hedges himself.

"The whole station is buzzing about it," Jordan coos.

Sparked by the beauty's attention, Roland offers up, "Really interesting what it took to bring it to air."

"I *totally* want to hear about it."

As Roland's liaising is taking shape, Arnett appears at the door. "We need to edit the piece for network."

"Don't know how in the world I can make it any tighter, Mitch."

"New York just previewed it. They want more minutes."

"I'm on it," Roland jazzily gusts.

Arnett disappears.

Jordan showers Roland with a gaze of favor before he debonairly suggests, "Can we talk more tomorrow night?"

"Of course. Email me your cell." The dating dance has joined.

"Great." Roland breezily exits to bask beneath the halo of impending television celebrity.

House, still with beard and cap but without fat-man wadding, swings out of the El Camino and strolls to a white Oldsmobile 442 parked among trees on a bluff overlooking a cluster of ho-hum, three-story, concrete office buildings and surface parking lot packed with an armada of commuter vehicles. At the wheel, Mario, squarely in the vice of boredom, is ecstatic to see House at the passenger's window. He opens the lock; House plonks down across from him.

"This buggy really caught my eye this morning. When did you score it?" House admiringly asks.

"Last month. Bought it from one of Capidonica's guys."

"Nice."

"Blow the doors off that GTO of yours."

"Could be you'll have your chance to try." The two exchange amused smiles. House looks around "Where's Jake?"

"His wife came by and took him home." Mario gives House the once-over and gently needles him, "You're a little thinner than this morning. What happened to the pork-chop look?"

"Wore my ass out lugging that shit around. Served its purpose."

"Who did your face… Lucinda or Coral?"

"Coral."

"Nice work."

"Yeah, holding up pretty good through a couple of mean sweats."

House hunts through the windshield, taking a reading of the site below. "What do you make of it?"

"From the cars and way people are dressed, looks like a production engineering outfit, back office of an insurance company, quiet government unit, something like that."

House screws tight his eyes, locking on the front of the buildings. "Don't see any signage. You?"

"Nope. What's your take?"

"If I could figure that kinda shit out, I'd be dangerous. How did it go on the way here from the casino?"

"She jumped around, slowed down, sped up… clearly didn't want to be tracked."

"Any problems?"

"She didn't suspect anything. It was easy enough to run parallels. Had to make up ground a couple of times, but nothing this baby couldn't handle."

"That's great, Mario. Really appreciate it. You guys are almost as good at this as at your stunts."

"You know how spotty work has been from the studios the last few years with all the runaway filming heading out of state. Have to keep the engine running for the family." Mario hands House a rough sketch. "That's where she's parked. Light brown sedan. Have the license plate number there, too."

House gives the paper a once-over, then pokes at Mario, "I see storyboards in your future."

"If you stay here as damn long as I have, I see NoDoz in yours."

With a cheered face, House reaches for the handle and opens the door. "OK. I'll take it from here. What do you want me to do with the El Camino?"

"Think you'll burn it before the night's out?"

"Might."

"Tully says to then just park it at the train station and leave it. We'll pick it up, paint it, and change out the plates. Make sure you leave the Leppard hat inside. Jake's kinda lost without it."

"Shall do. You'll be on time for the shoot, right?"

"Yep… half hour to spare. How did it go on your end?"

"Not what I'd hoped. After I took over for Tull, guy made a stop downtown. It had an underground parking structure with camera surveillance. Didn't want to get caught in the trick bag, so I stayed outside. He went from there to the federal courthouse, but then I ran out of time." House extends a hand to Mario. "Thanks, again."

"Any time, brother." All too pleased to be excused from dormancy, a stuntman's ultimate ignobility, Mario shakes hands with House and kindles his brutish motor, sending birds fleeing trees above.

Night has fully seized the Covarrubias compound. Argonauts Hopper and Trina, faces grim with dark camouflage cream and focus, have made their way from the mountain, slugged through dense, high brush, and crawled around several patches of bloated rocks to a position close to the air-conditioning plant and young tower guard. Hopper hands his Mk-11, archery case, tranquilizer gun, and machete to Trina, then peels off his vest. He removes several vials of clear liquid, syringe, and needle from a pouch, small wrench from another, and stows them along with a tin canister in his pants pocket. As Hopper checks his equipment, tightly secures his pistol and ties a long, thin nylon cord to his ankle, Trina attaches a suppressor and night scope to the Mk-11 and mounts the rifle atop a boulder. After she has sighted the scope, adjusted and zeroed it, and has the young guard's nose in her crosshairs, she ties the other end of the nylon cord around her wrist. She signals to Hopper, who immediately bellies toward a large duct bridged above ground between the air-conditioning generation equipment and residential structures and operations center below. When Hopper angles off, Trina lets the cord unwind from her wrist.

As Hopper is making his way, the young guard suddenly turns with lancing eyes toward Hopper's position. Trina yanks on the cord; Hopper stops and curls behind a cluster of large stones. The guard laces the rocky area with a powerful, wide-spectrum Xenon searchlight. Trina taps a finger on the trigger, ready to fire if a tincture of alarm crosses the youthful face. She discerns the guard's expression tensing. He concentrates the searchlight on boulders covering Hopper. Trina narrows her shooting eye. The guard brightens the beam. Hopper flips open the holster flap covering his pistol. A couple of fugitive varmints making residence under a crag in the rocks suddenly flee the glare. The guard shuts down the searchlight and rotates it to another vector. The gristly option having passed, Trina drops her head ever so slightly before tugging on the cord; Hopper continues on.

Once he has made it underneath cover of the duct, Hopper surveys the security platform. Seeing that the young guard still has a vantage to his location, Hopper grabs either side of the duct, bear-hugs it, and shimmies his way uphill to find a spot not clearly visible to any of the security platforms. Seventy feet later, Hopper's arms, brawny though they are, begin to quiver. Soon enough, his back muscles turn to mash. Feeling his body welshing on him, Hopper clicks on in his mind an image of Honorio's lying on a bed in a lonely barrack, cradling a football, crying himself to sleep. It takes no more for Hopper to press on to a point where he can safely take to ground. There he removes the wrench and undoes a rivet connecting sections of sheet metal. He injects fluid from the vials into the rivet hole and air blasting to buildings below. Once finished, he replaces the rivet. He then extracts from a pocket the tin canister which contains dusty particles and sprinkles them onto the dirt. Hopper gives himself a moment before braving the elevated course to Trina and schooling more punishment to his body.

Late into evening, Greta's beige sedan is one of few remnant cars parked in front of the largely darkened office buildings. House, humming what sounds to be a hip-hop cover of a medieval funeral dirge, waits in the El Camino on the bluff above. As yet another yawn stretches his jawbone, he spots Greta and Allan exiting a building. When she slides into the car Mario had marked, House starts his engine and tools down a curvy back road to a main thoroughfare where the parking lot dumps.

Once Greta turns onto the street, House waits until she is well away before dropping into light traffic behind. As he is trouping along, he sees her swing a sudden right at an intersection. House cuts onto the nearest side street, peels up several blocks, and shoots across to fall in a couple of blocks rear of Greta. He lurks along, texting a message.

Greta abruptly slows to a crawl. House steers into an empty medical-building parking lot, waits a ten-count, then jumps back onto the street. He soon again has her in his sights… but not for long. She brashly makes a clunky, mid-block U-turn. House instantly bails into a driveway, kills the lights, opens his door, and kneels on the front seat. When Greta passes, she sees only a driver, rear sticking out, reaching for something in the passenger's side. At the very next intersection, she makes a right and jams the accelerator.

House squeezes behind the wheel and surges onto the street. By the time he has rounded the corner, Greta's taillights are in the far distance. Not averse to taking license with road laws or an occasional brazen act of civil disobedience, House doesn't think twice about blatantly busting the speed limit, but knows that will likely only catch Greta's eye and send her off course. He texts another message as he inconspicuously tries to close the distance with the beige sedan. When Greta blows through a red light a couple of blocks ahead and streaks away, it appears that she has indeed given House the gate.

All at once, a motorcycle cop, red and blue lights beaming and siren shrieking, flashes by House in Greta's direction. The cars in front of House, including Greta's, slow; House dodgingly plugs along. The cop appears to be closing in on Greta, who starts to pull over, giving House time to slide within trailing range. Oddly, it seems, the cop zips by Greta and guns the motorcycle up the street.

As traffic resumes its flow, House enters a last text message, "Thanks, Galton." While Greta may have put House in check, she has him not without his queen.

Greta turns her sedan into the driveway of a high-security storage facility where a young armed guard in an entry booth smiles smarmily at her before opening the front gate. House watches the gate roll closed and Greta park in front of a far unit.

Promardie eyeballs through a telescopic lens and small window the lighted warehouse interior where the battered van and hearse are now indelicate heaps of parts. The processing table is being broken down by workers as others finish loading drugs sealed inside the small ice-cream-bar packages into a refrigerated truck advertising a Mexican supermarket. Promardie sets down the lens and turns to a dispatched Hispanic lookout bound with insulated electrical wire. Though there is little room inside the hollowed-out air-conditioning unit for skirmishing, the man tries to kick Promardie with tied feet. In recognition of the valiant and loyal effort, Promardie issues a due and fitting rejoinder: a crashing right that further flattens the lookout's pugly nose and knocks him out cold. Promardie rips off a sleeve of the man's shirt, stuffs it into his mouth, and bands him with yet more wire, this time around his head to secure the gag. He pulls a Springfield XDM 9mm pistol from his shoulder holster, ejects the magazine, checks it, and reloads. He collects a serrated combat knife next to a spool of electrical coil and secures it in a sheath strapped onto his high ankle. After a final inspection, he grabs the Hispanic's leather jacket and knit cap and then wriggles out of the tin unit.

Promardie efficiently makes his way through a rooftop hatch to a stairwell and retraces steps to just inside an exit door of the empty building adjacent to the Covarrubias staging warehouse. There he rings out on his cell phone.

Apostoli, busily studying data on McManus populating his computer screen, has budged not from the table at Marek's airstrip building. He checks his buzzing cell and answers. "Ready to move?" he asks without spare.

"Yep," Promardie replies.

"Go to the southwest corner of the lot of the vacant building. Fence has been cut at the bottom. There's a toolbox just inside with everything you wanted… including the pet. Your guy came through in spades."

"Great. How about Marek's man at LAX?"

"He has a small hangar clear for you in dead-air space. Directions are in the toolbox."

"Good enough."

"You can handle it alone?"

"No choice. Lance just landed at an unknown planet in his own universe."

Promardie pockets his cell, throws on the lookout's jacket and cap, and hustles through the night to the far end of the parking lot where he finds a sizeable metal toolbox inside an excised section of chain-link fence. He lugs the case to the other end of the lot next to the Covarrubias warehouse and removes a heavy-duty bolt cutter. Straightaway, he has carved a crawl space at the bottom of the fence.

Promardie retreats to the vacant building, snags a flashlight from the toolbox, and works his way downstairs and around the basement until he finds the emergency generator room. Employing a wrench from the case, Promardie opens a valve and exposes a pipe directly connected to the engine. He carefully extracts a chemical grenade from the toolbox, pulls the pin, drops it into the pipe, and hightails it out of the building. Just as he reaches the parking lot, an explosion rips off the roof of the vacant structure.

Promardie races toward the Covarrubias warehouse yelling, "*Fuego! Fuego! Fuego! Fuego!*"

As several exercised Hispanics jet out of the warehouse, Promardie pivots and sprints back to the burgeoning fire. When exiting men see the familiar jacket and cap, they head to the front gate and scurry to the blaze. When he is out of their sight, Promardie reverses fields to the fence, wriggles through the opening, latches onto the toolbox, and legs it to a far wall of the warehouse. Using the bolt cutter, he opens metal conduit budding from the ground to the roof. He severs electrical cable running inside the conduit; the warehouse immediately goes dark.

Promardie edges over to a side entrance. When a panicked Hispanic opens the door, Promardie coldcocks him. Promardie removes a small smoke grenade from the toolbox, activates it, tosses it inside, and once again bellows, "*Fuego! Fuego! Fuego!*" As white phosphorus burns into yellow flame, producing surges of smoke, all doors to the warehouse are thrown open. Promardie straps on night-vision goggles from the toolbox and sneaks inside. He immediately sees a Hispanic jumping behind the wheel of the freezer truck with the precious packaged drugs as another man frantically drags down a chain to open the large roll-up door for the truck to exit. Promardie spurts to the truck and hops into the passenger side. He points his Springfield at the driver's head, and, with his free hand, straps the man's hands to the wheel with plastic cable ties. Promardie draws the knife from his ankle holster, whips it past the Hispanic's ear, and sticks the driver's jacket collar to the seat. He slips onto the floor, cocks his gun, and orders, "*Conducir! Conducir!*" Though style points would not have been awarded for navigation, the cowed driver manages to guide the freezer truck out of the frenzied warehouse, through the motorized front gate, and onto the street without drawing undue attention.

In the ordinary course of events in the security monitoring sector of the Covarrubias operations center, one of the seated technicians would have instantly noticed the flare-up at the L.A. warehouse and exiting truck Promardie had hijacked. However, since the entire I.T. floor has been compromised by the improvident onset of fever, cramping, and hot-foot scampers to the bathroom, a number of chairs are empty. When the responsible overseer, pallid and perspiry, returns to his chair, the smoke-filled screen immediately captures his eye. He instantly signals to his supervisor.

As the freezer truck barrels west on the 105 Freeway, Promardie answers his cell.

"How we doing?" Apostoli fixedly asks.

Promardie scans the face of the jittery driver who seems to be contemplating a fate inside a tiger pit circumscribed by punji stakes. "One of us is doing OK."

"How's traffic?"

"Light. Some early aerospace commuters to El Segundo are kicking in, but that's about it. Everything good with the hangar?"

"Marek's guy is waiting. How far out are you?"

"Twenty minutes."

"If that truck is bugged, probably going to be close," Apostoli cautions.

"Don't I know. Call you when I make it there."

Promardie clicks off his cell.

The warehouse, now clear of smoke, workers, and, most critically, drug product, occupies the screen of a Campo Chana platform overlord, whose keyboard is a catch basin for sweat pouring from his forehead. An adjacent monitor shows a red blinking dot on an electronic map negotiating its way at a brisk pace on the 105 Freeway toward the Los Angeles International Airport. This night red is the color of a Pro.

It is a residential street much like any other in a working class neighborhood of Los Angeles, where many folks are rising early to reboot themselves for another day of supporting the family. However, the interior of one home on the block has anything but a family motif. Most demising walls have been demolished. Four-deep, brick-sized packages of white powder line those that remain. Several Hispanics from the soccer field are asleep on cots, automatic weapons a reach away; two snort cocaine at a kitchen table. A phone rings. Within moments, the house is abluster with men throwing on clothes, snatching guns, and packing themselves into the limousine parked in the garage.

Intently observed by the bald data kaiser on high, the monitor of the platform supervisor now displays an atoning blinking green light closing in on the red one nearing LAX.

As the limo bombs along the 105 Freeway, passenger Hispanics check magazines and slam them into AK-47s and FN SCAR 16S's.

Perceiving the freezer truck slowing slightly, Promardie's voice grows harsh. *"Conducir! Conducir!"* He orders as he nestles his pistol to the driver's temple. The directive immediately finds its way to the accelerator.

The pall of accountability has now ominously spread beyond the Covarrubias operations center. In a luxuriant compound office with a circus of inlaid wall terminals, a sickly looking lieutenant-in-command tracks the blinking-red-and-green-light saga on a large screen. He edges to the front of his chair when the gap between the two lights closes, then enters numbers into a phone. Another ashen Covarrubias heavy galumphs into the room.

As the drug ring's limousine approaches the western end of the 105 Freeway and noticeable air traffic, the Hispanic in the front passenger seat has a cell phone snug to his ear. The freezer truck, exiting toward hangars below, comes into view. While the man riding shotgun excitedly jabbers into the cell, the driver is bombarded from the crowded back with incitements of *"Acelerar!"*

The vigil at the Covarrubias office of grandees has now grown to three. The one on the phone switches to a speaker so all can hear the play-by-play from the limo. When the assiduously tracked red and green lights appear to be one, there is a mild show of deliverance. However, enthused expressions suddenly turn bleak when both blinking lights abruptly disappear from the screen, blanked by LAX-controlled airspace.

The freezer truck wheels from the freeway to a row of dark, still hangars with small offices in front, all showing the life of a Cistercian monastery. It speeds through an open gate (that automatically closes behind it) onto a remote LAX taxiway and spins into a small hangar space. A man with Eastern European features stands at electronic controls just inside, immediately closing the hydraulic door as soon as the truck clears. He quickly hits an automatic dial key on his cell.

Promardie jumps out of the truck, busts it to the front office, and sneaks a peek through undusted blinds. He sees a limousine creep along the street fronting the hangars. He retrieves a file from his cell. Yep, the limo plate is a match to the one from the soccer field. The Eastern European man joins Promardie. In an instant, an airport security vehicle whirls around a corner and is on the fender of the limousine. Pointing to the security car, the man brags in a burly Serbian accent, "He's from Belgrade. I got him the job." Promardie gratefully nods.

Fully appreciating that L.A. police can converge on a LAX location faster than a hobo on a hot plate, the driver about-faces the limo to the freeway.

Paulson and Arneston restlessly sit before a host of computer screens devoid of activity. Behind them technical sorts sleep on the floor of their cubicles.

Sounds of the dusky jungle are drenched by slapping waves taking lesser territory from the shore. A watchful Greg, sitting as still as a Petri dish, rests against a tree some 20 yards from the covered plane. Immediately before him is a M60 machine gun on a tripod with a long bullet belt extending from an ammo can. An intruder not to his liking would clearly be in need of a very viable Plan B.

Inside the Covarrubias residences and operations center, raging temperatures, cramps, blurred vision, tightening throats, and unslakable thirst devour all. A kitchen crew, battling duress, tears through shelves, food stock, utensils, and pots, searching and smelling for anything afoul. Another armed group treads room-to-room, unscrewing vents and filling ducts with flashlights and surveillance wands. A couple of Domingo Covarrubias's lieutenants, looking considerably less regal than in Paulson's photos, stalk the property perimeter, raging at cowed, sickly underlings to unroot the cause of the contagion.

In the dark outside, tower guards on high alert watch wobbly legged trackers trying to keep pace with a pack of Belgian Malinois sniffing out the compound. When the dogs near the duct area where Hopper had injected liquid from the vials and dusted the earth, they become sneezy and disoriented, which seems of little notice to their handlers suffering from worse.

Hopper and Trina, hiding behind a shed near the helipads, observe the turmoil about the compound. Hopper checks the time. "Ready?"

Trina offers a wry smile. "Yeah. Tired of slumming it here."

"Soccer goal at oh-five-forty?"

"Oh-five-forty."

After a knock of fists, Hopper takes to brush behind the shed and cleaves his way toward the dormitory. Trina rounds back toward the monstrous, thumping generator creating electrical power for the compound.

When Hopper reaches a clearing near the dormitory, he marks a nearby tower guard and two men on the ground packing assault rifles. Hopper unstraps the tranquilizer gun, verifies the hour, and waits.

A crouching Trina hustles up a narrow trough where electrical conduit runs from the generator to compound buildings. She stops at a complex of junction boxes, panels, and controllers, takes a diagram from her pocket, and, with a pin flashlight, compares it against the equipment configuration. She brings out a screwdriver to remove a panel plate. Within is a carbon tube identical to the one she has taken from her back pouch. Trina unlatches the device in place and immediately snaps in the substitute.

Within the operations center, a few scattered monitors in a couple of quadrants show instantaneous blips. Given the diminished capacity of operators and supervisors fighting reeling bodies and fatigued minds, it is little surprise that the ripple in their screens goes unnoticed... to them. The bald op don at the very top takes note of the simultaneous aberrations and is immediately on his phone.

In the San Diego office, screens around Paulson suddenly blow up with streaming algorithms, code, files, maps, phone numbers, bank accounts, and just about every electronic gift for which a government snoop could hope except the password to the Middle East mindset. Paulson stirringly eyes Arneston and motions to the bodies asleep behind them. "Rattle those yahoos. We hit gold."

Laker man and Apostoli sit in front of three laptops on the workbench in Marek's airstrip building. Their split screens show multiple shots of real-time video feeds from cameras in the Covarrubias compound and surrounding jungle. Laker man furiously works one of the keyboards.

As Trina replaces the cover plate amidst the electrical gear, she hears howling Malinois and bellicose handlers hurtling toward her. She rushes back through the ravine, leaving in her track the same powder Hopper had strewn below the duct. She dives into brush, clearing her pistol with one hand and machete with the other.

Confirming the time, Hopper scopes the tower guard with his tranquilizer gun and fires, lodging a projectile of hypodermic

needle, ballistic syringe, and tailpiece in the guard's leg. When
the startled Hispanic reaches to pluck the needle, Hopper hits
him in the side of the neck with another shot. The man tries to
draw the second stinger, but fumbles with it only momentarily
before an immobilizing agent crumples him to his knees and
knocks him out. As the ground guards try to discern what is
happening above, Hopper takes them down with like assault.

After clearing bodies into nearby bush, Hopper, pistol in
hand, eases open the door to the dormitory. Inside, an aisle splits
two rows of Hispanic boys asleep on barrack beds. Hopper's
cot-to-cot search is truncated when he sees a football on a ledge
above one of the beds. He steps lightly to Honorio and allows
himself a split second to thank his Lord for letting him once
again cast eyes on the treasured face. Hopper covers his hand
over Honorio's mouth, muffling the boy's gleeful yelp when
he awakes. Honorio squeezes his arms around Hopper's neck,
warming his rescuer with a current he had long ago thought ex-
tinguished by years of bloodletting. Hopper swivels on the bed
and signals for Honorio to latch onto his back; the youngster
jumps aboard.

Hopper carries Honorio from the dormitory to the edge of
the soccer fields. When Hopper kneels to let down Honorio, the
boy jumps in front of Hopper and hugs him with every ounce of
frayed, trembling fiber. "I knew you'd find a way here. I knew
you would."

"You OK?"

"I'm OK. They were taking me somewhere today. One of the
older players said he heard a guard say it was Columbia."

"You're not going to Columbia. You're coming home."

Hopper cups Honorio's face. "You've been very brave here. I
need you to be brave a few hours more." Hopper takes from his
backpack a black, quick-dry top and bottom, sock cap, and...
"These are your Our Lady football shoes. Trina, you, and I have
a lot of rough ground to cover."

"Trina is here?"

"Yes, she is."

"Where?"

Hopper's eyes pass over his watch. Hiding his concern, he answers, "Here, soon."

As Honorio is changing clothes and Hopper checking down his rifle, a shadow deftly moves toward them from the brush. Hopper pulls Honorio to ground and points the rifle at the figure. Honorio jumps up. Hopper tries to harness him, but the boy frees himself and rushes away. Ah, the blessing of young legs and keen eyes. Honorio ties Trina with a swarming hug before Hopper fully recognizes her. Honorio guides her to Hopper.

"How did it go?" Hopper asks as he throws the rifle over his shoulder.

"Device snapped right in, but it must've caused something on screens inside. Had Malinois on my position right away. Humped back through the ravine. Those dogs were coming down the barrel at me, but Banner's dust worked its magic... again. They were completely out of joint."

"How did the men sound?"

"Coughing, hacking, wheezing... like they'd been in a forest fire or something... exactly what Judson said would happen with the virus."

"Good. We need to hit it hard. Sun will up soon. No telling if one of the kids in there will have to take a leak and see the empty cot." Hopper brings Honorio close. "We're going through jungle to the ocean. We have a plane to take us back to Our Lady. We're not sure what's out there, but I saw a way through when we came in over the mountains. We'll stay close to a creek that runs to sea, so we may see animals watering. You'll be in back of me and front of Trina. We have guns and arrows; you don't have to be afraid. OK?"

Honorio enamels his face with a sure gameness. "I'm not going to die here like my father."

Color this boy gusty, Hopper and Trina conclude with an exchange of looks.

As dawn is cracking a dark sky and time passing with obscurity, Greg has budged not a whit from his position at the machine gun. Under another circumstance, with the placid aquamarine sea, pearly sand, and bold greenery, it would be the stuff of idyllic portraiture, thinks he, an occasion to craft a silvery, south-of-the-border aubade. So too evidently does a double-horned rhinoceros that emerges from the jungle and, as an apparent member of the area's higher estate, scouts the beach with a lordly sweep of its head.

Greg wonders what would next enter stage left onto shore: dancing polar bears, fire-eating baboons wearing puka shell necklaces, a two-head iguana, or Phineas T. Barnum juggling sombreros. What in the holy hell, thinks he, is a rhinoceros doing cavorting on a beach in Mexico? What if the beast spotted the plane and stamped it trespasser? Though this tropical setting offers a medley of singular features, the Delphi oracle is not one. Greg's mind races. While he has more than enough firepower with the machine gun to take down the animal, the heavy load might reverberate, electronically or otherwise, to the Covarrubias compound. If the creature reached the plane, Greg could release the canisters of fentanyl surrounding it, but he was not sure that the gas would drop the rhino before it might to do serious damage to the plane.

The rhino retreats to the jungle edge and, to Greg's consternation, tacks toward him. Greg removes his Beretta and slowly screws on a silencer. The animal stops and stares in the direction of the covered bright shell. Not only does it sense something is amiss, but ascertains it is its department to investigate. It heads directly toward Greg's position. When the rhino reaches the plane, it knocks away palm leaves with its snout. In rapid succession,

Greg fires at the fans atop the six canisters, knocking off each, releasing spurts of greenish gas. The creature is momentarily distracted by pinging noises around it. As the fentanyl descends and burns its breathing passages, the rhino pins immediate blame on the intruder plane. The animal gashes the fuselage with an angry swipe of its horn. Greg stands and unloads the last rounds of his clip into the facing eye of the beast. It grunts, staggers, and then turns toward Greg. Locating its assaulter, it charges.

Greg sprints through the jungle, branches whipping welts into his face. The snorting beast, blood gushing from its hollowed eye, crazedly mows down everything in its path. As Greg feels ground beneath him tremble from the pounding of the rhino's feet, he cuts behind a large palm. While this may have been a nifty move that swimmingly broke Gale Sayers free and impressed time and again in Soldier Field, it does not carry the day in Campo Chana. The rhino splits the base of the palm with its horn, nearly felling the tree on top of Greg. As the animal is at Greg's heels, its legs suddenly buckle. It tries to find its footing, but lists. Greg slams a fresh clip into his Beretta and unloads it into the creature's other eye. Whether it is the knockout gas or battery of bullets to the brain, the rhino crumples to the earth. It chomps on air until it moves no more.

Apostoli stands behind Laker man, watching him manipulate multiple screens. He points to a video of Hopper, Honorio, and Trina running on the bank of a narrow jungle watercourse.

"What are they seeing in the compound?" Apostoli apprehensively asks.

Laker man strikes a key. The monitor switches to an identical video of the area, but without human trace. "Their screens show that," he responds in a monotone, professorial voice. "I've looped the system back three minutes for all exterior-compound and jungle camera feeds… except the dormitory area. Since the switch was well before dawn, it would've been almost impossible to notice the cutover, particularly since you damn near incapacitated everyone in the data rooms."

"How about if they hit a snag?"

Laker man is clear with the calculus. "They have three minutes to be on their way." He glances at Apostoli. "That's the plan we all agreed on. If the loop's longer, there's a greater risk of discovery, particularly closer to sunrise when shadows move quickly."

Apostoli extends a finger to the bottom of the screen. "Are those reads from surveillance devices?"

"Exactly. They're signals from thermal imaging, lasers, motion sensors… anything within ten feet of a camera. I've blocked relays from all devices in the jungle to the operations center. They'll show negative no matter how many stations your people trip on the way to sea."

Apostoli bends to a screen where two guards stand near the entrance to the dormitory. "That the same time yesterday?"

"Yes."

"Which button do I push to show the live feed?"

"Alt-Z."

Apostoli performs the function. The same area is vacant. "Man, I hope this holds out," he hails more to the stars than to Laker man.

The petered-out, graveyard-shift security guard, eyes rebelliously blinking at first sun, cumbrously drags himself to the small parking lot at the rear of the storage facility. Before he can reach his car keys, a SIG Sauer reaches the back of his neck. He starts to turn, but a swift punch to the kidneys from House's free hand forecloses the notion.

"This isn't the time to earn that uniform," House, in beard and cap, toting a backpack and large, empty black athletic bag slung over his shoulder, admonishes the guard in a deep, disguised voice. "If the instructor who gave you your two hours of training told you one thing, it shoulda been this: brains do a lot more good inside your head than out. Nod if you understand."

The guard, suddenly very persuadable, emphatically dips his chin.

"Make this easy, nothing happens to you or the guy in the booth. Get the drill?"

The guard so signals.

"The good-looking blonde who came in early this morning… what's her unit number?"

"It's pretty far away from my station. I… "

House rams his knee behind that of the guard, causing the young man's leg to give. "Don't *even* try that shit with me, Romeo. I saw the way you were ogling her when she drove in. You not only know what unit she has, you've probably already been knocking around her file for a phone number. Am I right?"

"Unit twenty-eight," the guard quickly tenders.

"How often does she come here?"

"Almost every night."

"Every night the whole week?"

"I don't work Sundays. I have another job. I don't know about then."

Feeling the guard sufficiently softened, House clutches his shirt and pulls him upright. "Keep your eyes straight, don't turn around. We're going back to your station… against the buildings… under security cameras. When we're there, you're gonna have the guy who just took your place open the door. Say you left your keys… cell… Twister Board…whatever in the fuck you want to say… and that you need back in. When you step inside, turn out the lights and hit the floor. I'll take it from there."

"What are you going to do?" asks the guard, voice in a cinch.

"Shoot one of you in the leg so you won't be in trouble for not putting up a fight."

"*Oh, shit!*"

"No one'll be shot," Houses says, pleased with his put-on. "You have jumper cables for cars that are stalled inside the fence?"

"Yes, we do."

"I'll tie you both up with those. Have lock-cutters, right?"

"Yes."

"Point me to them and controls for the security cameras, keep your mouth shut, stay cool, and I'll let you go. Then you can make your normal stop at Circle K on the way home and light a candle to Bluto Blart, mall guard."

"You been following me to Circle K, man?"

House, even more delighted with himself and his on-the-spot profiling, instructs his subject, "Let's go, *and don't turn around!*"

Promardie sits on pallets inside the hangar, ruckus from jets landing at LAX stymieing the racket of the Eastern European man's changing with a pneumatic wrench a tire of a twin-engine plane. The sweaty driver of the freezer truck unloads cartons of drug-laden ice-cream-bar boxes onto the polished concrete floor. Pistol resting between his legs, toolbox to his side, Promardie scrolls through the driver's cell phone. His own rings.

Paula, phone to her ear, is seated before the same terminal where she had displayed traffic citations of suspect vehicles for Trina and Galton. She has on her screen a photo of a dingy, small meat-packing facility where the health code is apparently a piddling technicality. "Have time to talk?" she says sub rosa.

"Sure do," Promardie replies.

"The address you want is 5524 Ludemen Boulevard South. The feds have had it under surveillance for a month, maybe a month and a half. It's the biggest distribution point in the L.A. area for Salvador Quick—Covarrubias's main competitor here."

"That's great," Promardie appreciatively replies. "Can you text me information on it."

"Do you one better… shoot you an image."

"That'd be great. Thanks."

"How's it on your end?"

"Hoping we don't have to play this card."

"Keep me posted."

Promardie ends the call, points the driver's cell at the pile of ice-cream-bar boxes, and snaps an image.

Computer screens of Paulson and Arneston, as well as those in nearby cubicles, are raining data. Something in the blizzard of electronic print is troubling Arneston; this catches Paulson's eye. "What's up, Arn?"

"The download."

"Going to the wrong files?"

"No."

"Storage issue?"

"Can't say."

"If you sure we're capturing everything, move on. Don't know how much longer we'll have the door."

This Arneston does, though a nimbus of uncertainty hangs over his keyboard.

As the sun starts to take hold of the jungle, Hopper, Honorio, and Trina slog west through a creek dribbling to the ocean. Brandishing his machete, Hopper hacks away overhanging branches obstructing their path. Trina covers their rear. They slow while Hopper clears a particularly dense overgrowth of leaves. As the three swat through remaining foliage, a pit viper snaps out from a freshly cut branch and, with incredible striking speed, digs its fangs into the back of Trina's neck. Before the snake can recoil, Trina has grabbed its head, drawn her knife, and given the viper two new homes. "Hopper," she moans as she crumples to her knees.

Hopper turns and, spotting the severed snake, immediately extracts a vial, syringe, and needle from a pant pouch. He tells

Honorio. "Trina has a problem. I'll fix it. I need you look ahead, not at her. If you see anything move... I mean anything... holler. OK?"

Honorio mechanically nods.

Apostoli and Laker man sit at the work-bench terminals, watching Hopper take syringe and needle to the base of Trina's neck and inject a viscous liquid.

"What's he doing?" Laker man asks.

"Loading her with antitoxin," Apostoli doctorly replies.

"Can you tell what kind of snake bit her?"

Apostoli points to the severed head. "See the yellow markings. Mexican Cantil."

"How poisonous is the venom?"

"Extremely. It's a pit viper. If there was going to be a situation, we figured it would be either a Cantil or moccasin."

Laker man looks pressingly at Apostoli. "They have three minutes to move out of there."

"Hopper'll make the mark."

"Aren't you supposed to stay still after a snake bite?"

"He'll carry her to the beach."

"He can't stop for more than three minutes."

"He won't."

"Come on," Laker man checks Apostoli.

Apostoli stares squarely at the infidel. "We had a mission in the White Mountains of Afghanistan. Hopper and another guy on the team, Lance Errol, were separated from the rest of us by hostile fire. On the way to the rally point, they came across four wounded children... eight to nine years old. Hopper and Lance lifted a child on each shoulder and walked them for six hours straight to our chopper. In that whole time, the kids' feet never hit the ground."

Apostoli cements his jaw. "Hopper'll bring Trina to the beach. Need be, he'll hang a right at the water, carry her all the way up across the border to Coronado, and over the fucking bridge to a hospital… if that's what it takes."

Laker man considers not discrediting the settling chronicle.

At first light, the Covarrubias compound is overflowing with trade trucks and electrical, plumbing, and air-conditioning contractors, engineers, technicians, and repairmen handing back and forth enough rolled drawings to qualify for an Olympic relay practice. They work their way through a litter of putridly sick people.

Inside the operations center, the bald I.T. chief has come down from the pyramid top. Pistol now tucked under his belt, he stands alongside a platform supervisor, auditing video monitors. Seated operators, faces plaster pale, nervously absorb infrared stares from behind.

Boss man points to a screen showing a distant mobile camera shot of the row of LAX hangars where the limousine had followed the freezer truck. Voice Danish-thick, he interrogates his subordinate. "Where are our men?"

"On top an office building on Imperial Highway," the supervisor responds, the Rhineland saturating his syllables.

"Any movement from those hangars?"

"Nothing yet."

"How many planes do we have mobilized?"

"Two. One more inside an hour."

The tech honcho paces down the row of monitors, intently dissecting them as if they are Ouija boards in the Sumerian alphabet. He stops before one displaying two guards in front of the dormitory. "Any problems there?" he pumps the supervisor.

"None. We had bed check at 3:00 a.m. No one was sick."

"What time does the plane arrive from Barranquilla for the American kid?"

"Nine a.m."

"Send someone to make sure he'll be ready."

"Right away."

Branches and leaves cleared from the plane, Greg has a portable gas welding torch at full flame trying to close the deep puncture from the rhino horn in the fuselage at the pilot's seat. Machine gun nearby, he keeps an eye on the jungle for any more guest appearances.

Hopper, a barely conscious Trina draped on his back, her hands bound around his neck, trashes jungle leaves with his machete. His young myrmidon Honorio, quailing not, follows closely in the wake. Hopper's eyes are those of the underworld: dark, vacant, emotionless, hardened passages to a will without flex; his heart disengaged from any matter or feeling other than the task at hand. Air starting to salt his nostrils is dismissed an instant after it registers.

House powers his Pontiac to Marek's airstrip building, docks it near the front door, grabs the now bulging black athletic bag from the backseat, and charges inside. Apostoli and Laker man are parked at the workbench, pupils tattooed to laptop screens. House steps up behind them, diverting the attention of neither. "How we looking?"

Apostoli hangs his words like a black wreath. "Top's about to blow."

"Shit."

"How much did you nab from the storage unit?" asks Apostoli, doing his best to jigsaw thoughts.

House shakes the athletic bag. "Royal flush—disk drives, zips, even some hard copy… lot of pages highlighted."

"Much on us?"

"Looks to be a fair amount."

"Lose anything from the charge?"

"Some."

"My laptop's ready for you."

"Thanks."

As House makes his way to the long table, Apostoli hones in on a video feed of armed men sprinting from the compound dormitory, frantically chattering into headsets. Apostoli stands, paces behind his chair, stops, moors his arms to the chair back, and lowers his head. When he looks up, one of the screens shows a ground crew racing to the helicopters. Apostoli snags his cell phone from the workbench.

Inside the LAX hangar, the truck driver, hands tied behind his back, lies face down on the concrete in front of his self-constructed pyramid of ice-cream-bar boxes. Promardie finishes a call, takes his toolbox and the driver's cell phone, and makes a direct line to the prisoner. He places the driver's cell on the ground in front of him and feigns entering numbers. "You need to call to your people."

The man refuses with a dogged shake of his head.

"Realizar llamada telfonica!"

Again the man defiantly wags his head.

"OK." Promardie removes from his toolbox an aerosol can of cheese. He waits somewhat of a theatrical moment before next extracting a small cage holding a rat with chompers fit for snapping a Kryptonite deadbolt. Promardie bends over and, with the diligence of a single-minded otolaryngologist, checks the prone man's ear passages. When the driver realizes what Promardie has in store, he fixes eyes on his cell phone and animatedly nods as agreeably as a class toady.

Paulson and Arneston meticulously track data cascading down their screens. Much like a theatre where curtains unexpectedly drop in the middle of a matinee, their screens go black. They turn to see those in the cubicles looking futilely around.

The white plane, now uncovered, shimmers beneath the rising sun in a sky skimpily patched with blousy clouds. Greg is resetting strips of bark from the location of the plane to the damp stretch of sand on which they had landed. In the far distance he discerns Hopper, Trina drooped over his back, and Honorio plodding toward him. Greg tears to them. As he approaches, he notes Hopper's blank eyes and automaton feet in measured groove and Honorio's coaxing from himself as much courage as he can.

When Greg reaches them, an adrenalized Hopper veers not in gait or visual fix to the line ahead. "What is it?" Greg spills out.

"Cantil bite," Hopper raps back.

"Where?"

"Neck. She's on fire. Pulse is dropping fast."

"Shit."

Greg falls in step with Honorio and rests an arm over his shoulder. "How are you doing?"

The boy fights tears wanting to squeal through his eyes. "OK. Trina is real sick. She needs help."

"We'll take care of her, son. We're headed home."

Kingfish Mitch Arnett, togged out in a bright running outfit apropos of a Legoland Portofino, blows into a tony San Vicente coffee shop, past tables of aspiring entertainment types as if they are so many briskets of beef, and on toward the counter. There he booms an order for a coffee confection, sounding to be the caffeine equivalent of a Shirley Temple.

"What's the plan for the weekend?" the server, regrettably familiar with Arnett, asks. "Tracking stories?"

Arnett, drawing on his fund of camera time, raises Walter Cronkite into his lungs and harrumphs for all to hear, "We're airing a piece of investigative journalism that will open the eyes of the entire country. National news broadcast... 6:00 p.m." Arnett circles his hand over his head as if directing a cattle roundup. "Everyone here needs to see it."

"That's great, Mitch. I'll bring your order right over."

The clerk happily takes Arnett's money in exchange for a fresh, and certainly less blustery, face in line.

While Greg and Hopper are tying a rope to the tail of the plane to tug it onto the beach, Honorio tends to Trina, who is lying atop a blanket beneath the cover of a nearby tree. He swabs her griddling face with small, salt-water-soaked towels. Suddenly, the sound of whirling helicopter blades swooshes atop the jungle. Greg drops the rope, jumps into the brush, and slides behind the M60 machine gun. Hopper snatches the Mk-11 and ditches in back of the rhino carcass.

All too quickly, some distance away one of the Covarrubias Havoc helicopters zooms past them to sea. Since the plane's sheeny white fuselage shell has been fully exposed, it stands out like a neon Easter egg hidden on front porch steps. Once the helicopter turns back to land, it is on the plane's position in an instant. It hovers in front of the craft, its single gun in the undernose barbette and air-to-ground missiles in pylons beneath the stub wings now locked onto the plane. As the helicopter kicks out torrents of sand, Honorio throws himself on top of Trina.

"These rounds won't pierce that bird's armor," Greg roars above the din to Hopper. "Windshield is bullet-proof."

Faced with the menacing, swirling presence above him, Hopper claws to Honorio whose black, curly hair is capped with flecks of sand. Yielding to the governor in his brain, not protector in his heart, he coughs at the boy, "You have to go back to the compound."

Honorio chafes at the suggestion. "I won't go there!"

"You must go!" Hopper responds in a ripping voice. "We have no defense against that helo. One push of a button, and we'll all be blown apart. You have a life to live."

"There's no life with those people; they don't care about anybody but themselves."

Realizing there would be no adulterating this boy's pluck, Hopper hunkers next to him.

The large compound office walled with computer terminals is now occupied by virtually the entire leaderboard of Covarrubias's Campo Chana lieutenants, sickly though they are. As bubbly as a vespers assemblage, their eyes are fast on a particular screen—a video feed from the Havoc helicopter recording the outline of the white plane amidst a squall of sand. The bald man from on high in the operations center slips in the room and is greeted like the recently elected mayor of a penal colony. He drifts to a wall.

Momentarily, a mousy functionary, holding out a cell phone as if it is the devil's dance card, enters, buzzes to one of the lieutenants, and whispers to him. After a brief exchange, the lieutenant first points to one of the terminals and then motions for the bald man to take the cell. He servilely does. A couple of stabs to the phone and keyboard beneath the terminal by the man, and the voice of Quinn Promardie spirals through the room. "Are we having a conversation or do you want to kiss your product good-bye?"

The lieutenant nods to the underling who responds in fractured English, "We are here."

"Did you dive into a cave?"

"You are on a speaker."

"Are the people I need there?"

"Yes."

"Good. Just sent you an image," Promardie announces. "Did you receive it?"

The pregnant moment quickly passes. A picture of the stack of ice-cream-bar boxes on the hangar floor fills the monitor like so many insidious goblins at tenuous rest. The compound office is instantly rotten with stares of vicarious blame.

In the front office of the hangar, Promardie taps out another photo from the cell. "One more coming your way, and it's a beaut," Promardie snickers after sending an image.

Covarrubias's college of dark cardinals does not have to wait long before they are treated to the shot of the meat-packing facility Paula had forwarded to Promardie. The gallows moment takes on much more daunting proportions when Domingo Covarrubias, pale and cross, steps into the room. He needs little briefing to dimension his quandary. His foul look confirms to all present that there is indeed an entry in the annual operating budget for group castrations... followed by a random, ritualistic beheading or two.

Promardie has the stage. "Whoever of you hasn't had the pleasure of touring L.A.'s meat-processing plants, let me introduce you to one owned by Salvador Quick, though hear tell he processes more than meat there. Know him?"

Pagans in crisis, the room turns to their idol—Covarrubias. He nods as if acknowledging door clappers had just been successfully spot-welded onto his buttocks.

"Yes," the subordinate echoes.

"That's where your load is headed... Christmas come early for Quick, if you will, unless you cut the boy Honorio free. If he isn't in the States in two hours, the load goes out, and, believe me, those doofus motherfuckers in the limousine who trailed me will have no idea how it leaves LAX."

Again, floor to the *patron* Domingo Covarrubias, who stands impassive, unflappable, given not to knife-to-the-throat compromises.

Promardie hunches over the old, scarified metal desk and pours his ardor and imagination into the phone. "When we broke through your data security, we did a lot more than toy with pictures. We extracted everything you have on your clients. If I don't hear this instant that the boy and people with him have safe passage, then every single one of those clients will receive a holiday email, photo included, of product in your network being offloaded to a competitor. That should sit real well with the cartel whose merch I've lifted." Satisfied with his artfully crafted story, Promardie straightens.

At the compound, a virulent actuality slithers over Covar-rubias and his lieutenants as the bald tech guru looks for a piece of furniture with which he might casually fuse.

As Laker man packs his laptops and mandarin electronic equipment, Apostoli stands behind House, watching the big fel-low flip to a screen dense with data. With unerring eyes, Apostoli inspects the print. "So this is definitely the agency that fed the Irishman intel?"

"No doubt," House replies. "It's all here. You or Greg know anybody in this agency?"

"Know *about* them. What exactly do they have on us?"

"They haven't been able to knit together anything firm, but it's not for lack of trying." House rolls to a fresh screen. "Greg was spot on. They got a line on us from the mountain. Looks like a TV report-er, Mitch Arnett, who was also up there, sniffed us out, too. Best I can tell, a guy in this agency, think his name is McManus, has been spooning Arnett fake reports about us and has him hooked. Think the reporter's going to air with a huge piece... looks like tonight."

"What kinds of reports?"

"About missions we were never on."

"Why?"

"Haven't been able to tell yet."

"We can't let that happen."

"I know." House rewinds several pages; Apostoli appraising-ly follows. "People in this agency may be vulnerable. All signs point to their involvement in the extract of Honorio being of-fline... way offline; it's a very close-hold engagement. For some reason or other, Covarrubias is supposed to be outside the box for them. We could have real leverage here."

Two stony faces sense an opening.

Inside Storage Unit Number 28, Saturday morning win-ter sunshine is spreading little warmth. Greta is all triage as she stands before two medium-sized safes whose doors have been blown open. Outside, an older, apple-cheeked police detective of slouch demeanor, game-show-host sports jacket, and tie of misreckoned style, and two uniformed officers question the security guard House had commandeered and another. As Greta rummages through few remaining safe contents, the detective, tidying himself for the attractive blonde, drifts inside. "How much did they take?" he asks in a prairie twang.

In little mood for flabby chit-chat, Greta responds, "Quite a bit."

"Valuables?"

"Business records."

"Took a real pro to blow that door without smoking the inside. Opened it up like a pill box. Musta been something real interesting to draw that kind of boxman," the detective notes, dropping a scrupulous eye on Greta.

She wipes soot from the safe. "Yep. Drilled a hole near the lock mechanism, slapped on a small amount of what looks like 2,4,6-TNT, and *shazam*."

Not the sluggard his appearance suggests, the detective surmises, "I take it you won't be listing contents for a report."

Greta's snippet: "Correct." She gestures to the two unnerved security guards. "Anything from them?"

"The perp put the fear of God in those boys. If they know something, they're not owning up."

"Surprise. What about video?"

"Most of it's destroyed. Little that's left shows nothing of the perp. Stayed completely out of range the whole time. This guy did not fuck around."

"So it seems." Greta steps away to consider the gargantuan size of imbroglio in which she now indubitably finds herself. Her cell rings. She looks askance at the unrecognized number, then opens the call as one might a wedding present in black ribbon.

"Yes." As she listens, whatever hue Greta had in her face turns tapioca.

House stands outside the airstrip building, cell phone tight to scolding lips. "Know this, we took enough from your safes that we can make sure the only government job you'll ever have again is on Wrangel Island. If we clue in certain people in your agency about what you and your boss McManus tried with Domingo Covarrubias, this afternoon you and he will be on a military transport to D.C. featuring hemlock-and-soda high-balls. So you'll tell me everything... every single fucking thing... you've planted with Mitch Arnett for this broadcast tonight and why you're doing it. After we hang up, you're not going to say anything to anybody... and I mean *anybody*... about this until I tell you. Understand!"

Morning Mexican sun illuminates the white plane with radiant glow. Facing south on the beach, the craft sits at the northern end of the even swath of sand where it had landed... which now is not so even. Lathery sea water tumbling toward high tide is rapidly encroaching the takeoff area. After Greg gives the wheels a last inspection, he hoists himself into the cockpit. In back, Hopper has Trina's head on his lap. Breathing murmured and skin color cadaverous, she shows feint signs of life. A coarsened Honorio sits rigidly in front, looking glassily ahead, not at the inevitability he knows unfolding behind him.

As Greg locks in his seatbelt, he notices to his left curious animals stealing around the jungle periphery, evidently awaiting the next act in the gringo airshow. He then takes a pensive look-see to his right where the Havoc helicopter, forbidding metallic bird of prey, idles a mile offshore.

Hopper joins in the assessment. "What do you think? Will that bandit vaporize us once we're up?"

"No, if that was the plan, they would've done it when they came in hot. Judson and the Pro musta somehow got to them. Maybe it was House."

Hopper assays the squishy beach. Sensing a departure of some question, he asks, "We gonna be able to lift off this? We were pinned down a long time."

"We'll lift. Think we'll generate enough speed to clear that cove."

"*Think?*"

"We can't layover ten hours with Trina in that condition."

"What about the old man's chance?"

"Not sure she has it." Before Hopper can raise a responsive question, Greg imposes, "Let's get outa here; we'll talk about it up the coast. We don't have a clear path forever."

Congealing his rushing thoughts into single focus, Greg kicks over the engine. Reeling in any reservation, he blasts the plane south; wet sand spatters from the tires. As the craft draws perilously close to the cove's rock cliff, it is still slogging through mushy beach. Honorio silently prays for unspecified wind currents; Greg is intent on engineering what is increasingly appearing to be a miracle. Hopper, face business as usual, leans forward slightly. "Captain, think we need elevate this baby. Don't believe 'Open sesame' does the trick in this part of Mexico."

"We'll make it," Greg reassures himself more than Hopper.

At the point where a sensible person would either be bailing from the cockpit or issuing himself last rites, the craft's wheels finally find air. The plane takes a seemingly impossible upward angle. Against heavy odds posted by the jungle sports book, the craft appears to be safely scaling the steep stone. Just when it's almost clear, tires catch on an inhospitable ridge, casting down the left side. For a moment it seems a wing may be disemboweled by jagged rocks, but Greg neatly reels it in and levels the plane's trajectory.

Inside the cockpit as the three are shaking themselves free of the thrombotic moment, Hopper asks, "Did we knock on the bad wheel?"

"Yeah."

"What do you think?"

"Judson and I walked the dirt at the north end of Marek's airstrip. It's mostly sand... some silt. If we hit on the asphalt and the wheel gives, we'll have to jump and land on a soft spot there."

Hopper folds into his seat. "You're an expert in landing on that shit now, so I don't see a problem."

Greg holds a bated smile as he banks right.

The plane veers out to sea; the helicopter follows.

On that run of mountain ridge where he had left Hopper and Trina, Arturo, a long, whittled, sharp stick in hand, waves at the distant white plane circling north.

Paul Thornberg, wearing causal clothes and overarching grimace, surrounded by a flotilla of pleadings on the law library conference table, battles both brain shear and Saturday morning sun to fill his laptop with trial questions. Sutter Nance, dressed for a pending brunch on loping foothills of Mount Olympus, deposits several stapled pages in front of Thornberg. "We need to incorporate this into an exhibit."

Thornberg takes a quick read before looking dubiously at the senior partner. "Where did this come from?"

"Proctor's office just located it."

"How can that be? His secretary said she searched all his email folders, including archives, eight months ago in response to request for production."

"His administrative assistant found this, not his secretary," Nance regally pronounces.

Thornberg digests several paragraphs. "This contradicts the depositions of one if not two of Proctor's managing directors."

"As I read those depositions, questions were directed at actions of the Streeter project manager, not his imputed intent... which is a wholly different matter in terms of punitive damages," Nance commands his associate to consider.

In that ailing moment when a younger professional fully realizes that his employer's annual billings trump the perils of mendacity and the anointer of his bonus would suffer no opposition to expediency, Thornberg dismisses the fetching notion of integrity and gulps the company line. "Have it ready to go Monday."

"Good." Nance exits to let Thornberg, personal currency again debased, unfussily reshuffle the truth.

In a tower of a military base on the Baja, one air controller takes over the shift of another. Before the replacement is fully settled in, he spots an image on the screen that has him calling for a supervisor.

The white plane journeys north at an even clip above the sea off Mexican shore. Greg steadily pilots while Honorio sleeps. Hopper taps the shoulder of Greg, who looks around to his dour friend. Hopper shakes his head ever so slightly from side to side. Greg's eyes fall to Trina. She has lost the conflict with Cantil venom; life has left her. Greg returns a sunken face to sky ahead.

"Really think she used her chance at the soccer field or jewelry store?" Hopper searchingly asks.

"Jewelry store," Greg sterilely replies.

"Sound pretty sure."

"Had the Pro do a deep check on the two shooters. The guys were no flub triggermen. They were D.M.s with heavy fieldcraft training. Each had a bucket of kills. How do they both miss five to ten shots when Trina was exposed in that parking lot only seventy-five yards away?"

"Always a chance."

"Always a chance next time you watch *Titanic*, the ship won't sink. You and House came back quickly. We should know before long."

Hopper, a welter of emotions carved into his face, bends over Trina and prays.

A camouflaged F-5 Freedom Fighter, rudder colored with red, white, and green of the Mexican flag, screams north up the Baja coast.

In the San Diego office, Paulson and the project team stand behind Arneston who is analyzing his screen. From the pained, contorted look on Arneston's face, it appears all may be standing ready for a group Heimlich maneuver on him. He scrolls down a page, then shoots his cursor to a line of print. "There it is. Fuck me running, Pauly. How in the holy hell did we get hit with this? Didn't we just spend three million upgrading our elastic defense?"

Amidst the consensus of sudden confusion, Paulson arches forward to study the code. After a moment, he notes, "That's serious encryption."

"How many files are we losing?" one of the team asks in a dismayed voice.

"At this rate, everything we downloaded will be gone in a couple of hours... unless we break this." Arneston violently swivels in his chair. "Hit your fucking keyboards. We need to decrypt this. This shouldn't be happening." The chided programmers dash to their computers to get cracking.

Arneston, in the grips of free-fall despondency, turns to Paulson. "How can this happen? We worked for weeks on securing code in the plant device."

"The extract team brought in a stud hacker who aced our system and compromised the device. That simple," Paulson laconically replies.

"Not possible in the time they had. Someone not only had to blow through our security, but also create a program that deletes files once they hit our server and then sends them offsite to a box I'm guessing we'll never locate."

"No use fighting facts, Arn. What did they tell us at the academy? 'Ain't a horse that can't be rode; ain't a cowboy that can't be throw'd.' If there are guys who can infiltrate military data at rest, then there are guys who can do this."

"You seem pretty damn calm about the situation. With the hours we have on this assignment, the guys upstairs will barbecue our goddamn asses for coming up empty."

"No, they won't," Paulson blandly responds. "We'll just report that Covarrubias security automatically deleted files that weren't passed through to one of their servers."

A nodding Arneston quickly cottons to that solution. "Like that. Think the extract team wants to sell back data?"

"Maybe… could be looking to trade… for something. But as sophisticated as the work is, they could've done that more easily by bypassing us and directing files to wherever they're going now." Paulson deliberates the question lingering like a tax audit. "This work is precise, which means timing is precise. Why did they let us see data and redirect it now? What do they want us to know *now?*" Paulson's eyes bulge. "Shit, get on the line with *Direccion General.*" While Arneston frenziedly jabs keys on his phone, Paulson does the same to his.

On this Saturday morning, outside of a few rambunctious youngsters playing video games, some old-timers calling down faint thunder on a couple of lanes, and a shallow-eyed, shoestring staff, the bowling alley is largely deserted. In the cocktail area, a bartender, whose best art is either detachment or slyly nipping on inventory, serves a middle-age fellow in a discolored bowling shirt (that likely never had a better day) and drenching depression and Greta, who collectively comprise the drinking corner's paying-customer contingent. As Greta is working her way through a largely depreciated pilsner glass, her cell rings. After first ignoring it, she checks the number and answers. She tries a chirpy tone. "Hey, Paulson. Thanks for the texts. Are we storing everything we need?"

While Greta listens, her face tightens like that of a recipient of a tetanus shot administered with an elephant gun. "You mean they extracted it all from your server and we have nothing!" A skip. "Will have nothing? By when?" Another skip. "Well, that's just fucking great. I thought you had this crack team that made the device impenetrable." Greta waits an impatient moment before she adds, "I gotta tell you, sounds to me like we would've had better luck if we'd kissed off our security, put the damn device in a superhero lunchbox for protection instead of encoding it, and hoped for the best."

As she endures more conversation, Greta comes to sense catatonia might occupy a good part of her afternoon. She motions to the bartender for a beverage upgrade to the shot-glass-friendly family of very hard liquors. When she finally has the floor with Paulson, she advises him, "First, there's no doubt that if the plane doesn't make it back, we'll never see any Covarrubias files. Second, while I did say it's important we minimize our exposure to this team, I'm not as worried about that now as having a goose egg to show for all our work. So, absolutely yes, make sure *Fuerza Aerea* doesn't smoke the plane." An instant later, she adds, "You're not sure there's time! Jesus, Paulson." Greta absorbs several more seconds before she's had her fill. "OK, OK, OK. Make the call. We're burning minutes here." She signs off and flings the phone into her purse.

Father Raymond, face muddled, fettle meager, stops outside a small bedroom occupied only by crashing silence. He looks at shirts and pants of schoolboy uniforms hanging correctly in the closet, textbooks stacked on a study desk next to an idle computer, soccer posters of Messi and Neymar, and colorful action figures (that Honorio would never admit to being toys) on the window shelf. The saddened priest dips his head, then continues down the rectory hallway, accompanied only by choiring of fret and regret.

Inside the cockpit of the plane, Hopper dozes over a still Trina as Honorio continues to sleep. Greg is troubled by something beyond a growing stream of air leaking in over his lap from the failing weld of the slit courtesy of the promenading rhino. In the midst of bright, open sky, he senses a darkness descending. He immediately drops the plane toward a heavily forested canyon behind mountains fronting the ocean. The sudden plummeting rouses both Hopper and Honorio.

"What's up?" Hopper asks.

"We may have company. Check it out."

Hopper agilely rubbernecks to the window and searches above.

The Hispanic pilot of the Mexican Freedom Fighter closely follows the radar scouring airspace before him. Seeing the plane on his screen quickly descending, he immediately switches from scan to tracking mode and dives in pursuit.

Hopper comes away from the glass and pithily announces, "Bogey at two o'clock coming our way."

Greg plumbs the craft.

"Where are we headed?"

The aviator colors in the itinerary. "Judson studied that narrow canyon. It runs all the way to a couple of miles south of the border. If we work our way in there, only way a plane can lock on us is if it's directly overhead. Even then trees at the rim provide a lot of cover. When we come free, we'll almost be at the States."

"How did you guys figure out what's below the trees?"

"We didn't."

Realizing the remainder of the trip out of Mexico might prove to be quite the adventure in canyoneering, Hopper tightens his safety belt. Honorio turns to him. Hopper no longer sees the kittenish countenance he had first encountered at Our Lady. Honorio's florid face and downy cheeks have morphed into a front of bony determination.

"We'll be OK," Hopper assures the boy.

"I know." Jitters tangle not Honorio's voice.

Greg takes the craft deep into canyon shadows. As he maneuvers through the middle of the void, the jet whishes overhead. Greg drifts closer to a granite wall. Before the jet can circle back, the white plane has found cover of cypresses canopying the gorge. Greg throttles back on power. The jet passes by again, only lower.

"Next time, he comes right up our ass," Hopper austerely reckons.

"With our speed so slow, he'll have to recognize, lock, and fire in an instant, which will be tough as close as we are to the sheer," Greg replies.

Of suddenly greater concern than jeopardy above is one immediately ahead: a narrowing of the gorge that looks to scatter parts of an airplane like sons of Jacob.

"Oh-oh," Hopper utters.

"I can drop a wing and angle through."

Greg looks to Honorio, who shows little attachment to the concept. "Put your head into your lap." Honorio all too eagerly complies.

"I can do this," Greg declares over his shoulder.

Hopper nods ahead. "Then let it happen, captain."

Greg lowers the right wing. As jaws of the canyon walls close, dark shadows from trees above engulf the cockpit. Greg strains to read juts and overhangs. The plane's path bears too far to the left; the fuselage bounces off a protruding formation. Honorio grips himself into a tighter ball; Hopper clinches Trina. Greg steadies the craft. No more than 100 feet farther, the upper wing catches a ledge, thrusting it down toward the inky canyon floor. As Greg struggles to stabilize the plane and forge an upward course, a glint of light in the distance maps cragged sides of the canyon. Greg puts the craft through inventive gyrations to jockey through the recesses. Walls begin to peel back. Greg rights the plane. Gaining lift, he navigates toward a gap in protruding branches. Hopper immediately pans air above: the sky is absent clouds and executioner fighter jets.

Diane, wearing a straw gardener's hat and bulky U.C. Berkeley sweatshirt, hauling a hoe, treads on leafy soil past flowerless jasmines and gardenias browned by frost. Near the back wrought-iron fence, a saucy, scavenging squirrel seems genuinely aggravated by the infiltrator into his feeding ground. Showing its immeasurable fear, it stares down the woman bearing arms until she is a couple of feet away, and only then does it reluctantly withdraw to hills above. As Diane takes to weeds establishing a beachhead on the landscaped slope, her eyes wander to hydrangeas Greg had planted along the fence. She caresses them with mothering eyes and cries.

As technicians adjust stage lighting for the news set, the portly floor manager, an entertainment-type terrible decked out in a semi-safari outfit (for no stagecraft guru can accurately predict when he might encounter a crocodile-infested swamp in the middle of a sound set) directs them in sardonic timbre. While the remainder of the crew tries to avoid the roving, cussing bwana as best as their paychecks would allow, Roland, the lovely, vogue Miss Jordan swanning around him, slips in through a side door.

"We've never invested this much in a news set. The station is so *totally* behind your piece," she says in sugary voice.

"Mitch is pumped."

"If the numbers register tonight the way they're trending, no telling how many segments you'll have."

"We'll see," Roland responds, doing his best to hide his slobbering imaginings. "How about lunch?"

"Absolutely," Jordan agrees, surely drafted into the evening's glittery prospects.

House, Apostoli, and Marek stand in front of bollards separating the airplane warehouse from the weathered airstrip. Their eyes are fixed on the southerly sky, their faces tableaux of bare anticipation. Between that building and the next, Galton and Paula anxiously wait in front of a fully-staffed paramedic van parked next to a fire truck manned by four rugged fellows who are half-uniformed, but very much on duty. Across the way, a tall galoot in oily overalls exits his building to check the situation. Meeting stares of the brook-no-inquiry-or-interference gathering on the other side of the runway, he skedaddles back in his warehouse.

As House is replaying in his mind the stunt-car crash on the movie set, he spots a light speck in the distant blue. He takes a step in that direction. In but a moment, the entire group has the emerging white plane in their sights. Drivers start the paramedic van and fire truck.

Inside the craft, Hopper glances at Trina, whose silent features seem impossibly serene, and then squints out the window at the airstrip. "Appears we're covered down there."

"Yep. Trina's gal pals on the force pulled together top-flight guys that can keep their mouths shut. If something happens, it'll never leak outside the field." Greg puts an arm to Honorio. "We're almost home. You know we have a tire with a problem?" The boy forebodingly nods. "When we're about to land, want you to tuck your head like you did before."

"Can I sit with Brendan?"

"You're safer in front," Greg legislatively responds. He tightens a hand on Honorio's shoulder. "We'll make it through this. Need you to hang tough this last part. Can you do it?"

The task at hand flushes words from the boy; he bows his chin slightly in abiding acknowledgment.

Hopper moves forward to Greg's ear. "You had to swing major duty to take us to Mexico and back here. You've stayed frosty, and you'll be frosty now."

Greg tilts slightly to his apostle. "No script for something like this, compadre." He nods to air gushing in from the widening gash to his side. "With that weld giving way and the wheel, it'll be a chancy landing."

Hopper will not be deflected from his assurance. "We'll make it."

Greg grants himself a moment for a silent sidebar with a floating image of Diane before fixing on the airstrip.

House bends toward Apostoli. "When Greg radioed in, did he say how bad the wheel was?"

"No," a preoccupied Apostoli responds.

The plane descends. As it makes its approach, the wings begin to flutter, then pitch back and forth. Stationed behind House and Apostoli, who have edged closer still to the airstrip, Marek paws at imaginary aircraft controls. Just before the gleaming white craft is about to touch down, the wings steady some. All eyes are on the wheels. The moment they come into contact with the landing surface, a back tire breaks off and spits into brush. The craft immediately takes air. A pestilential coat of anxiety swipes faces along the airstrip. The fire truck moves out toward the runway; the paramedic van follows.

Once the plane has cleared asphalt, it lowers to dusty grub beyond. When it hits ground, rooster tails of sand billow in its trail. Paula and Galton jump in back of the paramedic van. The fire truck speeds toward the plane. House, Apostoli, and Marek hop onto its side. The van is right behind. As they both tear down the airstrip, the plane violently careens to the side of the missing wheel, flips over, and skids upside down. Gas sprays from a ruptured fuel line.

On this Saturday, a large open floor of unadorned cubicles is left to a few ambitious sorts trying to squeegee an advantage from their computer screens over their off-the-clock peers, others gaining lost ground in a war of attrition against unrelenting government forms, a couple of fidgety sorts making ample use of copiers (probably for resumes), and Allan... clearing out his space. It takes no prophet to foretell from his tranquil expression he is headed for a calling more his liking. As he loads belongings into a couple boxes, McManus looks over the top of a partition and tries to cast lightheartedness. "I guess this means you're really doing it."

Unfortunate partner to a conversation he had not particularly expected or craved, Allan bypasses superfluities and elusory, satiny banter. "Yeah, think the opportunity to do research for a private agency is a really good one."

"You certainly know your way around documents... and how to put them together." Expressions of congenial departure not his best friend, McManus purposelessly looks about the cubicle. "You did good work in here."

"Wasn't the doghouse all that many times."

McManus allows a fugitive smile. "Read your exit interview. Textbook stuff. Thanks for the nice words."

"You taught me a lot."

"Off the record, anything in particular about the job stick in your craw?"

Allan searches for a diplomatic answer, yet one without contrivance. "I think sometimes it was hard to see a positive purpose of some projects. Makes it tough to stay motivated."

"I can understand that, but it becomes clearer as you work your way up. Remember my telling you when you first joined what can happen here that can't most anyplace else?"

"Yes. If you're successful, you become a one-call guy: you can accomplish things with one call that it takes even very important people outside a helluva lot more time."

"That's right, but to reach that point, a lotta people in the system need confidence in you. You earn that early on by *your* having confidence that they're heading in the right direction... though you might know the why... might not even be allowed to know the why... of what they're doing."

"Think that would become too complicated for me."

Awake to a distance that clearly would not be bridged, McManus winds it down with a dollop of good cheer. "Not much a guy with your talent won't be able to eventually figure out. Good luck to you, Allan."

"Thanks."

McManus leaves his erstwhile report to gladly move onto a life of fewer deceptions and blinds.

Black. The color of much with redeeming value, but not the most comforting herald when one is hoping for salvation. Perhaps it is just a funereal dream... like tormenting nights between days of fighting butchery in malignant pits of unabated conflict. Greg tries to stir himself from the eclipse of consciousness, rouse a chowdered brain. In an effort to pry himself from this altered state, he must have moved, for he feels the touch of a hand to his forehead. Maybe, just maybe he has foiled the gods and not suffered the Kamikaze fate he thought certain when the plane somersaulted beyond the high-plains airstrip. He forms a slight slit in his eyelids... to view an angel—Trina... alive, alert, face a blossom of vibrancy, pink with health. Is this the greeting to life everlasting or has indeed death been put in a holding pattern? He reaches for Trina's face and runs a finger over her cheek. Greg's heart flutters at the summery warmth.

She breathes into his ear. "We made it. We all made it." Trina shows a smile that could direct a man home from a most sinister darkness. Greg examines his body and then hers. They are as fresh as those in a First Communion line. He hunts for signs of blood. Nowhere to be found.

Confounded, he mutters to Trina, "Did everyone walk away without a scratch? House was so banged up after that stunt."

Trina raises Greg's head. In a mess of brush 40 yards away, the twisted, mangled plane might well have been snagged, gargled, and spewed by a passing, fire-eating asteroid. Much nearer stands an immaculate Honorio, smile salt-flats wide, in between Father Raymond and a loose, limber, unmarked Hopper; each man has an arm around the boy's shoulder. Off to their side, House and Apostoli, eyes anchored on Greg, radiate relief. Not too far beyond them Galton, Paula, the paramedics, and firemen are taking in the scene as though someone had just come down from the hills surrounding the airstrip with a third tablet that had escaped Moses. Several fringe spectators shake their heads in disbelief.

Trina helps Greg to his elbows. Logic finds further footing in his mind. "We all still had our chance... even you, I guess," Greg says in an undertone. "But how did the boy make it through the crash?"

A nonplussed Trina can only wiggle her shoulders. "We have to drive to Los Angeles. You need to start walking and shake this off. Not sure how many answers there are, but we can talk about it in the car."

Finding life somewhat a strange bedfellow, Greg, now fairly certain he would not soon be occupying a split-level in eternity, follows Trina's lead to his feet.

At the far end of the runway, barely detectable is a figure sitting atop a bollard. Close inspection would reveal the aged man, wearing a white Mexican guayabera shirt, linen pants, and expression of gratifying accomplishment. Tucked in his arm is a football... the one that had been above Honorio's cot at Campo Chana.

Diane sits at the patio table outside her kitchen, staring at a phone, distress working its way to heartbreak. The phone rings. She clicks it on faster than a politician's excuse. As she listens, her face brightens into a blush of relief.

Mitch Arnett, wearing camera-ready dress shirt, tie (that colorfully mirrors the brainwave pattern of a dysfunctional T. rex), loud suit, and makeup applied with a Faberge touch (for all the benefit it conferred), takes pompous steps toward a corridor leading to a spruced-up broadcast studio for the about-to-be-knighted; he savors every stride to the dizzying fame awaiting. Before he reaches the door, a page in her twenties stops him, hands over a business card, and points to the parking lot. Ushered by sudden unrest, Arnett makes his way down the hall and outside into winter twilight.

In a plaza area where Christmas lights outline a complex of surrounding buildings, McManus stands with a foot on the base of a fountain gushing a symphony of jet streams and spray. Across the water stands a stumpy man with a snarl of black hair and splotchy beard that, from a distance, makes it appear his aftershave had equal parts Indian lime balm and watery charcoal. His dark trench coat hangs like sackcloth.

When Arnett exits the studio building, he is stalled by the sight of McManus, then put dead in his tracks by that of the other man. McManus extends a Caesarian hand to the blue service van parked at the curb. Kiefer steps out; the Mick remains in the passenger's seat. Arnett's stunned face reflects the trifecta of doom now before him.

McManus casually strolls to Arnett, allowing the newsman ample time to contemplate his imminent repose. He takes a satisfying moment to relish anguish roiling Arnett's face before plucking a cell phone from his pocket and holding it before the shaken reporter like an implement of hara-kiri.

"Do I need to put Vertain and Montrose on the line," McManus caustically tees off on Arnett before pointing to the pudgy man and then Kiefer like prized zoo exhibits. "Or are Palladian and my Irish mole here enough for you to realize the shit hole you're in?"

Arnett shakes his head as might a reconciled convict on the hanging platform refusing a hood. McManus waves off trenchcoat man Palladian, who exits the plaza, and Kiefer, who slips back into the service van.

"I don't have a lot of time. I'll lay it out so even a half-wit motherfucker like you can understand. That's not my name on the business card. I'm not with that bureau. My agency makes them look like a bunch of broomstick cowboys. You became seriously sideways with me when you burned one of my snitches."

Arnett starts to contour his mouth with a question, but McManus rules against that option with a derisive shake of his head. "You're here to do one thing, clown: listen. You've been under blanket surveillance since the siege in the mountains... phones tapped, electronic comm intercepts, high-tech ghosts all over you and that flunkey of yours Brandt. When you went out to Montrose and Palladian, I told them if they took your assignment, they wouldn't work again in this town. To stay on my good side, they put you onto Kiefer… who's on my payroll."

Slightly behind cue, Roland, the arresting Ms. Jordan at his side, emerges from the studio door as McManus is knifing down Gypsy death cards on a hump-shouldered, dispirited Arnett. It takes but a moment for Jordan to realize there would likely be few garlands this evening for the limp reporter… or her now inconvenient companion Roland. She pirouettes back inside (to undoubtedly fertilize the set with dramatic, freshly pulped gossip), leaving Roland alone to weather wrath being rained on his boss.

McManus continues his cudgeling of Arnett. "Vertain's story is a total plant. He has nothing… never did. The reports Kiefer spooned you are bogus. One of my people put them together. His hobby is creative writing. Pretty good at it, right?" McManus waits not for a response before galloping on with his plot. "But there *are* facts in there… you'll just never know what part. And some facts are so sensitive that if you release them, you'd be in line for a treason charge. We have videos, photos, transcripts of conversations… Kiefer was wired the whole time, you know… of you paying out serious money to breach this country's national security. There's enough to lock you away in military stir for the rest of your sorry-ass life. I guess it could also be a problem for Kiefer if he wasn't headed to Amsterdam in a few hours… no return flight booked."

A gutted Arnett, his professional life now a cadaver before him, gropes for a response. The best he can offer: "What do you want?"

"You and your caddie production assistant are going to work for me—just like Vertain. I feed you stories no one else can source, you take them to air with the slant I want, your ratings go up. You come onto something of value, I'm the first to know. What you do with it… that's up to me. You agree, and your New York bosses will receive a call in five minutes that the piece they're about to run isn't in the best interest of the country... that there are larger issues at stake. You'll be credited for stellar, clever investigative work. You shouldn't be much worse for the wear."

"Nothing else?" Arnett meekly replies.

"That's it. Money you paid Kiefer is your loss. Price for fucking with one of my canaries." McManus swills Arnett's pain a long moment, then concludes, "Do we have an agreement?"

A broken Arnett nods.

"Good. I'll be in touch."

McManus sheds Arnett with a nod to the studio building. Arnett, joined by Roland, scuffs inside to come to grips with this disastrous undoing.

Still outside the TV studio, McManus brings out his cell phone and speed-dials a number. When he raises his head, he sees spotted around him at some distance Trina, Hopper, Greg, and House... all standing unnervingly still. McManus signals to the blue service van. As the Mick is about to open his door, the rear view mirror on the driver's side and then on the passenger's side explode. It takes but an instant for both the Mick and Kiefer to raise their hands and sit absolutely still... wisely so. Parked a hundred yards away is Promardie's white Volvo station wagon. The Pro holds a Remington PSR sniper rifle to the circular hole in the back window, while in the driver's seat Apostoli vigilantly scans the parking lot.

Torso now fossilized, McManus waits for these cataclysmic figures to set the hours of his judgment day. None of the four twitches, which further burrows into McManus's splintering psyche. After a few more moments, vigilante law is set into motion—Trina and Hopper walk to McManus; Greg and House take several paces in.

"Hope you weren't trying to phone your errand girl Greta, because we have her under a gag order," Trina cold-bloodedly announces.

"We blew your two safes in the Valley storage unit. We have all the dirt you can't afford anybody else to see," Hopper joins in, "including hanging us out to die on the way out of Mexico." Hopper parks his face against that of McManus. "I hold a real grudge against people who don't want me or an innocent boy around for the next sunrise."

Realizing there is no visa out of this fix, McManus simply stands for his sentence. Trina does the honors. "All your files are on the way out of the country courtesy of a Polish friend of ours... you know his name, right?" McManus risks not an answer. "That's where they'll stay... in our custody. If you want them kept locked away, you and your tool Greta erase any mention of our names at your office and dump anything else you have on us. Forget who we are, that we know each other, that we exist, and you can go about your business. Are we communicating?"

"Yes, we are," McManus says to the marriage of appeasement.

"Every now and then, we may need assistance," Hopper adds. "Only question will be the color of the butler vest you wear."

"Anything else?"

"No. Do the right thing, and we might just cut loose some of that Covarrubias intel to you."

"OK. I'll be leaving then," McManus says in a quietened voice.

"You may have a good idea there," Hopper remarks.

McManus cannot quickly enough make himself scarce from this trade show of requital. As he tries to come to grips with his enfeebled situation, he thinks of the warning against tangling with this bunch that he'd been given at the USC library. Why had he turned a back to such damn sound advice? Had hubris once again ensnared its carrier? Quite possibly.

The blue service van starts and pokes toward an exit. Soon enough, an additional ticket to Amsterdam would be procured. Like many before, these vanquished had learned their fate all too swiftly and starkly.

Trina and Hopper turn to Greg and House. Their eyes show the promise of the one blessed life they have to live.

———

"How much truth can... a mind endure; how much truth can it dare?"

Friedrich Nietzsche
"Preface"
Ecce Homo: How One Becomes What One Is (1908)
Translated by Anthony Mario Ludovici

ᕤᕦ

"... [C]ruelty and intolerance to those who do not belong to it are natural to every religion."

Sigmund Freud
"Two Artificial Groups: The Church and the Army"
Group Psychology and the Analysis of the Ego (1921)
Translated by James Strachey

www.ingramcontent.com/pod-product-compliance
Lightning Source LLC
Chambersburg PA
CBHW021510240626
47154CB00002B/574

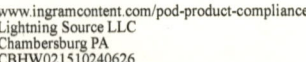